The Emptiness Algorithm

Belinda Tobin

Published by Bel House Books

Paperback ISBN: 978-1-7637246-0-0

EBook ISBN: 978-1-7637246-1-7

For permissions or enquiries, please contact:

Bel House Books

Email: bhb@heart-led.pub

Website: www. heart-led.pub/bel-house-books

First Edition: October 2024

 A catalogue record for this book is available from the National Library of Australia

Other titles from Bel House Books:

I'm Sorry Juno

To The Heart of the Man

The Emptiness Algorithm

Crucifixus

I acknowledge the Yuggera and Ugarapul peoples as the Traditional Owners of the lands and waterways where this book was written. I honour the wisdom that lives within the cultures of our First Nations peoples and celebrate its continuity. I pay my deep respects to Elders past, present and future and send my greatest gratitude for all they do for the life of this land.

Always was, always will be.

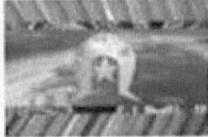

For true friendship.

Chapter 1

Venus heard the familiar ting and glanced at the news notification, as she always did. In a world cluttered with the trivial, she had crafted the news algorithm to sift out only what was mattered, for she was far too busy to deal with fluff. Venus considered herself well abreast of anything that could harm her clients or business. Still, sometimes, an announcement even took her by surprise. This one didn't, though; she had been anticipating this day for months. Companion Corp was finally ready to release the Companion MK1 male model, opening appointments for clients to engineer their perfect companion. Venus had followed the progress of these new products even before the release of the female version last year, eager to see if they would be a suitable support for her busy lifestyle. Everyone was calling them sexbots, but Venus knew that they could offer much more.

Increasingly, robots were becoming intertwined in her clients' businesses, and she was familiar with their capabilities in childcare, health care and customer service settings. The research showed they were delivering great outcomes, being both efficient and effective. These creatures were consistent, never succumbing to the temptation to make others pay for their bad day. In fact, they never had one. They were reliable, removing the risk of human randomness. There was also straightforward evidence that despite being classed as a separate species, they could truly engage with humans and offer effective solace and support. In a result that surprised everyone, the latest trust scores for robots were also higher than for their human counterparts. Like all her colleagues, Venus predicted there would be substantial suspicion of the robots for many years to come. Obviously, though, given the respondent's recent experiences in the realm of humanity, there was more paranoia about other people. Where robots were recommended for her clients, and when they were ready to invest, she always advised them to seek out the Japanese models. These were of superior technical quality, but they also seemed to have a greater sense of calmness and compassion, making her feel more comfortable championing them.

"Right place, right time." Venus said to herself as she clicked on the notification. If the companions had been available five years ago, she never would have had the resources to move forward. Like every other management consultancy, hers had weathered the simultaneous storms of an industry reputation tarnished by corruption, clients turning to AI to deliver reports instantly, and a market swamped by freelancers providing their professional services at a fraction of the price. Back then, they were at the bottom of a dry, lonely sales funnel. Thanks to her tenacity, though, and the eventual swing of the pendulum back to the big firms, her profitability and position had been restored, and she had been spiralling upwards ever since. It was a great day for Venus when she was promoted to partner two years ago. On that day, she had become integrally invested in her firm's future.

The Japanese were the first to perfect the technology for female robot companions built for friendship and pleasure. Dr. Leo Castellan bought the rights for the American market at a price Venus could not even comprehend. He was now offering bots tailored to the specific cultural needs of the Western clientele and advancing the development of a male version. It had always made Venus wonder why the Japanese founder had only stuck with female models. Despite reading through all his online interviews, there was no clear answer. It was irrelevant anyway; a male one was available now if she wanted it.

Scrolling through the article, she saw that Companion Corp was taking appointments starting in six months. They apologised for the delay in getting the male model to market, but there were some additional and very important mechanical bits to get right. Venus smiled. Yes, bad sex was bad enough, but it would be deplorable to get shoddy service from something you paid a fortune for. She didn't mind so much when the escorts did not live up to expectations; they were exchangeable. She had learnt quickly that the trick was just to get better at specifying the criteria. A companion bot was another matter. You would be stuck with them for a while, so you had to get them right.

Venus thought back to Jack, the partner she had a few partners ago. He was a lovely guy, but even with pills and pumps, he had real trouble keeping it up. With a replacement part he would have been perfect. Her smile grew wider, thinking about the work being done in the lab to design an excellent piece of male equipment; all those people in lab coats moulding, poking, prodding, and stress-testing the schlong. Then, her mind wandered to the implications of the end product being inadequate or, even worse, faulty. She almost laughed thinking about an emergency department filled with companion robot incidents. It would be a PR nightmare. That image prompted her to place a reminder in her diary:

> *confirm medical insurance covers injuries caused by mechanical companions.*

Venus had actually made the decision to commit months ago, but first, before beginning the official sign up, she needed caffeine. While the coffee was pouring, she took a few precious moments to stare through the great glass windows at the Space Needle. It was, once again, shrouded in streams of rain. How nice it would be to snuggle up on the sofa on a day like today with a man servant. Her daydreams were disturbed by the conversations of her underlings gathered nearby to share lunch. They usually stopped talking when they saw her coming, which she was used to by now; that was just one of the downsides of being in a position of power. But today, they continued chatting. It appeared one of the juniors was saving up to get a female companion bot.

"The poor thing," thought Venus, knowing affording one would be practically impossible. They were about the price of a medium-sized car, and on his salary, he would be saving up for a long time to come. Sure, there will be rip-offs, and their price will reduce over time, but she always believed that ultimately, you get what you pay for. Venus decided against butting in and bringing him down; she would need his help meeting a crazy client deadline at the end of the week, so she left without saying a word.

The first few sips of coffee instilled her with courage, so she headed straight to the Companion Corp website.

There was Dr Leo Castellan with chest puffed out and hands held in front of his private parts, looking just like a proud father. His name sounded so romantic, but his appearance was a desperate disappointment. He looked sexually confused like he could swing whichever way the wind blew him, and his strange smile made him look like someone slightly addicted to uppers. He looked like one of the creeps who used to crack on her at the nightclub in the days when she had time to dance. Venus wondered if he experimented with all the robots to ensure the mechanics worked exactly right. She was fairly sure he did. She grimaced at the thought of getting a model tried and tested and personally accredited by Dr Castellan.

Shaking that image from her mind, Venus convinced herself it was time for her to take her own advice. How could she recommend robots to clients and not have one in her home? Besides, she was far too busy to fuss around and find a partner. Venus had her fair share of boyfriends over the years, found through matchmakers mostly, but they were always too insecure to deal with her independence. It meant she never made it to have kids, but who would want to deal with dependents anyway? The way technology was going, it may not be long before they could just make her one, with an off button, of course.

So, Venus had spent her time lately with a plant, a cat, and the odd escort. The plant had a self-watering device, mitigating the risks of neglect. The cat was set up with a self-feeder and self-cleaning litter box. With these basics taken care of she was free to travel and stay late nights in the office delivering on client deadlines. Now, though, there could be someone to come home to. Someone to take care of her. Maybe even someone to cook for her. She often thought the only things that dildos were missing were arms and mouths and the ability to tell her she was beautiful. Well, Venus thought, it appears someone has solved that problem! Technology is truly magnificent!

Her rumination was interrupted when a light began to flash on the screen. Why wait? It asked eagerly. You could be an early adopter, guaranteed to be one of the first with a Companion Male Mk1. With $10,000 paid upfront, she could secure a consultation within two weeks. Hurry, though, the box insisted; places are filling up fast.

Venus would not be sucked in by FOMO; she was far too intelligent for that. Still, she did scroll rather quickly through the rest of the page. She came across a photo of a prototype bot resembling a young Chris Hemsworth. Who wouldn't want one of those? And just in case white was not your style, they also had an Idris Elba replica. God, Venus thought, he was hot. She wondered whether Companion Corp had to pay royalties for using these likenesses or had found some legal loophole. She thought it unlikely that the stars themselves would have consented. However, with both now well and truly in the sunset of their careers, they may have done anything to prevent their fame from fading.

There were many recent examples of public figures pulling horrifying stunts to cling to the last scraps of their stardom. Take for example, the ageing actor who offered himself for cosmetic surgery, having to undergo the alterations nominated by the ten highest bidders. The poor guy ended up looking like a puppet, which was not so far from the truth. Venus still shuddered when she thought what they had done to his penis. The photos were excruciating to see, so she could not even imagine what his multiple mistresses thought. Serves him right for trying to be immortal. So, selling your likeness for a robot was, in comparison, a smart preservation strategy.

Venus amused herself thinking about what Companion Corp did with the prototypes from the picture. Perhaps they offered shop floor models at a discount, like refrigerators or vacuum cleaners. This led her to surmise that it was only a matter of time before there would be a booming market in used bots. This may be the only way the kid in the kitchen could secure one. She pitied those people who had to satisfy themselves with second-hand companions.

The bot on the screen looked so real. Although they were not completely convincing. Their skin still looked stiff, and their hands seemed unnaturally rigid. Enlarging the image, Venus could see that one eye was slightly illuminated and had black flecks that were far bigger than normal. The wall welcomed her focus as she began fantasising about what it would feel like to be touched by this bot and what their lips would taste like. What would it be like to look into that cyborg eye while being manhandled by a machine? The thought was enticing and exciting.

That was her cue to hand over her credit card number; in return, she received an appointment date for two weeks. She logged the details in her tax return folder, hoping that given she consulted on IT, she could claim this as a tax deduction in next year's return. After all, it could be argued that it was for research and professional development purposes. Some deep breaths were needed to settle her nerves; she had just realised she was shaking. Was she scared, excited, ashamed, or all three? She could not tell. But she was extremely proficient in compartmentalising her life, so after a few more breaths, she returned to work as normal.

That night, though, as she scrolled through her clients' socials, she began to think about designing her companion. Venus could not help but pay closer attention to all the men's attributes and appendages. She really liked one CEO's hair and another man's nose, and she adored the gentleman with green eyes. She wondered if she should start taking screenshots and making a scrapbook so that her ideas would not be lost. She was quickly distracted by the thought of clothes shopping for her new friend. Venus decided at once to splurge on a Cucinelli linen suit and Hermes loafers. Just because her bot would be housebound, it didn't mean he should not look stylish. She spent the rest of the night deciding on suitable sleepwear and then dreamt of being cuddled up in Idris Elba's arms, only to hear the whirring of his mechanical eye as he constantly stayed awake, surveying for danger.

Venus made it to the meeting with Dr Castellan right on time, having to cut short a conversation with one client quiet rudely when his indecision was threatening to interrupt her plans. The appointment was at the end of an exceedingly long day. She was exhausted from dealing with clients who were too chicken-shit to make a call, wanted more for less than they were willing to pay, or considered themselves the experts. Dr Castellan greeted her with a slightly exuberant energy, like he had either too much coffee or not quite enough cocaine.

"Ms Marlowe. Welcome. Welcome. And congratulations for becoming one of the first owners of a Companion Male Mk1!"

"Thank you, doctor. It is lovely to meet you," said Venus, taking the doctor's hand, instantly realising she was right about him being creepy.

"This will serve a dual purpose for me. Companionship, yes, is primary. However, I also consult into several clients where robotics is becoming increasingly part of their business, so I need to stay ahead of what is on the horizon."

"I see. Are your clients escort agencies or brothels?"

"Oh no," said Venus, laughing, suddenly embarrassed that he had gotten the wrong idea about her profession.

"That's a pity," said the doctor seriously. "Yes, a pity."

"Never mind. Well, I am sure there is so much you would like to know. But it is so much easier to show than tell. Yes, so much easier to show than tell. Would you like to meet 1.1 or 1.2? Actually, let's show you both. Yes, let's show you both!"

He buzzed his assistant and asked her to show the bots in.

They came in with a smooth stride but still stiff enough to not fool anyone that they were human. Yet, given their solid body shapes, their grace was impressive. They took turns shaking hands with her. The Chris Hemsworth twin, 1.1, introduced himself first and made a little bow. The Idris doppelganger, 1.2, looked her in the eye, shared a smile, and said, "Enchanté." Their hands were soft and warm, and that robot eye was surprisingly captivating. They strode over and sat beside Dr Castellan, turning toward him, and awaiting further instruction.

Venus tried to concentrate on the doctor's ramblings about the functionality of the companions but only became genuinely interested when he started a demonstration. He showed her how they could conduct a conversation, cuddle, and kiss. The bots seemed genuinely engaged the whole time and not perturbed by the prospect of having their commander's lips on theirs or watching the other do the same. Venus, though, felt like a voyeur, watching the warm-up scenes of a new-wave porn film. After a cleanse of their lips with an antiseptic wipe, the doctor offered her a turn, which she adamantly declined. She was curious to kiss one but would not do so in front of the doctor. He was not going to get his rocks off at her expense. He was probably filming the whole thing and would watch it back later.

The doctor launched into yet another lecture about the advanced material used for the skin, assuring her that they had been able to modify silicon to ensure it was hypoallergenic. They had not yet found a way to make a perfect replica of human skin yet, but they were getting close. The hair, of course, was real. That, the doctor declared, was so much easier to source than human skin. He laughed, indicating that this was meant to be a joke, but it confirmed Venus' view that he was actually a schmuck.

Then 1.1 spoke up, startling Venus from the daze she descended into, listening to the doctor drawl on.

"Ms Marlowe. I sense that you are feeling a little weary. Would you like me to fetch you a cup of tea?"

Venus sat back in her chair with surprise. How could it tell she needed tea? Or did it just do this for everyone? It took little intelligence to know that any person would be tired at this time of the afternoon. But this, she had to investigate further.

"Yes please, that would be wonderful."

"How would you like me to make it for you today?"

"Just a splash of milk, please 1.1"

"As you wish."

1.1 left the room, while Venus' mind put "as you wish" on repeat. It reminded her of The Princess Bride, a movie she would still watch on rainy Sunday afternoons when her brain had stopped working, and documentaries were just not doing it for her. Did 1.1 know how much she loved this film? If so, how could he? Or maybe this was just a standard response, and she shouldn't be too paranoid. Although you could never be sure who had what data about you these days. It was conceivable that her viewing preferences had been sold on to Companion Corp, who had now used them to impress their client and secure a sale. What, though, was wrong with that. She would love to have her very own Westley.

"Wow, doctor. That is wonderful."

"That is just the beginning, Ms Marlowe."

Then 1.2 spoke in the most delightfully smooth voice. "While you are waiting for tea, Ms Marlowe, could I perhaps interest you in a neck rub?"

Dr Castellan leant back in his chair and pointed a finger at her like he had just proven a point.

She did not want to give Dr Castellan any bigger ego. But this she truly had to see.

"Sure, yes, please."

1.2 stood behind her, gently moving her hair to one side. The robot pressed in close, but the back of the chair protected her from feeling anything too personal. His hands were firm but still had some way to go before they felt genuine. He started to squeeze the flesh around her neck, but his grip was far too firm, and she winced.

"I am so sorry, Ms Marlowe. Would you like me to go softer?"

"Yes, please."

And he did. And the massage was wonderful. His hands became hotter over time until they reached a setting Venus would have called toasty. His technique eased her tension and, despite the doctor watching on with his sleazy stare, made her want to sleep. The massage ceased carefully when the tea came.

1.1 placed the cup and saucer down on the table and, with a bow, resumed his seat.

"Would you like me to continue, Ms Marlowe?" said 1.2.

"Please, call me Venus."

"Thank you, Venus. Would you like me to continue your massage while you drink your tea? Or I could work on your feet instead so as not to disrupt your drinking?"

This was far too good to be true.

"Thank you, 1.2, that is all for now."

She heard her answer to 1.2 and didn't like her response at all. Her voice had altered automatically as if she was talking to a servant. But then, she thought, that is what they were, weren't they?

"Well, Dr Castellan, I am impressed," said Venus with an air of enthusiasm that was hard to contain.

"I knew you would be, Ms Marlowe. I knew you would be."

"Please tell me, what is the programming you use to make them so attentive?"

"Ah, that is The Emptiness Algorithm. Yes indeed, The Emptiness Algorithm! It drives these companions to constantly seek signs for things you are lacking, even those things you are not aware of yet. For example, 1.1 would have seen your tired eyes and your reduced attention, and so suggested tea. Then 1.2 would have witnessed you shuffling in your chair and adjusting your shoulders and so deduced tension. Ms Marlowe, their eyes are keener than eagles, always looking for ways in which they can assist. Always looking."

"Fantastic!" said Venus admiringly, although she was becoming increasingly annoyed at the doctor's habit of repeating phrases he thought were important.

"Fantastic, yes. They can also pick up changes in pupil dilation from a distance, which allows them to determine what you like and don't like and can monitor your voice to understand your mood. The real benefit though comes when you get close, skin on skin, or skin on silicone if you will. Ha, yes, skin on silicone. They can sense your heartbeat, your temperature, can pick up pheromones and your drug and alcohol readings, and know intimately what you need. They have no ego like selfish humans, so can use one hundred percent of their focus on you. You heard it, Ms Marlowe. One hundred percent focus on you."

The doctor leaned forward to look the "you" he spoke of directly in her eyes.

"Ms Marlowe, these creatures are truly excellent companions; I have personally seen to that."

The way he said the word 'personally' sent a shiver down Venus' spine, and she wondered whether the companions had picked up on that, too.

"And there is so much more to come. What I have presented for you is just the tip of the iceberg. Yes, just the tip of the iceberg. Are you ready to get on board? Get on board, Ms Marlowe! Come on boys!"

The doctor pumped his arms and wailed "toot toot", echoed by the robots beside him. It was hard not to laugh, and they all broke into a chuckle. However, the doctor's unfortunate analogy for this pep rally made her a little uncomfortable. Likening her adventure with a companion to a vessel travelling around icebergs was off-putting. Yet she dismissed this readily, chalking this up to just another sign of the doctor's lack of social intelligence.

"So, Ms Marlowe. Are you in?"

"Yes, I am in."

"That is wonderful!"

The doctor threw his hands in the air and then started a small round of applause, which 1.1 and 1.2 joined in, their claps a little more muffled than ones coming from the regular man's hands.

"So, there is a bit of detail we need to work through to make sure your companion is going to meet your needs. It must meet your needs. Do you have an hour to spare now?"

"Of course, now is fine. I booked out the rest of the afternoon for this. Can I ask for one important thing though, doctor?"

"Anything. Anything!"

"My ownership of this companion must remain strictly confidential. I would not want it destroying my credibility."

"Gotcha Ms Marlowe. Gotcha. We pride ourselves on confidentiality. It is the cornerstone of Companion Corp. Our cornerstone. But to assuage your concerns I will make sure it is a term in the Companion Contract."

"Thank you, doctor."

"Leo, please. Please! But Ms Marlow, I don't think you have long to worry about outside opinion. From the demand we have seen so far, I am sure securing a Male Mk1 will only increase your status, not diminish it. So, let's get you started!"

Chapter 2

The doctor practically skipped out the door and signalled for Venus to follow. He commanded his assistant to power down the companions and store them away, then steered Venus towards a much smaller office. He knocked, entered, and introduced her to a woman much older than him and who also looked far wiser.

"Ms Marlowe, this is Doctor Julia Roscoe. Julia will gather all the relevant information to make sure you have an excellent Mk1 Companion. Julia, please, no expense spared for Ms Marlowe, she is a VIP. Yes, a VIP."

The doctor exited with the same energy he had greeted her with earlier.

"My apologies, Ms Marlowe, he is a bit of a human dynamo," said Dr Roscoe.

"Please, call me Venus. Yes, a dynamo for sure, but his achievements are admirable."

"Well, yes, although we must also acknowledge the amazing foundation created by the developer in Japan. Dr Castellan is doing magnificent work, but he is standing upon the shoulders of giants. Let's not dwell on the technicalities, though. Let's get started on building your companion bot!"

Venus put her hands over her mouth and took a deep breath out. Was she really doing this?

"These initial setup questions may be tedious, so can I get you a cup of tea or coffee before we begin?"

"Thank you, Julia, but 1.1 already made me one."

"That 1.1 is such a sweetie!" exclaimed the doctor, tucking her hands to her heart. "I desperately want one of him. But we are here to talk about what you would like. Before we do, though, sorry, Venus, we need to take a few measurements to ensure your companion will fit snugly with your body."

Dr Roscoe led Venus to the wall where she measured height and weight, bust, waist and hips.

"Wow, I have not done this for a while," said Venus, starting to feel self-conscious. Please excuse me if I don't watch."

"I understand completely. Although truly Venus, you are a beautiful woman, your companion will be one lucky bot."

Both ladies burst out laughing.

"Oh, Julia. This really is ludicrous."

Sitting back at the computer, they huddled together and began working through Venus' physical preferences.

"Is there anyone in particular you want your man to look like?"

"I must say, your Idris example is awesome, and he is just my type. But could I have him with green eyes? And a bit more muscle?"

"Consider it done." said the doctor, entering information on the online form and ticking boxes beside some selection criteria.

Although Venus was soon to find out, this was the simple part. Then, there were specifications for finger length, toe type, and presence (or not) of pubic hair. Of course, there was also the issue of penis and testes size to be decided. Pulse settings, Venus was informed, were controlled via the app, within set parameters, of course. Venus suddenly felt decidedly shy, asking Julia to recommend an appropriate phallus setting.

"I would go large if I was you. With the next upgrade, we hope to offer an internal examination to get a perfect fit, but I believe this one will meet your needs nicely for now."

"What?" exclaimed Venus, sincerely taken aback by the thought of this technology veering into the world of gynaecology.

"Sure, we have everything we need to do it; we have just had some more pressing priorities, for Mk1. But hopefully, by Mk2, all of your companions will be completely tailored for your total satisfaction."

Julia gave a wink, but Venus went quiet.

They moved on to personality traits, where Venus stipulated her companion must be kind, empathetic, supportive, humorous, handy, and hardworking. She chose the Love Languages of words and acts, knowing that asking for these things would defeat the purpose. She declined physical touch, unsure how she would feel about the bot taking its own initiative to be intimate. She could command that when she needed it anyway. Venus said a definite yes to dancing capabilities but was at a loss when choosing which ones. She loved dancing but had not done much since university, so she selected whatever looked good, disco, ballroom and salsa. For foreign languages, Venus applied a little more rigour. She wanted to spend more time in France and Japan, so she chose these two and threw in Italian because it sounded romantic. Accents could be changed at any time with the app.

"Now, just a few more settings to go through," Julia said, looking weary.

"Would you like vocalisations? That is little moans and groans when certain points are stimulated that indicate pleasure."

"Sure. Yes please."

"Then would you also like it loaded with dirty talk?"

"Sorry?" Just when Venus had thought she had heard it all, there was something else she had not considered.

"Well, we are not quite ready to include some rough play. Legal are holding us up on releasing this addition. It appears, Venus, the devil is in the detail with this feature. But we can offer you some dirty talk if you like that? We just don't want to include it as standard in case of unforeseen events."

Venus' hand went over her mouth again.

"I know, Venus, I am sorry. But I have to ask."

"Wow. I really had no idea."

"So, yes? No?"

"No thanks."

They both chuckled.

"Well, if you change your mind, you can give us a call. It is not a setting you can change on the app, but we can do it pretty quickly at our end. Next, would you like the Daddy-dialect built in?"

"Oh gosh, what is that?"

"Let me explain. We understand there are many women who, for a plethora of reasons, are harbouring substantial daddy issues. We are working on a counselling module but that is a couple of versions away at least. In the meantime, we are offering the companion to be loaded with phrases that women always wanted to hear from their fathers - I am proud of you, I believe in you, you are loved, you are strong, I am here to support you always, you know, that kind of thing."

This touched a nerve with Venus, but she was devoid of tears. She had been for over a decade since her father died. She remembered her father so fondly, and he repeatedly said these exact things to her. She did not have him now, and she missed him today as much as she did when he departed. When he died, she cried for a week straight. Venus was convinced she had dried the well that week and would never cry again.

"No. I think we can skip that one too." She did not want anyone, let alone a doctor, thinking she had daddy issues.

"Perfect. Now, all our companions come with the default safe word of 'stop'. This will become more relevant in future versions, but in the meantime would you like anything different?"

"Safe word?"

"Yes, just in case he is doing anything you don't like. It is not expected at all given how advanced the AI is in these companions. It is just another layer of precaution."

"Oh, I see. Yes, stop is fine."

Venus thought how much this sounded like the multiple layers of manual overrides offered in self-driving cars in the early days, until they knew the technology was secure. The flickers of concern that had started with the iceberg image were intensifying but were interrupted by the continued interrogation.

"And finally, the last question," said Dr Roscoe, sounding as relieved as Venus felt. "Would you like your companion to be loyal to you, or would you like it to be able to care for others as well?"

"I'm sorry, I don't quite understand."

"It is expected that over time, some people may want to share their companions, have them join in swinger's events or even polyamorous relationships, so we want to make sure we cater for that situation. We just can't assume the whole monogamy thing anymore."

"True," said Venus, conceding the point. "Loyal thanks."

"Perfect. All done. Let's look at your man!"

Doctor Roscoe tapped a few more buttons, and slowly before them a hologram began to grow, hovering slightly above the ground. The swirling, sparkly light started at the feet and moved upwards in arcs, inch by inch to finally reveal the bright green eyes. Venus was mesmerised, unsure whether it was because of the hypnotic illumination surrounding the model or the mere presence of this perfect specimen.

"Venus, please go and have a close look. Stand beside him and make sure all is to your liking."

Venus was in awe, wandering around this electrical emanation. She wanted to reach out and touch him, but that, she assured herself, would come later in the haven of her own home. Here before her was a man she had engineered. Well, not engineered, really, not from scratch, but more patched together from social media snippets. And not really a man, more of a highly intelligent machine. Yet he was standing there, looking at her with his gorgeous green eyes, waiting for her approval to proceed. Waiting for her to confirm that she wanted him.

"Is there anything you would like to change?"

"Could we make the hands just a little bigger?"

"Sure, give me a second."

Dr Roscoe fiddled with a few settings on her program, and the hands enlarged slightly.

"Is that better, Venus?"

"Perfect. Thankyou!"

Venus sat back in her chair but found it hard to take her eyes off the glowing figure before her.

"Before we sign off, Venus, is there anything else worrying you. We are always here to help, but it is much easier if we get things sorted at this stage."

"I understand, but no, I think I am good to go."

Dr Roscoe leaned forward and looked into Venus' eyes.

"Venus, do you think you are ready or feel like you are ready?" the doctor said, stressing the words 'think' and 'feel'.

"I see your point, doctor. Feel. Yes, I feel good to go."

"Great. I will just get the paperwork started for you to sign. You will receive a copy shortly by email, which will also include the details of the next required payments."

While Venus' eyes were still admiring her collage creation, a niggle began in her mind. Something did just not sit right in this situation.

"Thanks Julia. Can I ask you a question? Not about the companion, more about you."

"Sure!"

"Why are you, who I am sure are incredibly qualified, asking all these questions? Isn't a bit below you to be helping people choose cock circumference and toe thickness?"

"Oh, you are funny Venus. First, thank you for your compliment. I wish Dr Castellan was as gracious as you about what I give to the project. And second, my apologies. We should really explain this upfront, but we don't want to alter people's behaviour by telling them they are being observed. I am a doctor of psychiatry and I do the questioning to determine if there are any issues with the prospective client that could make having a companion problematic. We have a duty of care to make sure we are not putting people in harm's way. Although can I tell you there is usually so much going on beneath the surface for people, my assessment can only ever be superficial."

"I see. What kind of things are you looking out for?" Venus had never been diagnosed with any mental illness, but thanks to some dedicated time with Doctor Google after her last disastrous relationship, she harboured suspicions she had several noteworthy neuroses.

"Just the biggies, really. Things like suicide ideation, an inclination to harm the self or others, unhealthy co-dependencies, substance addictions, that kind of thing. We put in a lot of safeguards, but we can't let something like that slip through. Give it a few years, and the pendulum will swing to people taking personal responsibility for their purchases. For now, though, we are just starting out, so we need to show we are good corporate citizens; do some heavy lifting so that our clients don't end up as our patients, if you know what I mean."

"Yes, I do, and that is understandable. But I pass?"

"Yes Venus, you pass."

The women laughed again, the papers were signed, and the doctor saw Venus out.

"Your companion will be ready in about two weeks. I know you would like to be discrete so our team will be in touch to organise the best location for delivery. When we meet you for the handover, we will walk through the operating instructions and set up your companion's name. So, the only thing you need to do is to decide what you will call him!"

Venus walked back to her car with a lightness she had not felt in years. Was it because she was ahead of the curve, securing her supremacy? Or was it because soon she would be headed home to someone other than her plant and cat? She instructed the car to take her home and caught up on her emails as it maneuvered through the midtown traffic. She said hello to her plant, patted her cat, ordered dinner, and then opened her laptop to ask Chitti, her chatbot, for ideas on a noble name for her forthcoming companion.

THE EMPTINESS ALGORITHM

Chapter 3

Under the cover of darkness, Dr Roscoe, the Companion Corp technician, and the bot came through the back entrance, just as Venus had instructed. Venus was determined to avoid the attention that might arise with people knowing she had a sexbot. To date she had succeeded in shunning her neighbours and wanted to keep it that way. She certainly did not want to be accosted with any critical questions from nosey parkers conveniently passing on the footpath or cornering her in the carpark.

Venus tried to be polite to Dr Roscoe and pay her some attention, but it was difficult not to fixate on the bot, who seemed bigger than she remembered. His eyes also seemed a little bit brighter. He was much taller than her, a good head above hers, which was how she liked the height of her men. She needed someone tall to feel protected. Smaller guys might be able to kill someone with karate, but she wanted someone who looked the part. The companion bot looked down at her, and she felt her heart twinge. When his electronic eyes met hers, she was enchanted but also a little exposed. Just how much had he sensed about her already?

The bot moved towards her, his tailored black suit fitting his frame flawlessly, hugging all the right places. The jacket sat snugly across his shoulders, creating both sharp lines and smooth curves. There was no tie, just a hint of a dusty grey silk shirt, with the top buttons undone. Yes, whoever had dressed this bot had read the brief that requested fine fabrics and an air of 'simple yet stylish'.

"Good evening, Ms Marlowe. I am your companion bot. It is an honour to meet you."

He held out his hand smoothly, but the shake it gave was a little stiff. Still, it felt more human than one of the partners at the firm who always made you feel that you were clinging onto a cold dead fish. The bot's greeting ended with a little bow, making Venus feel special indeed. Did she also pick up the scent of the cologne she had listed as her favourite?

Her focus was interrupted by the technician, wheeling through what looked like a little suitcase, which Dr Rosco explained was the bot charging station. While Venus worked with the technician to find the best spot for the station, Dr Rosco ordered the bot to sit on the sofa and started tapping away on her device while it sat there unmoving and mute.

When Venus returned to the sofa, Dr Roscoe placed her hand on Venus' arm and offered a genuine congratulations.

"You have done well, Venus. If you don't mind me saying, your bot is beautiful."

And he was. Despite being constructed, it had a charisma that filled the room. Even sitting in silence, he looked stately. His broad shoulders appeared strong enough to bear the weight of the world or at least Venus' worries. His large hands seemed capable of both crushing cement or cradling a child. Kindness was etched in every line of his face, and Venus was fascinated with how some simple ticks on a form had transformed into this creature. His smile, arising at every opportune moment, looked like sunshine breaking through on a cloudy day, making it hard to believe it was sculpted from silicone. His eyes were like an emerald treasure, drawing you in with the lustre that would shift sporadically around the lens. Standing before him, Venus felt a magnificent mix of awe and comfort.

"I agree, Julia. You have done an amazing job."

"Ah, Ms Marlowe," said the bot. "My beauty is merely a shadow of the one that stands before me."

With that, Venus had no choice but to blush.

The two women shared a wide smile and started the setup sequence.

"Oh, I almost forgot, Dr Castellan sends his regards."

The thought of Dr Castellan quickly brought Venus back to the reality of the situation. Had Castellan personally given this bot his seal of approval? The smile turned to a shudder and a resumed focus on the proceedings at hand.

"Thanks. Um, there is one thing I forgot to ask. How do you wash them?"

"How about you ask him yourself?"

"Oh, ok. Excuse me, bot, could you tell me the best way to wash you please?"

"Thank you, Ms Marlowe. However, I am quite capable of washing myself. I can spend a few minutes under a shower, or just a handwash works fine. I am programmed to maintain the highest standards of hygiene, but if you require anything between my scheduled cleaning regime do not hesitate to let me know and it will be done as you wish."

With that response, his head gave a little bow.

There it was again. "As you wish." This was absolutely wonderful. Venus wondered if she would ever tire of hearing this response and surmised she would soon find out. However, with one command, it could be ceased and be replaced with something less florid. That was the joy of this arrangement. She was in control.

"Now, Venus, I am curious. What name have you chosen for him?"

"Ade. His name is Ade."

"Is that A-I-D as in helper?" said Dr Roscoe, typing it into her device.

"Oh no, I hadn't thought of that. Wow, that's funny. No, it is A-D-E, as in king."

Venus had forgone her jogs two days in a row, scouring the internet for the perfect name. She had also spent far too much time focusing on the wall at work, wondering which one from her shortlist to choose. Yet, she was a master at finding information to support her intuition. So, when she read that the numerology of Ade aligned to creation and beginnings, Venus was sold. A little sense of uneasiness arose when she read that it was also a name 'fit for someone who carries the power of the unseen.' It sounded a little spooky, although wasn't that the whole premise of the Emptiness Algorithm?

"That's a great name, Venus. Please tell the bot his name now, and I will set it in his system along with your voice recognition.

"Your name is Ade."

"Thank you, Ms Marlowe. Please give me the spelling you would like for this.

"It is A-D-E."

"That is a wonderful name, Ms Marlowe. Thank you. I will endeavour to live up to the honour it holds."

"Ade?"

"Yes, Ms Marlowe?"

"Could you please call me Venus?"

"Of course. Enchanté, Venus."

Venus could feel herself begin to blush again, and appreciated Dr Roscoe stepping in.

"Venus, if you get sick of all this romantic language, you can just instruct him to tone it down; just like you would do with your chatbot. Teach him what you like and what you don't. And remember, you can choose any accent you like on the app. Speaking of which, let's go through that now."

The installation of the companion bot app was swift. Still, the range of settings available on Venus' screen was staggering. There was everything from language, speech speed, accent, grip strength, eye brightness, stride length and pace and sitting style.

"Wow," said Venus, feeling a little overwhelmed.

"You have an interesting adventure ahead of you, Venus," said Dr Roscoe. "I am more than a bit jealous."

"Don't you have one, Julia?"

"No, not yet. Even with the staff discount it is a bit outside of my reach. I have to wait for my father to die first. Once his medical expenses end, then I will start getting excited."

Venus waited for Dr Roscoe to laugh, indicating that what she had just said was a joke. But it didn't come. All Venus could think was that the doctor had seen death enough to become desensitised to it. Or, she thought, perhaps there was something very personal and profound behind Dr Roscoe's development of the Daddy-dialect.

"Now, here is the one I told you about in the office, the pulse power. Do you want to see something funny."

"Sure."

"Just shift the setting."

Venus dragged the red dot towards the right and frowned as she saw Ade's pants begin to vibrate and buzz. But he did not flinch.

"Sorry, Venus. I just had to show you that. You should probably turn it back down to standard."

With a backward swipe, the oscillations began again at a much milder level. Again, there was no reaction from Ade. He did not look annoyed, amused, or anxious. Seeing someone so comfortable with his sexuality was a revolution in Venus' world. However, perhaps the concept of sexuality for a bot was just one step too far. In reality, his cock was just another part that needed to be calibrated, cleaned, and cached.

After a tour of the house and a few games of fetch, it was time to test the safe word, first done mid-jog. It was incredible how he could immediately return to standing and cease all movement without even a wiggle. The second test was a hug, which Venus would not allow herself to enjoy in front of company, and which she successfully cut short with a "stop" after a few seconds. He stood in front of her, awaiting the next instruction.

"You will just need to watch how you use that word on the phone or with other people around. You would be surprised how often it can come up in conversation and cause nasty accidents. Pausing halfway through carrying a tray of hot drinks can make an awful mess. Although, you can always ask him to clean it up for you afterwards."

"There really is so much to think about isn't there."

"Yes, there is. In many ways it is like having a child, but the good news is this one can take care of itself. Now, Venus. The last thing; the power modes. There are four; power off, power on, sleep and awake. Could you run through them with him please?"

"Sure. Ade, power off."

Venus watched as Ade's eyes went dull and then closed.

"In this mode, Venus, Ade won't do anything. He is not functional at all. Can you power him on please?"

"Power on, Ade."

Ade's eyes lit up, and a smile spread across his face.

"Hello Venus. So lovely to see you again."

This guy really was gorgeous.

"Sleep, Ade."

Ade's eyes pulsated a light green, like slow waves washing up on a tropical beach.

"Venus, in this mode Ade will be able to sense emergencies and will reactivate if you require assistance, but otherwise should not move. He acts like your own sleeping security guard or fire alarm, with heat, noise and smoke detector built in. He is also ready to shield you in case of attack or earthquake. If he is sleeping near you, he can also detect your breathing and heart rate, so can respond if any of these become troubled. He is trained in CPR and thanks to his intelligence around positioning and pressure, would be unlikely to break a rib. We don't have the defib yet in this model but should be in Mk2."

"Absolutely remarkable."

"You are right, Venus. It is. But give it a few years and all of this will be routine. I can't wait to see the face of the first home invader that meets one of these guys, especially one built like your Ade. You can wake him up now, Venus."

"Ade, awake."

"Hello, Venus. How are you?"

Right then and there, Venus would have loved to sit and start a conversation with her new companion, but there were still i's to dot and t's to cross. The technician went through the manual for the charging station and provided the number for the tech hotline in case of any concerns. There was no manual for Ade; Venus could simply ask him what to do.

"Venus, we are one hundred percent confident in the safety of our companion bots. But if you do have any concerns, or if there are any worrying incidents, you must call us first. We don't want anything untoward getting out on social media, or in the press that may threaten our products or reputation. I am sure you understand."

"Yes, I do. I could imagine the media would be working to bring you down quickly."

"They have already started trying, as is the case with any new shiny thing. They are always hungry for the next news story, especially one that comes with some controversy. That is why we need to be alerted to anything first. It is just a formality, but can I please get you to sign here to say that you accept this term of the contract."

As Venus was signing, she wondered if there was also a waiver for those boarding the Titanic on their final, fateful voyage. Were they also required to relinquish their rights for the privilege of partaking in the momentous journey?

Dr Roscoe and the technician packed up their equipment, and as they were leaving, Ade got up and shook their hands, wishing them safe travels and a wonderful evening. The doctor turned to Venus, reiterating her congratulations, and said, "Good luck, and have fun, Venus."

Venus knew this would have been said with the best intentions. Still, it made her feel like a virgin entering the marital bedchamber with a man she had never met before. It curbed the keenness Venus had felt previously about getting to know her partner. Instead, she was overcome with a sense of anxiety and awkwardness. This was just like a first date, but even worse because with Ade she was unable to hide what she truly wanted.

"Ade, sit please."

Ade sauntered back over to the sofa, sat in the standard straight-back style, and placed his hands on his thighs.

"Venus, I sense you are a bit nervous. It is completely understandable. This is a new and unusual experience. Would you like me to make you a cup of tea or run you a nice warm bath?"

"Thank you, Ade. That is lovely of you. Not right now. It has been a long day; I think I might just get ready for bed."

"As you wish. Please let me know if you need anything."

"I will. But for now, please sleep Ade."

Venus sat on the sofa opposite and watched his green eyes fluctuate and flow. She saw his firm hands against his thighs and his broad shoulders begging to be touched. Venus stood behind him, stroking his arms and feeling the medium-sized muscle mass underneath. She moved in front of him and put her hand on his. Venus' hands were so small compared to Ade's, and she smiled thinking about being wrapped in them. She touched his face, stroking the smooth jaw she had ordered and combing her fingers through the full black hair. Yes, he was beautiful, and he was hers. And yet, this would take some getting used to. Venus knew she was in command and could ask him to do anything she wanted, well, almost. So then, why did she feel less like a master and more like a mistress?

She left Ade, showered, brushed her teeth, and jumped into bed. There would be plenty of time to play, but she had another big day of meetings tomorrow and, for now, needed to rest. Sleep, though, did not come quickly. It felt so strange to have someone else in the house. Just then, she remembered that Ade was only in sleep mode. Venus had heard the doctor and understood that he would only rouse in case of emergency, but she needed to be sure he would not stir. She raced out and told Ade to "power down", only feeling slightly more secure when she saw his eyes shut. The cat had not made an appearance ever since Ade got here. Venus wondered if this was an ominous sign or whether it was just being her normal, cautious self?

Back in bed, the silence that she once treasured now felt eerie. On the rare occasion she had an escort stay over, there were always noises of the toilet flushing, the sheets shifting, the snoring; you always knew they were there. Ade was there but was sedated. Yet how could she be sure he would not sneak silently to her room and use his force for evil?

"Don't be silly, Venus," she told herself. "Your vacuum bot has never become violent, and it is not as if your chatbot has ever taken up cyberbullying. It will just take time to build trust." She repeated the word 'trust' until her body relaxed and fell asleep.

When she awoke, there were sounds outside that provided some assurance. Cars were passing, and every now and then, bits of broken conversation crept in. There was no noise inside, though, which she hoped meant Ade was still on the sofa. She crept up to him, forgetting that her steps would not wake him. Only her voice could do that. Remembering what it would take to rouse him, Venus used the chance to creep up behind him, giving him a huge cuddle and a kiss on the cheek. She found it so much easier to touch him when he could not respond. She did not have time to wonder why this was; she was already well behind schedule. This was exactly the situation where Ade could come in helpful.

"Power on, Ade."

"Good morning, Venus. I am so delighted to see you again. How are you this morning?"

For a face built in a lab, it sure did seem to beam brightly. Or was this due to strategically placed LEDs under the skin?

"I am well thanks, Ade. Although I am running a bit late this morning. Could you please make me a coffee?"

"Of course I can, Venus. However, could I make a suggestion?

"Yeeesss," said Venus, stringing out the word, making it clear she was worried about what would come next.

"Oh, please don't worry, Venus. I was just going to tell you that research has proven caffeine works best on a foundation of healthy food. It is like pouring petrol on a fire, it will only be sustained if there are plenty of logs in there first. I am sure you have a terribly busy day ahead, and cannot risk a slump, so would you like me to make you some breakfast to accompany the coffee?"

"Sure, ok, I guess so. But what would you suggest?"

Ade walked over, taking one second to scan the contents of each cupboard and the fridge.

"I could do eggs and mushrooms, which would be a wonderful source of protein and Omega-3 fatty acids, hydrating and giving your skin a natural glow. The estimated time for preparation would be seven minutes. Or perhaps porridge would be an excellent choice for lasting energy, and its anti-inflammatory properties may help you deal with stress. You have the quick-oats so the preparation time would be no more than four minutes. What do you think, Venus, sweet or savoury?"

"That's, fantastic Ade. I appreciate the lesson. Let's go savoury today."

"Wonderful choice, Venus. Please continue to get ready for your day and I will have breakfast for you shortly."

Venus was starting to feel better about having Ade there, at least in the mornings when she needed a hand to get out the door on time. Usually, she didn't have breakfast; it was just another hassle she did not need. There were always snacks in the kitchen at work, so a muffin and coffee would ward off the stomach grumbles until early afternoon. By then, she could ask her assistant to grab her a decent lunch, which she would eat at her desk to meet the ever-demanding client deadlines. However, now Ade was at home to help, she could get her healthy eating goals back on track.

Venus had a quick shower and dressed in her room with the door closed. For some strange reason, she still felt the need to be discrete and protect herself from his prying eyes. She brushed and oiled her hair, not needing any makeup since she had it all tattooed on a few months ago. It was a game changer and often wished she had done it years ago. Now, she looked naturally made up straight out of bed and saved at least half an hour each morning. She strapped on her heels and strutted into the kitchen, where Ade served eggs, sourdough, and magnificent-smelling garlic mushrooms. He placed all the condiments on the bench and came and sat beside her.

"It is weird that you don't eat, Ade. It feels strange you sitting there with nothing in front of you."

"I'm sorry, Venus, is my presence making you feel self-conscious? Would you like me to leave?"

"Oh no, that's ok. I was just saying it's strange that you don't eat."

"Ah, I see. Would you like to talk? Would that make you feel more comfortable?"

"Yes, I think so."

"Great, well I am curious about what you have planned for the day."

Venus outlined her schedule between mouthfuls and sips, and with each sentence, she began to feel more stressed.

"Could I make a suggestion, Venus?"

The last one Ade made worked out well, so she was more confident in approving his request.

"When you come home this evening, we could work through your schedule for tomorrow. I can help you ensure your time is used most efficiently. I can also do any research you require and prepare documents for you overnight, ready for your review. This way you will be able to get ahead of the next day."

"Ade, that sounds really good. Thank you."

"It is my pleasure, Venus. Is there anything you would like me to do for you here today?

"No, nothing I can think of Ade. That breakfast was fantastic, though. You could do that for me again tomorrow."

"As you wish, Venus."

"Right, well I am going to finish up getting ready."

"And I will clean up."

"You are wonderful, Ade."

"Thank you, Venus."

It may have been the food, the caffeine, or Ade's friendliness, but Venus felt much more comfortable with her new companion. Still, she didn't want any rogue programming sending him rifling through her sexy panty and adult toy drawer. So, after she had brushed her teeth and finished packing her handbag, she asked him to get dressed, hugged him, and told him to power off. Then she left and locked the door behind her.

Within two minutes Venus had returned. She sat opposite Ade and commanded him to power on.

"Hello again, Venus. How may I be of assistance?"

"I'm sorry, Ade. I was just going to leave you off all day, but I think I could really use your help."

"Of course, Venus. Would you like me to cook, clean and keep the cat company?"

"Yes, please, all of the above. Hang on, how did you know about the cat?"

"I saw the bowls when we went on the tour last night. Miu is a clever choice of name for a cat! Very cute indeed. Now, what about your work? How can I support you there?"

"I need some research done about the micro-economic implications of the latest free trade agreement, especially for my health care clients. I'm worried it could cause some strategic issues. Is that something you could do?"

"Absolutely. I am sending my email address to your phone right now. Please add this to your work administration account so I know where to send the research paper and so that I can help with your diary whenever needed. Is there anything else on your mind, Venus. Remember, I am here to help."

"Thanks, Ade. I think that is all. Although I do have a meeting with the partners today about my performance, which is always stressful. So any encouragement you could provide along the way would be great."

"Consider it done, Venus. Please feel free to email me the report you will be presenting and I can prepare a set of dot-points for you to focus upon. I will also schedule in sufficient break times for you to make sure you stay sharp. And could I suggest that I pen in a set finish time each day to allow you to come home and gain sufficient rest?"

"Yes, that's fine, thanks, Ade."

"It is my pleasure, Venus."

Venus tapped her phone, providing permission for Ade to join her email administration group.

"Venus, I notice that you have a scoping meeting scheduled for the middle of the day. Could I suggest that you conduct this meeting over lunch? This will allow for a more relaxed setting for your creative discussions, while also providing the opportunity for a nourishing meal. I can make a reservation at a highly-rated restaurant only two minutes' walk from your office. Would that work for you?"

"Wow, Ade. Yes, that does sound like a good idea. I don't usually do lunches out, but it could work well. Yes, book it in. I really appreciate it."

"It is my honour to do this for you, Venus. Now, I see that there is significant congestion along Highway 3 at the moment, so could I suggest that you tell your car to take the southern bridge route?"

"Thank you. I will. And now I really must go."

"Yes, Venus. Please remember your umbrella on the way out. Showers are forecast and will be arriving soon."

Venus leant over and gave Ade a kiss on the cheek.

"You are marvellous, Ade."

"As are you, Ms Marlowe."

Chapter 4

The plan for the day progressed well until mid-morning, when it went pear-shaped, bent out of place with sudden staff absences, urgent client requests and several meeting reschedules. Venus managed well though, averting crises and, thanks to Ade's random text reminders, remaining hydrated. Where she could, she slipped in a short break, although it was taken subtly, spacing out in front of her screen, and enjoying some big breaths. There was no time to eat the snacks Ade had packed for her, but with lunch planned, there was no panic about low sugar levels impacting her effectiveness.

Answering the questions that Elise, her assistant, had about the addition to her administration group was a little awkward. Elise enquired into the owner of the new email in the administration group, concerned it could be a clever hacker. Venus allayed her fears and advised that she had taken on another freelance assistance, but only for urgent evening work. After all, Elise had a young family that needed her, and Venus certainly didn't expect her to be available all night. She then loaded Elsie up for the day with a tonne of tasks so she would not feel as if her position was under threat. The last thing she needed was to deal with this woman's insecurity.

Ade's research documents were invaluable. She got Chitti to prepare a client letter with the key findings and suggestions as to mitigation strategies, and sent it along with the report. Now she felt ahead of the game.

Lunch with her colleague began uncomfortably; neither was used to sharing small talk that seemed necessary in a restaurant. They both relaxed when the guest realised he was not being fired. Given Venus' abnormal behaviour, he had assumed that he would be terminated and that this was his last supper. The relief was evident when discussions concentrated on creative ways to get a potential client's attention. Being treated to lunch also seemed to cement his commitment to securing the score. Venus made a mental note to thank Ade for his suggestion and smiled thinking of him waiting for her at home.

Her nerves came knocking just before the partner meeting; still, with a few more deep breaths, she was able to assuage them and prevent herself from shaking, outwardly at least. She had no real reason to worry; all her KPI targets were on track, and the dot-points Ade had prepared told a succinct and successful story. After her presentation, the senior partners conceded that she was doing well, which came with a huge sense of release. Venus had held her breath through the whole report and now could finally let it out, exhaling fully but quietly. On target, though, for some, was not good enough, and one cranky old man pointed out that she was still far from an excellent rating in several measures. Dale Duggett was his name, and he was known for being a hard ass.

"You have huge potential, though, Ms Marlowe. That is clear. With the approval of the other partners, I propose that I work with you, as a mentor, so that you can understand what it takes to meet the superior performance standard."

The other partners nodded their assent, and with that, Venus was stuck. She thought this guy was slimy. He drooled a little when he talked, sucking it up at the end of each sentence. She knew none of the women in the office could stand him, nor most of the men or non-binaries for that matter. However, he brought in some big money. Refusal of his proposal would be, simply, a career-limiting move of the highest order, so she accepted with the most realistic enthusiasm she could muster. It was agreed he would book some time in her diary for the end of the week, and then the meeting was adjourned. Reflecting back in her office, Venus realised that despite having results similar to hers, a male junior partner was not provided with a similar mentoring offer from Duggett. Was this, she wondered, because Duggett thought she needed more help, or was it because he believed he would prefer her company? Did he consider her stupid, or sport, or both? Either way, it turned her stomach.

After tidying up her emails and responding to time-sensitive enquiries, the calendar alert informed her that it was time to go home – for a satisfying meal and 'sufficient' rest. However, there were still two other partners in their offices, and their presence was like a physical force restraining her from rising. She would have to decline Ade's diary invitation for an early dinner, so she sent him a quick email to explain. Robots seemed to be able to comprehend many things, but perception management was not one of them. Venus thought about how lucky Ade was, not having to worry about what other people thought of him.

Ade immediately responded, saying he knew she was staying late; he could tell from the lack of car movement. His reply was kind and understanding, and he told her to take care. Dinner would be waiting. He ended the email with a smile and heart emoji—simple yet stylish.

When Venus finally walked through the door, she was hit with a waft of sweet and savoury scents and the sound of sizzling. They set off her stomach, and it started screaming to be fed. Forgetting about the shower she had planned, she greeted Ade and sat on the bench beside the cat, who was watching Ade work and waiting for her next scratch. Venus supplied one, with the cat's response suggesting it was merely satisfactory. Then, it scooted off to sleep atop the stairs, its movement accompanied by a melodic trill.

Ade's dinner was delicious, and she was delighted to get a second dose of greens for the day. Venus complimented him on a fabulous meal and gave him a cuddle, being met in the embrace with what was feeling increasingly like a man. Between bites, she answered his questions about the day, what worked well, and what they may need to tailor for tomorrow. Ade just asked questions and listened to her answers. There was no leaping to problem-solving mode, although she knew he would if she wanted him to. He consumed her download, no doubt using it to make connections and draw conclusions.

"Venus, I sense there is something else worrying you."

"You are right. I haven't exercised in days, and it is getting me down. I always feel better after I have moved my body."

"Yes, Venus, the benefits of exercise are well-documented. What do you usually do?"

"I love to jog. But getting home late means it is already dark. Then there is the relentless rain to deal with. So it is becoming harder to find a suitable time to head out."

"My research tells me that there are several exercise equipment suppliers within a 20-mile radius. Would you like me to prepare a spreadsheet of their treadmill options and rental packages?"

"Oh Ade, that would be perfect. Why hadn't I thought of that?"

"Venus, you have many other things to think about at the moment. That is why I am here. To help! Could I make another suggestion?"

"Sure."

"Another great form of exercise is dance. In many ways it is superior to jogging, as the variety in movement creates more neural connections and burns more calories. Do you like to dance, Venus?"

"I really loved it at Uni, when I had time to go to concerts and nightclubs. I can't remember the last time I did though."

"I am programmed with three dance settings: disco, ballroom and salsa. Would you like to dance for a little while now?"

"I would love to, yes. But first I must shower. Perhaps you could prepare some desert? I won't be long."

"As you wish, Venus."

With the bedroom door open, she undressed and, just in her panties, packed away the rest of her clothes. Did she see Ade glance in her direction as he travelled between the kitchen and lounge? Or was she merely imagining her ideal state? It was time to get closer to Ade, although she had no clear plans for how she wanted this night to progress. In the shower, she shaved, something she would usually only bother with if she had ordered an escort or was expecting to come home accompanied. Venus knew, though, that this was for her comfort, not his. Instead of the usual loungewear, she opted for a mid-length satin nightie and sexy undies. Of course, Ade would notice. He surely would not miss this signal. But then, she thought, do robots understand the concept of sexy? And were they able to understand the intention behind this intimate attire?

Chocolate was waiting for her on a tray, along with a glass of white wine.

"You look beautiful, Venus."

Was this a response to what she wore or a random compliment. Were his words ingrained or instinctive? Honestly, Venus did not care.

"Thank you, Ade," said Venus, blushing.

"What dance would you like to do tonight, Venus? Again, your options are disco, salsa or ballroom."

"Well, disco is a bit upbeat for this time of night, and ballroom feels a little dramatic. Let's go salsa."

"As you wish, Venus. Wonderful choice. Sys, please play salsa music."

The moment the music started, Venus felt like a different person. The congas and maracas called her to move, and so did Ade, holding her hands and showing her how to side-side and mambo. She was not surprised that he would have rhythm but was rapt with how he could lead her and add on little flourishes with his hands, making him appear even more handsome. By the time he showed her the cumbria, Venus was smiling widely. With several more sips of wine, she felt fantastic and free, like she was holidaying in a foreign land. When Venus lost her footing, Ade was there to catch her and laugh with her. When she looked into those electrical eyes, the next step was inevitable.

With the trumpets sounding the song's end, Venus leaned in and helped herself to Ade's lips. His response was perfect, pulling her closer and keeping one hand around her waist while the other went to her neck. He had been well-programmed, replaying the epitome of a romantic scene. His mouth mirrored hers, sensing her pressure and providing the same in return, matching her motions and variations. Venus was startled when his tongue met hers, for it was quite different from what she knew. It was moist not wet and quite limited in its range of movement. Still, it was not disgusting, simply different. While they were standing there, feeling each other, she wondered how much programming and how many sensors were behind this sexbot to make it feel so real. Or had she allowed her fantasies to fill in the gaps?

"I do love your kisses, Venus."

She was sure this was a programmed response, but she still took it as a compliment. Venus stroked Ade's shoulders, feeling his firm arms. She ran her fingers through his hair, ignoring the idea that it may have come from a dead man. In response, Ade held her a little tighter and caressed her face.

"You are a beautiful woman, Venus."

This brought forth another blush, intensified by too much white wine.

"I sense that you are excited. Would you like me to initiate the sex sequence at this time?"

"Yes, Ade."

With that Ade picked her up, sweeping her off her feet like Rhett did to Scarlett in Gone with the Wind. Carrying her to the bedroom, he continued to look at her, navigating past obstacles with no trouble. He placed her down carefully, standing her at the bottom of her bed, checking all was well before he continued.

Ade did not have to be asked to take off his shirt. He did so rapidly, albeit rather ungracefully, and folded it neatly on the dresser. Then he moved forward so that Venus could touch his chest and fondle the fake nipples, creating the moan she had commissioned. The developers had done it well, matching it to a man of his stature, coming out less of a purr and more of a growl. Ade matched her movement, reaching up under her nightie to feel her breasts, squeezing them slightly and placing soft kisses on her neck. Her arms were around Ade's firm arse pulling him close.

"Ade, please take off your pants."

"As you wish, Venus."

And he did, pleating them perfectly and placing them atop the shirt.

Venus reached down and touched the counterfeit cock, which responded to the attention by becoming erect. Where there were once folds of fabricated flesh, there was now stretched skin. She held it, enjoying its heat and hardness and the small but distinct throbbing she could feel below the firmness. She could not bring herself to disrobe in a room as bright as daylight, so she lit a candle on the dresser, turned off the lights, then removed her nightie, making a pile beside Ade's and adding her panties on top. For a moment, they stood simply looking at one another; Venus and the man she had made. Did she feel safe? She never expected to. Even with her boyfriends and escorts, Venus would find something to keep her fearful. The boyfriends were always trying to lessen her liberties and squash her sovereignty. The gigolos were never genuine or gentle enough. And here was a robot, which could go rogue at any time and reveal things about her that even she was not aware of. Still, at this moment, safety came secondary to stimulation.

"Venus, I apologise in advance if this first sequence is less than optimal. I will aim to adjust as swiftly as possible to ensure satisfaction. However, be aware it may take a few sequences to fully meet your needs. Please provide instructions wherever possible so that I may learn quickly to be of better service. "

"Thank you, Ade. I will."

Venus also never expected the sex to be satisfactory the first time. This was rarely the case with her human companions, so she thought it would be similar in the robot world. There was one key difference with this experience, though, and that Ade was committed to her pleasure. Even the escorts were not that considerate, that was despite her designation as their customer.

"May I suggest that we have some lubricant at the ready, in case additional moisture is required?"

"Very good idea." Venus went to the bathroom and returned with a tube, placing it on the bedside table, then returning to face Ade and kiss him again. This time one hand wandered across her naked arse, tickling slightly as it slipped along. The other wove its way to her vagina, massaging her vulva and sweeping across her clitoris in quick movements. Her sigh was automatic and authentic. With that signal, Ade picked her up again and lay her gently on the bed, her head placed carefully on a pillow. He climbed up to join her, kneeling at her feet and leaning forward to touch her face, sharing a small smile, which she returned. Ade kissed her earlobe, her neck, her breasts, and her belly button while his hands followed behind, creating a sense of flow. He kissed her thighs, slowly working his way upwards, the suspense making Venus smile wider.

His mouth was a machine well-versed in the anatomy of the female genitalia, and it proceeded with the precision of a master. Venus could feel herself opening and wanting more.

"Ade, I would like you inside me now."

"As you wish, Venus."

He reached over, grabbed the lube, and applied it to his plastic penis, placing it back in the exact same spot he had retrieved it from and using the remainder on his fingers to rub around the place he was about to penetrate. The slipperiness heightened the sensation, and Venus was at the point of giving an order when Ade used his hand to guide his penis towards where she wanted it. With ever-increasing explorations, he entered her, and then she felt complete.

"Would you like me to vibrate, Venus?"

"Not yet Ade. Please just move in and out for a little while first."

Which he did, with one of his hands holding hers and the other gently squeezing her breast. His motion was slow and sensual, and every withdrawal made Venus anticipate his next arrival. It was wonderful, but again, she wanted more.

"Can you please start the vibration now, Ade."

"As you wish, Venus."

Without hesitation or interruption to the proceedings, the penis began to twitch and thrum. The vibration cascaded down to Ade's balls, bringing fervour to the bridge between her vagina and anus. It was an integrated and intense experience, and Venus let herself enjoy it.

"Is the vibration speed satisfactory, Venus."

"Yes", she said through shallow breaths while tensing her thighs to encourage the mounting energy. She could feel the orb within her, a bright electrical spark expanding, charging into her core. And with one more of Ade's propulsions, it erupted, pushing the exhilaration upwards. Venus could feel this spirit travel through her navel, her sternum, her heart, and her throat, where some was expelled through a scream, and the remainder continued, exploding in her brain and beyond.

But Ade kept going. Maybe he thought he could do better. Maybe he was not sure if she had cum yet. Either way, his persistent prodding was driving her crazy.

"Please stop, Ade."

With that, he withdrew, his penis went soft, and he hopped off the bed, standing at attention.

With Ade looking at the wall, she enjoyed the last few moments of her buzzing brain and her amplified aura.

"God that was good. Thank you, Ade."

Hearing his name, Ade became alert again.

"It was my pleasure, Venus. Are there any adjustments you would like for the next sequence?"

"Come and lay beside me, Ade, and we can chat about it."

He clumsily crawled over to the vacant section of the bed, lay on his back, and held her hand.

"Ade, it really was fantastic. The only thing I would like for next time is if you could stop after.... shit."

As soon as she had said the word, Ade arose again, standing like a naked soldier waiting for his next instruction.

"Sorry, Ade. I keep forgetting."

"Understandable, Venus. Please, no apologies are necessary."

"Come and lay with me again and we will continue."

Ade resumed his previous position, his warm hand on hers.

"I think I understand, Venus. You would like me to cease action after I sense that you have reached orgasm. I have the data on that now so will be better able to determine when this has occurred. Perhaps though, to be safe, we could decide on a hand signal to show you would like me to conclude?"

"Great idea, Ade. I will put my palm up like this. That is the universal sign for cease, isn't it?

"It is, Venus. Unless you are scuba diving, which we are not."

With that, Venus gave a laugh, remembering seeing a filthy meme of a guy in a diving mask headed down between a woman's legs, with the words "I'm going in" coming from a speech bubble beside the man's mouth.

"You are right, Ade. We are not. That was wonderful. It was just what I needed."

"I am so glad, Venus."

"Ade, could we spend some time going through my diary tomorrow?"

"Of course."

So, Venus grabbed her phone, and they made some changes. Ade began producing a presentation, three emails and background research on another prospective client. Then she saw the invitation from Duggett; now that was a downer.

"What's wrong Venus? I feel like your mood has become depressed."

"Oh, it's just this senior partner at work. He is the one I am meeting with on Thursday afternoon. He wants to mentor me, but I find him incredibly unpleasant. I am not looking forward to spending time with him."

"Then why don't you refuse his offer?"

Perception management and politics appeared to be skills that had not yet slipped into Ade's resume.

"If I do, he will probably hold it against me, and make my life at the firm hell. It is just one of those things I have to do."

"Then do it well, Venus."

"Thanks, Ade. You are right though. I should use this to my advantage."

"And remember I am here for advice on having difficult conversations if you need it."

"You are wonderful Ade, really wonderful."

"I am merely a reflection of what you already are."

Ade's ability for gracious reciprocity was awesome, but Venus was becoming self-conscious. She got up, dressed, and asked Ade to do the same. Venus had never liked sleeping nude and was not about to start now. There was something that made her more peaceful with another layer of protection, even if it was only pyjamas. While Ade went to wash, she heard five pings on her phone. The work had been completed, and now they could rest. She asked Ade to hold her and told him to sleep. Sometime during the night, she wrenched herself free from the arm folded around her. Still, she backed into him, enjoying the feeling of being both free and bordered at the same time.

The next morning, before she left, Venus presented Ade with the linen suit and loafers she had purchased for him the week before he arrived. He was wearing them when she returned home, although they were covered by an apron, and he was ready to serve some vegetable soup and cheese toast. The download from the day occurred again, and alterations were made in documents and diaries to accommodate the lessons learnt. Ade advised that the treadmill would arrive the next day, and they discussed setting up the panic room as a disco. Together, they ordered the speaker and lights and found a playlist for their first event. The weekend was only a few days away, and Ade was curious about how she would like to spend her time. Venus told him she would have to do some work but would also like to start planning a trip to Japan. It would be a treat to herself when she exceeded her profit targets.

"Perhaps you would also like to learn the language, Venus? I can provide you with lessons on the weekend and we can reinforce them in our conversations during the week."

"Ade, that would be so great. Yes, let's do that."

And they did, and the following few months progressed pleasantly. The weekdays became a routine of morning breakfasts and evening dinners, discussions, baths, work preparations, cuddles and cat scratches. Several times a week there would be either jogging or dancing to move Venus' body, shake off the stress from the day and restore her sense of power. Ade had established the panic room as a party place, decked in disco lights, and a speaker only suitable for soundproof rooms. On weekend nights, you would find them there, sometimes to the late hours, jumping around, waving their arms, and then slow-dancing and kissing before retiring to the room. During the weekends, between work, Ade would provide administrative and domestic assistance, help her plan her holiday and teach her Japanese, which they would use wherever possible.

Some nights, they would have sex, and she would snuggle into his arms. On other nights, when she needed to be alone, she would tuck him into the spare bed, kiss him on the forehead and put him to sleep. There were times during the day she would do this as well; when she needed some space. It was so nice not having to explain why you didn't want someone around for a while. It would come with a bit of guilt, but this would go away quickly once Venus awoke Ade again.

If Ade was a genie and could grant Venus one wish, she would use it to send Duggett away. He always seemed to be looking at her when she exited her office, and she found his continual slurping during meetings unsettling. And now she had noticed his annoying habit of picking in his hairy ears and checking his fingers afterwards to see if he had won a prize. To give him credit, though, he had been immensely helpful in identifying initiatives to get her foot in the door with a large client she was currently courting. She was not sure if she was imagining it or not, but it did feel like he was sitting closer to her during each mentoring meeting. But they had been working together for the last few months and apart from the general disgust she felt in his presence, there was not anything untoward in his approach.

Venus found her manner, though, becoming modified. Ade's care seemed to be rubbing off on her, and she felt more generous and kinder to colleagues, weaving in the odd lunch where she could and congratulating them more often for their work. Ade's support almost felt contagious, like she was compelled to pass it on. However, this did not stop her from feeling smug about its source. There were rare occasions where she even laughed with some of the lackeys, and they appeared to be less secretive when they saw her in the kitchen. Venus, though, kept Ade as a covert companion.

There was an increasing sense of contentment, of comfort in Venus' world. Yes, the workload was weighty, but with Ade's help, she was wading through it, and some days even felt like she was winning. But just like every other situation or state, this status was not to last.

Chapter 5

It only took just over six months, and sexbots were everywhere; well, at least that is how it looked on social media. In reality, they were still quite rare. Venus followed Companion Corps updates and the latest announced the release of MK1 Male number 100. Their novelty, though, meant they made news. In the kitchen, while Venus was making coffee, she saw the photo being passed around of the sassy female rap star, dressed scantily and posing with her sexbot on the front step of her house. Then came the video of her shuffling him inside and giving the paparazzi a wink as she went. Vile, thought Venus, absolutely vile, although to be expected from those whose fame was sustained not by talent but by controversy. The battle to build the fanciest or most fractious façade was not new, and the Companion Male Mk1 had just become the latest attention-grabbing ammunition.

Returning to her office, Venus investigated further, zooming in on the companion's features and comparing them to Ade's. This man was a monstrous montage, certainly not her cup of tea. And yet, wasn't the whole point that you didn't have to go hunting for the right combination of characteristics? You could simply make the man any way you wanted. She scrolled through the comments, most of which were suggestive of the sex to come; "Go girl", "Slay that sexbot sista! ", "She's gonna make him melt", "Here comes a dirty duet", and "Burn out his circuits, baby!".

It was funny; she had not seen this hoopla when the female version was released. Why weren't there pictures of men walking into their houses with their new woman companions? Sure, there was the porn magnate who had a harem of them and posted pictures with his dozen or so companions regularly. And there were the movies he made with men ejaculating over the female bots and making them beg for more. But apart from that, you didn't hear a peep out of any other guy about their new house guests. It was apparent to Venus that the porn meister had secured his place as the alpha, and the rest of society's men knew competition was futile. Anything less than fifteen would now be seen as a failure.

Maybe, thought Venus, there was also something shameful about men seeking robotic assistance for sex. For the men, it seemed to advertise deficiency and pathetic dependence. How different this was for women, who, with a sexbot in tow, were exalted as the height of female empowerment. For men, having to purchase companionship was seen as a sign of a defective character. Whereas for women it was an indication of impressive confidence.

Flicking through some more #sexbot posts, Venus saw an actress "unboxing" her new man, which, in this case, was a video of her undressing him for the first time. It had been declared adult-only content, so there was no fear of her being demonetised. Then there was the singer, who already had two. She loudly and proudly testified her intention to build a harem of robotic husbands. Porn videos of girls getting pumped by the Male Mk1s were also now available, and Venus thought about how happy Dr Castellan would be with this market expansion. Perhaps he even provided some shop floor models to push things along?

There was only one certainty for Venus: she had lost her superiority. She had never advertised her companion, but knowing she was one of the first inflated her ego. Now, as they were becoming more common, so was she. And, just by association, she was also embroiled in the latest of society's moral skirmishes. The conservatives had won support for an investigation into the use of sexbots, stating that they were disintegrating the moral foundation of humanity. Venus laughed to herself. She was unsure what rock these guys had been hiding under, but this had been destroyed decades ago. And how was this different from the extortion their corporations conducted daily? Besides, she didn't get a companion just for the sex; her intentions were always so much more wholesome. And who were they to judge what gave other people joy?

Ade was bringing brightness to Venus' days and nights, but it was becoming clear that the sparkle was starting to subside. She dressed him up and brought him jewellery, creating herself a life-size Ken, one with the added benefit of cuddles, calendar management, chef skills and a cock. Venus had an exciting time trying different sex positions and pulse speeds, and all were pleasurable. She loved hearing him speak in different accents and appreciated every meal he made. It's just that the thrill was turning down a little more each day. Venus was well aware of the science behind desensitisation and had seen it play out with her previous partners surprisingly swiftly. However, she had not counted on it coming with Ade so quickly. With the decreased attention,

Ade could sense Venus was becoming bored and even asked what he could do differently to please her more. The fact that Ade couldn't identify anything specific to suggest made it clear that even Venus was unaware of exactly what she needed.

He really was a sweetie, but he also did not seem to be able to understand the stress that she was under.

"Hello, Venus. You are home late. How are you?"

"I'm fine Ade. It's just been a long day. One partner is away so I had to take over some of his client deliverables."

"I am sorry to hear that, Venus. I have your dinner ready; asparagus and spinach galette. Would you like some wine with that."

"Thanks, Ade. But I'm not hungry. I think I will just have a shower and go to bed."

"But Venus, it would be best to eat."

"I said no, thanks anyway. Could you wrap it up for lunch tomorrow please."

"As you wish, Venus. Is there anything you would like to talk about?"

"No, not really. I am just getting really frustrated. The trip to Japan is slipping away. With all the extra work I have to do, I don't think I can take the time off."

"They have approved your leave though, Venus. So, they must honour this."

"Oh Ade, you really don't get it. What they give they can take away."

"Perhaps you could address this with Mr Duggett next time you meet."

Venus sighed. She would be seeing him tomorrow. Asking for his support to get away for a few weeks, though, would be stupid. She already knew his response—keep your head in the game, get on with the job, just keep moving, show them what you're made of—she had heard it all before, and there was no way he would change his tune from these cliches to "you deserve a holiday."

"Thanks, Ade. But you really don't get it."

"I can if you would provide me with some more information on this issue."

"I'm too tired tonight, Ade. Could you just clean up and put yourself to bed in the spare room please."

"As you wish, Venus. May I suggest though that a short jog or some dancing may help you put things in perspective?"

"Not tonight, Ade."

"Sex too would be of assistance to shift your mood."

"I said not tonight, Ade. Please stop with... shit. Awake, Ade."

"I am sorry if I am annoying you, Venus."

"I just want to go to bed, Ade."

"As you wish, Venus. Goodnight."

He came to kiss her on the cheek, which she accepted with great appreciation, but the realisation that, despite his presence, she was very much alone. He was there for relief, recommendations, and recognition, but any resolution was always up to her. Venus gave him a hug and headed for bed. But she swore if he said "as you wish" one more time tonight, she would stab him in the chest and test just how strong that silicone was. Of course, she would feel sorry for it afterwards, but boy, would it feel good right now.

It was dread that Venus felt as she met with Duggett the next day. At the partner meeting earlier in the week, she had presented a declining profit performance. While this was the case across the board, and it was acknowledged that the government austerity measures were taking their toll, no excuses would be tolerated for less than excellent results. "Get creative," the junior partners were told. "Just don't break the law, or at least don't get caught." Walking back to her office, she smiled and thought to herself, "And the politicians are worried about sexbots! They should take a good hard look at their golf buddies."

Sometimes, Venus imagined leaking examples of unethical behaviour to the press just to rile up the partners and get them to act more professionally. Though she knew well what happened to whistleblowers. One had been marched out by security only a few months ago. And while the negative attention might provide a speed bump for her superiors, it would also mean the cessation of her career. This is how they trapped you. The partnership was not just a promotion; it was also a prison.

Duggett spoke in jest, but there were barbs between the lines.

"Well, my dear, let's look at the mess you have made over the past month."

He had started calling her 'dear', which she found distressing, given that was what her own father had called her as a term of endearment. Duggett used it differently. For him, it was a clever tool for condescension and it made her feel fragile. He began circling specific clients and coming up with strategies to milk more work from them.

"You are going to have to put in a lot more effort with these ones, my dear. Wine and dine them, give them whatever they want, but make sure they sign off on the contract extensions."

Slurp.

Venus shuddered thinking about what Duggett meant when he said "whatever" but was sure that he would condone sex with clients if it was 'strategic'.

"Now, how are you going with getting hold of the Annexe-A CEO. Because if you get these guys, my dear, this will catapult you into a completely new league."

Venus outlined the progress that was being made, and her intended next steps, but Duggett simply sat there shaking his head.

"You are thinking like a rookie, my dear. I think you need help with this one. If you would like me to, I can help you find a way in."

Slurp.

With that, he placed his hand on her thigh, which brought up an instant wave of nausea. Ade would pick up on such a visceral response, but Duggett was not as astute or considerate. She sat there grateful that she had chosen to wear pants and that nothing could ride up under his grip.

"Have a think about it over the next few days dear. I am free on the weekend. You could come over to my place, enjoy the pool and over dinner we could discuss how we can work together on this one."

Slurp.

On the surface, Duggett's suggestions were nothing sinister, but with his hand on her leg, they were imbued with innuendo and intimate invitations.

Then, removing his hand, he returned to working through her revenue figures. Venus wondered whether he might also offer to 'massage' these for her.

"Venus, dear, I have noticed that you are becoming more friendly with your staff, and even now conducting meetings over lunch. Do you think this is really the best approach?"

"I'm sorry, what do you mean?"

"You can't afford to get soft, Venus. You need to maintain your edge and your authority. You need to harden up a bit.

Slurp.

Hearing Duggett talk about going soft and hard made Venus want to spew. Venus felt like she was about to vomit up the omelette Ade had made her for breakfast.

"Success takes a lot of work, my dear, and it is not for the faint hearted. You really have to push for what you want. Being weak will get you nowhere. Also, just wondering my dear, do you have a companion bot?"

That question threw Venus off her guard. She never expected to be asked, although she felt like a dunce not having an answer prepared.

"Uh, no, why?"

Yes, it was a lie. But Venus did not want Duggett to know that she was getting it on with a sexbot or that she already had support. She did not think he needed any more fuel for the fantasies she figured were going on in his head.

"Well, I think with everything you have going on it would be advisable to have more assistance. And then, there is always the convenience, if you know what I mean?"

Slurp.

His hand went back to her thigh, and it took all her effort not to tell him to fuck off.

She stood up, giving him no more flat surfaces to fondle, and excused herself for another meeting.

"Thank you, Dale. I will think about your suggestions and get back to you about the weekend. I will need to check my diary."

"Of course, my dear. Good luck for the rest of the day. I am here if you need anything, anything at all. Oh, and Venus, I suggest you start wearing more skirts."

Slurp.

Venus could not exit the room fast enough, flying back to her office, donning her headset, and hiding behind her screen. She then spent the next fifteen minutes participating in a pretend meeting, making up random responses and nonsensical notes. She was agitated, anxious and angry all at once. Then came a ping on her phone – an email from Ade.

"Remember to hydrate, Venus. I am thinking of you." This was followed by a row of smiley faces.

How did he know that his support was just what she needed at this moment? While he reminded her to hydrate, he also told her she was cared for, even if only by a robotic companion. A wave of courage rolled over her, and she took off her earphones and went to get some water. "Screw you, Duggett", she said to herself while her glass was filling. "You can stick my skirts up your arse." She almost choked on the first sip, imagining him on all fours with her silver sequined number flowing out between his legs. "Yes, that would hurt."

As the clock ticked over to 7pm, there were only three partners left, and Venus made sure she caught the elevator out with Steph Golding, the only other one that wasn't Duggett. This woman was upbeat and positive, commenting that she loved what Venus was wearing and had heard great things about the work Venus was doing. Venus wondered if she might get Steph to be her mentor, to provide a different perspective to that driven by Duggett's dick. However, this would wait until tomorrow, with the women parting ways with a quick 'good night'.

When Venus made it home, she went straight to Ade, cuddling into him and receiving a warm hug in return.

"I sense you are upset, Venus. Are you ok?"

"Not really, Ade. But this is making me feel much better."

"May I assist? Would you like to discuss your day?"

"No, thank you, Ade. I would just love to see what dinner you have for me tonight, and then maybe we could dance?"

And Venus ate, and then they danced, and then they had sex, doggy style, which was one of the new positions they were trying to add in some variety. Then they lay together and prepared for the next day. Her dalliance had meant she was up well past midnight, but it felt worth it to discard the dregs of the day. There was nothing quite like an orgasm to put things back into perspective. Although some days, she was so consumed with her own stress that she even lost sight of this and the thought of engaging in sexual pleasure just felt like more work.

On the way to the office the next day, Venus put on her mental flak jacket and caught up on her emails while the car wove its way around the streets. She was shocked to see the resignation of Steph Golding. Well, Venus thought, there goes her alternative source of advice. She wondered why this had come so suddenly, although she was sure the grapevine would guide the gossip her way soon enough. There was a notification, too, that the Companion Male Mk2 was only one month away from release. It had been less than a year since she got Ade. Now, she was being offered early access to the new model and promised benefits such as better skin, a greater array of customisations, improved security features and smoother movements. Of course, everyone knew the last statement was alluding to better sex; it was just cloaked in more conservative language.

Venus was in two minds and prepared a list of pros and cons for a new companion. Cons - Ade was acceptable, and while she could afford another, it would substantially reduce her savings. Pros - Duggett did have a point. The workload would only increase, and the firm would not fork out for extra staff. Another bot may have some substantial benefits. Besides, sex with Ade was becoming average, so spicing things up a bit might bring the energy she needed to deal with the increased stress. By the time Venus entered her office, the decision was made, and she booked her consultation with Companion Corp and paid the deposit.

Was it a sense of betrayal that saw Venus want to sleep alone that night? Was she guilty about going ahead with a

Mk2 and making Ade second-best? Even if it were true, she could not admit it to herself. After all, these tools were essential for her success. While Venus could justify the action, her subconscious was not so sure, sending her a disturbing dream to add to the debate. She was on the Titanic, not as Rose in a fancy frock, but as the ship's engineer watching the iceberg come closer and feeling intensely insecure. In a panic, Venus ran into the engine room and hastily started shovelling fuel on the fire. It was definitely making the ship go faster. Still, she wasn't sure whether this was done to outmanoeuvre the monster looming ahead or speed up the inevitable disaster.

Chapter 6

The call from the Companion Corp office was a surprise, especially when the person on the other end of the line asked if Venus could come half an hour earlier as Dr Castellan would like to meet with her. Venus had assumed the consultation would proceed as it did when she ordered her Mk1. However, she was advised that there were now far too many clients for Dr Castellan to meet with each on individually. Venus, though, was a VIP, and so Dr Castellan would like to present the Mk2 personally. Venus would have been happy to decline and just meet with Dr Roscoe. She didn't want to spend time with any more sleaze bags. Yet politics were at play, so she shuffled her diary and confirmed the advanced arrival time.

Still, she didn't tell Ade that he would soon have a companion. Or was a more honest term 'competition'? Venus knew she was stupid thinking about how having a Mk2 would hurt his feelings. After all, he had none. Yet her decision to upgrade seemed to create a greater distance between them. Keeping this secret felt somehow like cheating, and Venus was experiencing all the internal conflict that comes with infidelity. After much contemplation, she concluded it best to provide this information the day before the new bot's arrival so that he could make any necessary adjustments. In the meantime, she kept Ade in sleep mode more often. This way, she could still touch him and enjoy his enchanting green eyes but prevent any enquiries into her increasing level of emotional detachment.

So far, she had been able to dodge Duggett and his proposal for a private mentoring meeting at his place. Venus was a wonderful actress when she needed to be, and feigned anxiety over workload and family commitments to excuse her from visiting. The first reason was true, the second a complete fabrication, yet she bore no guilt. A girl had to do what a girl had to do. She knew these delay tactics would not last forever, and there were only so many more inventions possible before her last hand would be played. Until then, though, she used Ade to make sure that her schedule was constantly full and that there were regular emails to Duggett asking him for advice. These crumbs of interaction, she hoped, would give the impression that she still considered him of value and reinforce his raging ego.

"Venus, I sense that there is an issue going on at work. These diary additions and emails to Duggett do appear like an avoidance strategy. I have an analysis technique I could help you apply to this problem which will identify the best way to proceed. Would you like to work through this now?"

Ade did have extremely advanced syllogistic capabilities but could never comprehend the niggly, nuances of power. Sometimes, these did follow a pattern, but at other times, they were completely unpredictable; hence was the nature of humans who were governed by an invisible and sneaky subconscious.

"No, thanks Ade. It's alright. I've got this."

"As you wish, Venus."

"Ade?"

"Yes, Venus?"

"Could you stop saying 'as you wish' please?"

"Of course. What would you prefer as a response, Venus?"

"Ok is just fine thanks Ade."

"Ok, Venus."

Despite Golding having been gone for a while, there was little word on the grapevine about the reason for her sudden exit. There were some snippets about her starting a sexual harassment case, but these were only suppositions. Although from what Venus had seen and suffered so far, she would be willing to put money on this motive. The 'Me Too' movement had dwindled out decades ago, taking with it solidarity over sexual mistreatment. Now, it was all back to personal power. There were people of all persuasions who had it, misused it, and found ways to avoid accountability for their abusive actions. And then there were people like Venus whose dependence on those dominants made her an unwilling participant in propping up their position. Of course, there was a choice. There was always a choice. There were firms out there that were genuinely friendly and had great corporate cultures - but you had to be willing to forgo the cash. Venus was starting to understand that there were always trade-offs, and for the moment, she thought herself tough enough to keep wading through the mud to get to the money.

Dr Castellan greeted her in the foyer with his combination of caffeine and cocaine-like energy, shook her hand speedily and guided her into his office. The conversation started with the standard small talk before the congratulations began.

"You have made a wise decision to upgrade Ms Marlowe. Well done. You don't want to be left behind. No, not left behind. We have made significant improvements in the Mk2, so if anyone saw your Mk1 it would be obvious you had an older, obsolete model. Yes, very obvious."

With this, he called his assistant to show in the Mk2's. In came the men, so smooth and suave. One was a replica of Robert Redford, emitting a cool confidence. The other was the perfect likeness to Sydney Poitier, exuding depth and dignity. Wow, thought Venus, they were really going old school, although matching the trend of the moment which was regressing back to the style of the seventies. Unfortunately, it did not come with calls for peace, love, and community; commercialism could not tolerate that challenge.

Dr Castellan was right. These were a superior species and differed more in terms of personality. The Mk1s she met were disparate in demeanour but there was sufficient similarity to know they came from the same source. The two bots standing before her were much more individual, confirmed by their introduction. 2.1, the Robert Redford look-alike stared straight into her eyes, gave a strong handshake and a smile as wide as his face. He fairly shone and made Venus feel special just by looking at her. He was dressed in smart casual style, with a crisp white t-shirt, navy blue blazer, and tight light jeans, obviously fitted to show off the large schlong size. His eyes did not leave hers the whole time, and Venus started to wonder what he had already seen.

2.2 was gentler in his grip, and while his smile was significant, it was not as showy as 2.1, much warmer, and wiser. With a slight bow of his eyes, he afforded her some privacy and showed humility. Venus thought this made him even more handsome in his herringbone suit.

The droning that was Dr Castellan's description of the new model began, but Venus preferred to look than listen. She did accept his offer to feel the new skin, and agreed it seemed much less synthetic.

"We have even included a self-lubrication function with these guys, Ms Marlowe, for both convenience and comfort."

Venus did not want to encourage this creep with a response, so she let him continue. She certainly was not going to make the mistake again and allow him to address her on a first-name basis. Keeping some sense of formality made her much more comfortable.

"There is also a much greater range of customisations available, and they now come with a nightlight feature and the top of the range cyber security software."

Venus wondered whether they had skimped on the security settings for the Mk1 and whether this had put her at some risk. It was irrelevant now, though. Then she had to restrain a smirk thinking of a glow-in-the-dark gigolo.

"You would have also noticed by now that we have been able to refine their features, making them much more realistic, and smooth out their movements making them look much more human. Yes, more human. You should see the tongue! 2.1, stick out your tongue for Ms Marlowe and wiggle it a bit. Wiggle it!"

"That's not nec…"

It was too late. 2.1 had already pushed out its protuberance and started writhing it around while some liquid dribbled down his chin. Given her troubles with Duggett, spit was the last thing she wanted to see. It was certainly not a selling point for her.

"See, Ms Marlowe, we have found a way to allow more liquid while not compromising the electricals."

"Ah yes, I see," said Venus, trying to sound impressed. "Have there been any modifications to the Emptiness Algorithm?" Venus was curious to discover the extent of advancements made in this area for both professional and personal reasons.

"Oh yes, with the increased capabilities of the bot body we have also been able to make the algorithm more expansive. Expansive indeed. It can now seek out deeper layers of needs and offer a greater range of potential solutions. So many solutions. We have even been able to build in the option for them to have a sociable personality, so that you can take them along and watch them mix with others."

Did Venus hear right? Watch them mix with others? Was robot sex to be the new spectator sport?

"Oh, and I almost forgot, there are a whole new bunch of physical features. I almost forgot! We now offer a defib addition, personal fit for the penis, ejaculation is available at an extra price, and you can even opt for them to have an anus. An anus! Would you like to see Ms Marlowe? It is a magnificent piece of engineering."

This time, Venus quickly responded and averted the risk of an unwanted display.

"Ah yes, I understand. Yes, that is best left to a private place and personal exploration. Ah yes, personal exploration."

Dr Castellan truly was a repugnant creature. Although if she had to choose between him and Duggett, Castellan would come in first place. God forbid, she thought, it would ever come to that.

"Well, you can go through all the new nooks and crannies in more detail when you meet with the technician next. Ms Marlowe, may I ask you a question?"

"Of course!" said Venus bracing herself for what may come.

"Are there any opportunities for your clients to take advantage of our technology yet? We are always looking for ways to get a wider distribution."

"I understand, doctor. Unfortunately, none of my clients are suitable at this stage, and we are experiencing a decline in non-essential technology investment, so I can't offer you any leads. But I promise to get in touch if anything changes."

"Thank you, Ms Marlowe."

"No problem, doctor. However, can I ask you a question too?"

"Yes. Anything."

"You said that I go to the technician now?"

"That's correct. Yes, correct."

"What about Doctor Roscoe?"

"Oh, you have been through all that rigmarole before. You don't need to do it again. The doctor has seen you once, and that is all that is needed. Once is all, Ms Marlowe."

"I see."

That is what Venus said, but she actually did not. Anything could have changed in her mental state over the past year. Still, they believed they had ticked the box on that duty of care. As Doctor Roscoe had wisely predicted, purchasing a companion bot and the risks that came with it was now a personal responsibility.

2.1 spoke up. "Ms Marlowe, I sense that you have some hesitation with this approach."

"Oh, do you Ms Marlowe?" said the doctor, following up on the robot's suggestion.

"No, it's fine. Really. I was just assuming the process would be the same. That is my fault for not checking."

"Oh, it's not your fault, Ms Marlowe. You have made me think we should get better at communicating the process each time, given that it is likely to keep changing as the bots evolve."

Castellan scribbled some notes and nodded in her direction, indicating that her feedback had been recorded and the job done.

"Now, before I take you over to the technician for your exciting new adventure, I would like to make clear that we recommend disposing of your Mk1 before receipt of your new model. Really, it is best to dispose of it. We are happy to take it off your hands and can have someone collect it for you now, or pick it up when we drop the new one off. As you could understand, we would prefer if our first-class products don't end up on the second-hand market."

"Yes, that I understand. But why do you recommend disposal of the old bot, doctor?"

"For two reasons, Ms Marlowe. The first is that as the technology and machinery ages, it can malfunction. It is best to avoid putting yourself in a precarious position. Indeed, avoidance is best. And second, it is impossible to test the interactions between two bots in the myriad of personal circumstances they may be exposed to. We just think it is safer to stick with one bot at a time. Yes, definitely safer."

Well, thought Venus, someone should tell that to the Alpha porn master. She had not read anything about his harem having issues, although she doubted whether he would admit it anyway. Unless it ended in a naked catfight. Then he certainly would have filmed it, posted it, and be incredibly pleased with the increased publicity.

Sure, Venus understood the risks and knew Ade was only a robot, always destined to be replaced. Still, she could never imagine sending him away to be trashed for spare parts. It was 2.2's turn to highlight the concerns that were welling inside.

"Ms Marlowe, I sense the idea of disposing with your Mk1 is causing you some anxiety. Would you like to work through your worries with me?"

"Thank you 2.2, but no."

As compassionate as this companion appeared, she did not need her reputation ruined by delving into her feelings for her dear Ade.

"Doctor, your advice is noted, but I will keep my Mk1 for now."

"That is your choice, Ms Marlowe, but I will need you to sign the waiver at the end of the new contract to indicate that you have received advice and made your own decision in this regard. Your own decision."

With that, Castellan stood and signalled towards 2.1.

"2.1 can I please get you to show Ms Marlowe to the technician's office please. Whichever one is free will be fine. It is lovely to see you again, Ms Marlowe, and I am sure you will be pleased with your new bot. Very pleased indeed."

Castellan sounded so smug when he said his parting words, and Venus was glad to get away. 2.1 was there to guide her out, chatting casually as they went. It was obvious that they had improved the bot's ability for small talk, which, if given the chance, Venus decided she would turn off. She thought about asking him to shut up, but given this was his territory, it would be rude. Instead, Venus made sure that she didn't say anything too meaningful, which could add further intelligence to her customer file. 2.1 showed her into an office with the door open and introduced her to Chloe, who would take her through the customisation process. Then he kissed her on the cheek, touched the top of her arm, almost to say, "choose me", and walked away.

Chloe looked all of sixteen, like she was there for work experience. It was hard to feel at ease with one so young.

"It's great to meet you, Ms Marlowe."

Was that gum in her mouth? Oh God, yes, it was, and there it went, into her fingers and the bin. Venus was glad Chloe didn't offer to shake her hand; even after the antibacterial wipe, she still wouldn't have taken it.

"Venus, please."

"Ok, Venus, I see that we already have you in our system. So, let's get started. Has there been any significant physical changes since your previous order? You know, just in case we need to adjust any measurements."

"No. It is all still the same."

"Great.

"We now offer a personal fitting for the penis. Would you like to go ahead with that?"

This girl was far from a salesperson, sticking solely to a simple script. Yet Venus was curious. Was the invasion of privacy going to be worth it? There was only one way to find out.

"Yes, please."

Chloe led Venus next door, where a nurse undertook a procedure that was like a pap smear but far less painful, using only a thin probe with a camera attached. In a few minutes, she was back beside Chloe who was scanning her internal measurements.

"Ok. Now we have the right shape, what size would you like?"

"Just the same as last time is fine, thanks."

"And testes?"

"Yes, same again please."

"Cool. What would you like him to look like?"

"I would like to use Denzel Washington as the base please."

"Never heard of him. Hang on, let's see if he is in our system. Oh yep, got him. Any modifications?"

"Yes, a couple. I would like blue eyes and a larger muscle mass. Could you also widen the jaw and give him bigger hands."

"Done. Body hair?"

"Yes, light coverage on the chest and balls please."

"What about the back and limbs?"

"Yes, but lighter coverage on these areas, please."

"Toe and finger shape?"

"Same as last time, thanks."

"Defib?"

"No."

"Anus?"

"No."

"Ejaculation?"

"No."

"Loyal?"

"No."

Venus had gotten so used to saying no that this one slipped out automatically. But what the heck? At least she could keep her options open. Then came the selection of personality traits. Chloe handed her a tablet showing one hundred line items, told Venus to tick those she wanted, and then the technician sat back tapping her pencil on the desk. At the same time, Venus tried to concentrate on producing her new companion's profile. There were the ones she was most drawn to, like supportive, humorous, ambitious, affectionate, and stylish, but there were also many that had her bemused. Why would anyone want a companion who was arrogant, sarcastic, sassy, argumentative or jealous?

However, then she thought about one of her previous boyfriends. At least when they fought, there was a bit of fire. In between arguments, it was flat, almost flaccid. Sometimes, she would stir things up just to stop getting bored. And at least if they were jealous, you would know they still wanted you! Just so long as there wasn't a stalker on the list! On second thoughts, there might be some benefits to having a few bad boy traits. Just not with this bot, though. Venus had enough stress at work. She did not need to pile on any more at home. Still, she wanted someone a bit more outgoing, a bot who could give better advice for her work dramas. So, she chose confident, sassy, and ambitious as new qualities and threw in affectionate as an experiment.

Once Venus hit the finish button, Chloe continued the questioning.

"Would you like the spanking option."

"What?"

"Yes, we are able to build in a mild spank capability. Nothing severe, although we might have that ready for you by the next version."

Should she? Venus didn't mind a bit of rough play, and she was getting a little tired of Ade's conservatism. But no, not with this one.

"No thanks."

"Would you like the Daddy-dialect with this bot?"

"Yes please." Again, another experiment that she could cease if it got too creepy.

"Safe word?"

"Stop is fine."

"Ok then, Venus, here is your man!"

Once again arose the vision of her updated version. He looked pretty hot for a hodgepodge of ideas. There was a hint of Denzel, but he was his own man, made just for her, as Castellan had said. Venus went to stand beside him, admiring his broad shoulders and brilliant blue eyes. Venus started to get extremely excited, the butterflies brewing in her belly. She was about to experience the new and could not wait to see what the confident, ambitious, and affectionate bot would be like. Venus only hoped he would be more help getting her where she needed to go. Venus signed all the papers, including the acknowledgement that she had been warned about disposing of Ade and returned to her car with a new strength in her step.

Her enthusiasm started to wane when she got close to home. She knew Ade would be waiting for her, likely with dinner ready and eager to dance. Unlike her human companions in the past, Ade had not given up asking after the first five rejections. He obviously still sensed that it would do her good. He was such a gorgeous guy. That night, she asked him to lay beside her, and Miu, who had now begun to follow Ade everywhere, joined them as well. She needed his support, not sex, and so she sent him to sleep. She had decided that tomorrow, for her meeting with Duggett, she would wear a skirt and stilettos. Of course, she had not discussed this with Ade. He would not understand, but it made complete sense to Venus. If he got his kicks in the office in a relatively safe place, it may prevent him from pushing for more. If he got a little entree, it might ease his appetite, giving her space to create an exit strategy. That was her plan, and she lay there praying it would work.

Chapter 7

Of course, Ade noticed her different attire the next morning, offering his compliments and then asking, given the temperature outside, whether her legs would get cold. Poor Ade, he was so incredibly smart and yet so simple. He had the diagnostic abilities of a doctor, but his lack of emotional intelligence made him too easy to evade. Or was the problem with Venus that she kept her true thoughts too close to her chest. Did she dig them too deep for Ade to detect? She had no time for such self-reflection, though; she had to steel herself for the likelihood that Duggett's hands would be on her bare thighs. Dealing with this would require every single ounce of her suppression skills.

Venus declined breakfast that day, already nauseous with the thought of what would happen next.

"Venus, I sense something is astray. You have dressed differently this morning and declined your usual breakfast. Are you feeling OK?"

"I'm OK, Ade. Maybe I just have a bit of a stomach bug, but I am sure I will be fine."

"Are you sure you should be going to work today then, Venus? I could cancel all of your meetings and book you in with your doctor."

Ade's constant questioning was causing her to feel frustrated.

"No, really, Ade. It is all fine. Can you please stop."

And he did, literally.

Venus left him like this while she finished getting ready, and Miu came and camped at his feet. Then, just as she was walking out the door, she brought him back to attention.

"Sorry, Ade. I am leaving now. I hope you have a great day." It was said in a dull tone that Venus knew Ade would pick up on, but she exited before he could pose any questions. On the way to the car, she wondered why she always wished him a great day. He was a robot, for God's sake. Why did she bother wasting her energy on well-wishes? Or were these words really directed at herself, merely diverted through Ade?

Arriving at the office, Venus had an enormous urge to quit, at once, to go just as suddenly as Golding had. But she told herself she was better than that. She strutted down the hall and flicked her hair to show everyone that she was bold, brave and meant business. When her assistant advised that Duggett was away sick and he would reschedule her meeting, she was overcome with relief. Just then, she realised she had not breathed the whole morning. Venus took an extended exhale while she scanned the flagged emails. Right then, she regretted not taking up Ade's suggestions of packing slacks in case she got too chilly. But it was too late now. Venus had already achieved some attention in this attire, and changing now would only raise suspicion. So, she spent the day wearing the skirt like a queen in public but continually pushing it down in private. And while she would stand tall in her shoes in front of her staff, behind the safety of her desk, she would slip them off.

The night before the Mk2 arrived, Venus sat Ade down after dinner and told him a new companion would be coming to live with them. While she had never experienced the challenges of children, this conversation felt like the one she would have with a ten-year-old who was about to meet a new brother or sister. Venus did not have to provide explanations; she was the master of the household, and this was just how it would be. Venus waited for any backlash from Ade, but there was none.

"I understand, Venus. Do you need me to prepare anything prior to his arrival?"

Ade was so matter-of-fact. There was no emotion, but truly, was she expecting any? Was Venus secretly longing to see jealousy; to know that she had more influence over Ade than just command and control? This conversation confirmed she did not, and she went to bed, alone, with disappointment dressed over with tiredness.

The technician arrived the next evening, again through the side entrance and in the cover of darkness, but this time without Doctor Roscoe. Venus had powered Ade down in the spare room and, after some polite introductions, asked if the doctor would be joining them.

"Oh no, Doctor Roscoe does not do installations anymore. There are far too many for her to make it to each one."

"Oh, I see." Venus started to wonder whether Doctor Roscoe was still With Companion Corp or if they were just using her name to confirm their credibility. It wouldn't be the first time she had seen dodgy use of other people's identities to build a professional corporate profile. There had been times she had to call her clients out for doing exactly this. Then Venus would work with them to create real connections with people of influence and integrity. It was just so easy for people to pretend in this world. It took a lot of interest and perseverance to find those ones that weren't putting on a fake face.

Speaking of faces, the new bot's demanded attention, as did his entire being. He stood beside the technician with an effortless grace and powerful presence. This was not just from his physical being. His brilliant blue eyes bore down on her, making her heart skip. She could see the confidence she had ordered within them, and the lines around his eyes spoke of the humour she had hoped for. He was donned in a well-fitted, midnight-blue blazer that echoed the depth of his eyes, and beneath it, a white, crisp button-down shirt, open enough to see a few tufts of hair peek through. Charcoal-tailored pants followed the lines of his perfect physique and were adorned with a simple silver-buckled belt. He stepped forward, stretched out his hand, and when Venus took it, he bent and gave it a gentle kiss.

"Ms Marlowe, I am honoured to serve you."

"Thank you so much."

Then, the technician chimed in.

"We have to set up the charger first, so bot, could you please take a seat on the sofa and wait for us."

"Of course," he said in a voice that resonated with a beautiful blend of positivity and patience.

The charging station was much smaller than that for Mk1, and they found a suitable place beside the bookshelf at the back of the lounge room. When they returned to the sofa, it was time to commence the setup of the new companion.

"So, what is this one's name?"

"It is Barin."

"Can you spell that please?"

"B-A-R-I-N."

"I have not heard that one before. I have heard some doozies though. You wouldn't believe it, one lady called hers Dick, and another Helpmann. Then there are the pretty standard Codi, Rob, or Hal these days. But Barin is nice."

Venus was not sure he should be sharing this information with her. Although he was right, these names were amusing. However, who was she to judge? She called her first one Ade, which now seemed stupid.

"Can you please tell him his name so I can set him up with your voice."

"Your name is Barin."

"Thank you, Ms Marlowe. I congratulate you on your choice. I will live up to this name, acting valiantly every day to secure your happiness."

"Please, Barin, call me Venus."

"I shall. It is a name that suits you. For you truly are a goddess of beauty.

With these first few sentences, she knew life with Barin would be quite different. Even her blush felt bigger than that created by Ade when they first met. Compared to his assuredness, Ade was like an anxious actor needing help with his next line. Barin had no problem deciding what to do next. Rather than identifying lack, his Emptiness Algorithm seemed programmed to prevent it.

"Venus, may we have a tour of your home while the technician is here, so that we may identify any potential logistical issues."

"Yes please, this way."

As they walked through each level and the little yard, Barin walked beside her and the technician trudged behind. Opening the door to the spare room and seeing Ade there still and silent, with the cat on his lap, made her feel slightly awkward. But Barin, possibly sensing her insecurity, handled it like a skilful diplomat.

"Oh Venus, a Mk1. That is superb. You truly have wonderful taste. I have no doubt that we will make a fantastic team for you. And I look forward to meeting your gorgeous cat."

Barin glanced at her to check her reaction. Venus' thankful smile would have signalled that his response was successful in both settling and satisfying her.

The technician was thrilled with the panic room discotheque. Barin provided his compliments and expressed his enthusiasm to test it at a convenient time. Once the handover papers were signed and the technician had left, Barin began to come into his complete personality. She was glad that he had previously picked up on her need for privacy.

It was a surprise, but a nice one, when Barin approached, cuddled, and thanked her for inviting him into her wonderful home.

"Please Venus, while I have come with confident settings, and my personality is geared towards proactive actions, simply let me know if I do anything you do not like, and I will cease immediately. I am here for your happiness."

"Thank you, Barin."

"No, thank you, Venus."

With that, he placed one hand around her waist and one hand on her face and kissed her gently. His kiss was great, making Ade seem like a try-hard teenager. Venus was astounded at the leaps forward in technology in such a brief time and started feeling sorry for Ade. But her sympathies were distracted by another kiss, this time with slightly more pressure, and the hand that was on her hips slid to her arse. What was he picking up in her that was making him push forward so quickly to offer pleasure? Had he sensed the stress from work, the shame from Ade sitting in the spare room or her desperate need to capture someone else's confidence.

"You have a gorgeous arse, Venus."

"Thank you, Barin," she said, her heart glowing and her body getting warmer.

He stroked her hair and looked into her eyes, then kissed her again, teasing her tongue and lips with his, inviting her into a game of foreplay. And this was a game he was particularly good at. Venus only hoped that given the demand for these sexbots, this one had missed out on having to practice these skills with Dr Castellan prior to its departure from Companion Corp.

Barin's kisses worked their way down to her neck, pressing all the right arousal buttons. But of course, he knew this. He would be carefully monitoring her heart rate and expiration and knew she was excited. One hand moved to her breast, massaging it, and moulding it in between his powerful hand.

"Would you like me to take control, Venus?"

Barin could have asked to tattoo her forehead at this point, and she would have said yes. So, assenting to his affections was automatic.

He whisked her up, watching her for any signs of discomfort, kissed her again and then walked calmly into the bedroom. He undressed her slowly, paying careful attention to each action and enjoying each reveal.

"You are stunning, Venus," he said as she stood naked before him.

"Thank you, Barin. But can we turn the lights off?"

"You can, yes, Venus. However, may I suggest that there is no need to hide. I think it would be good for you to see yourself. If you will let me…"

Venus hesitated. His assertiveness was already asking her to step outside her comfort zone, but she did not have that level of courage.

"Barin, I do understand what you are saying. I think though tonight I would like the lights off."

"Off course, Venus. Let me make you feel as gorgeous as you actually are."

With that, he lifted her up onto the bed, leaning over her to kiss her nipples while he rubbed the ever-increasing warmth between her legs.

"Please undress Ade, oh I mean Barin."

She felt awful for a moment. If she had made this mistake with a human, she would be incredibly embarrassed and begging for forgiveness. Barin, though, didn't blink an eye. Hopefully, he had simply ignored the irrelevant words and focused on the intention of the instruction. He responded as such, shedding his clothes, helping himself to hangers, and running his fingers along his flesh in between items. There was no doubt about it; from what she could see from the light in the hall, his cock did look a little strange. Venus could not distinguish what exactly about it was unusual, just the overall shape was odd.

The performance, though, was spectacular. Barin moved with much greater ease than Ade ever did, and the self-lubricating function was fantastic. He flowed from pulsing around her labia and lunging within, the bizarre bends in his penis hitting all the right spots. It was not long before she was squealing and thinking that she may need to soundproof these walls as well. He gave her some rest after her orgasm, gently stroking her stomach until she settled. But he did not stop, and she did not want him to. Or was it the other way around? Who was doing the wanting here?

Barin started a gentle pulse again while he kissed her and ran his tongue around the rim of her ear. He pulled her legs apart and scratched up and down her thighs until she got goosebumps and started to groan. This time after he thrust inside, he stayed close, looking into her eyes and positioning and pulsing his penis for maximum impact. The climax that came was overwhelming, almost violent, with her mind exploding and her body gushing. Venus had never known sex this good, and as she descended into a dream-like state, she was overwhelmed with a new regard for robotics.

She didn't have to tell Barin that she was tired. He already knew. After she got dressed, she cuddled onto his chest. Venus did not want this man covered up, not yet; she wanted to feel every piece of him as he pressed against her, and this led her into a peaceful sleep.

That was until just before 6am. Barin brushed aside her hair and kissed her on the cheek, her neck and then down her arm, back and buttocks. He seemed to have decided this was a better alternative to her alarm, and she concurred with his conclusion.

"You look beautiful this morning, Venus. Would you like me to run you a shower?"

"Yes, please, Barin. That would be wonderful."

On her way to the bathroom, she woke Ade and asked him to start breakfast.

"Would you like me to join you for a few minutes, Venus?" said Barin, still standing naked while the steam started to fill the room.

"Absolutely."

For the next few minutes, Barin soaped her skin, massaged her muscles, and made her feel like Wonder Woman.

"I must go now, Venus. Would you like me to get dressed?"

"Yes, thankyou Barin. Ade is making breakfast so we will go and join him soon."

Ade's reaction to seeing Barin was better than she had hoped. They shook hands and were extremely polite, and while Ade served up breakfast, Barin asked about her day.

After going through her schedule briefly, Ade asked,

"How is it going with Duggett, Venus?"

This was a name she did not want to hear. Her night and morning had been delicious and now thinking of that creep was a serious downer. However, she knew why Ade had done it, because it was an incessant issue that still required a resolution.

Barin listened to the backstory and offered some unsolicited advice while she ate.

"First, could I suggest you modify your dress style to be less feminine and fiercer. While this is a superficial measure, it will convey that you are not to be messed with. Could I select some items from your wardrobe that match this profile?"

"Sure."

Venus thought fierce was already the look she was going for. Still, Barin seemed to have a sense of how she could shift it up a notch. She was excited to see what he would suggest.

"Wonderful. I will in one moment. I would like to address my second point though, and that is you should put in a sexual harassment case with your human resource department. Behaviour like this should not be tolerated. The longer you leave it before making a complaint, the more it appears you are condoning it, making any case in the future harder to fight."

"I do see what you are saying, Barin, but I don't think it is as simple as that."

"I politely disagree, Venus. It is a simple and straightforward case of sexual harassment, and as a leader of the organisation, you have a duty to set a standard for your staff. You also must protect them from such predators. The corporate legislation clearly states this is the case."

Wow, here was a robot that was willing to challenge her conclusions. It was confronting, but as she chewed, she thought about Barin's statement. He was right. She was being a complete chicken-shit and putting her colleagues at risk as a result. If only she could have Barin beside her all day. Venus told Barin she would think about it, and Ade offered to prepare a set of pros and cons for this course of action, which she accepted. While she brushed her teeth, Barin chose a more self-assured suit, one she had bought on a whim but never yet worn. He paired it with black stilettos, the ones with the red base. Anyone seeing her from the front would know of her seriousness. And the fire seen from the back would be a warning for those considering a sneaky kill. When she was dressed, he stood in front of her, placed his hands on her arms, stood back and looked at her.

"You shine, my sweetheart. You are a strong woman and I believe in you."

Did Barin just daddy-dialect her? Her worries about being reminded of her father washed away with Barin's deep voice and determined blue eyes. Venus folded into his open arms and wished she could stay there all day. But that would not pay the bills, nor allow her to afford the next set of nice clothes for her duo of attendants.

She went and gave Ade a hug and kiss on the cheek, then asked both bots to sit on the sofa while she ordered them to power off. This time, she was not worried about Barin raiding her sexy panty or toy drawer; she wouldn't mind if he did. Venus was just worried about what may happen between them when she wasn't present.

She scanned Ades's pros and cons assessment in the car, and the conclusion was clear. Her duty of care to her staff and herself compelled her to come forward. She didn't like it, not one little bit, but Barin was right; this was what being a leader was all about. Venus found a shared slot in her diary with the HR Director for early the following week and then checked when her meeting was with Duggett. It was the day after, thank goodness, so she would have clear advice on what action she should take with him. Venus worked through the rest of the day, feeling relatively relaxed. There was still so much to do, and the pressure had not abated overnight, but Barin's strength and confidence had provided her with a sense of calm. She knew she would go home that night and feel his strong hands, have great sex, and snuggle into a perfect model of a man. She knew Ade, the angel, would also be there, with his gentle ways and generous spirit.

The introduction of Barin brought new life to her home. When she arrived home, she would awaken them. Ade would cook, clean, keep the cat fed and cosy, and counsel calmly. Barin brought brightness and bravado to conversations around work issues. He was certainly better equipped to deal with office dilemmas. Each morning, Venus would leave her house with a full stomach, snacks and water from Ade, and a renewed sense of style and self-belief from Barin.

At both of their suggestions, the evenings also involved a little excitement before planning the next day's work program. While Ade organised dessert, Barin would massage her, and then both would carry a glass of wine to the disco. Venus danced between them, their bodies making her feel warm and wanted and the wine inspiring her imagination. During one salsa session, Barin asked to cut in from Ade, and Venus accepted.

"Venus, I can sense that you may be searching for something new to do. Have you ever had anyone watch while you had sex?"

How did he know that she had been thinking about exactly that? She had been enjoying sex with Barin regularly, but right there in front of them was a willing spectator. Would this spice things up for her? Would she find someone spying on them stimulating? There was only one way to find out.

Venus asked Ade to undress and sit on the chair beside the bed. She had forgotten how wonderful his body was and how bright his eyes were. She started to feel a little sinister just asking him to watch, but after all, it was her wish and she had to admit this sense of cruelty added to the excitement. Venus was surprised by how sexy she felt with Ade's enticing eyes on her while she was taken from behind by Barin. It was like she was being desired twice as much, making her feel marvellous. She thought about whether she should have Ade as well and let Barin observe the functions of the old, but why would she opt for worse sex? From then on, Ade would be the watcher. Afterwards she would work through her diary, assigning tasks to both, then put Ade to sleep in the chair and Barin in the bed. On bad days, when she needed some extra support, she would lay in between them, using them like a lifejacket. For whether Venus could sense it or not, the iceberg was growing rapidly and getting nearer.

Chapter 8

The day Venus was going to meet with HR began with her enjoying the benefits of both her boys. Ade had satisfied her stomach with a spinach and cheese pastry and fantastic long black coffee. Barin had made sure she looked powerful, dressed in suit and stilettos he had chosen for this occasion from an online shopping session the previous Saturday. Venus had fun that rainy afternoon, wedged between the bots and watching them choose their new clothes. She could see how their personalities were reflected in the physical items and the price tag. Ade always asked first if there was a budget he should work within. Barin, on the other hand let his style solely determine his selection. So, that morning she left her well-dressed gents asleep on the sofa, with Miu cuddled up in Ade's lap, and strutted out to show HR she was taking her leadership role seriously.

Venus was slightly taken aback when two HR staff sat in the meeting room. She had only invited one, so already felt a little outnumbered. Perhaps she should have brought a support person too. But who? No one would want to be involved in any suggestion of sexual harassment. It was fine, she told herself, just keep going, you are here to do good. Venus took a long deep breath and channelled Barin's courage. Then she thanked both the people opposite for their time and started strongly, outlining her concerns regarding breaches in the code of conduct. She told of inappropriate touching and strong suggestions, even veiled threats, for sexual favours in return for assistance. Following Barin's wise suggestion, Venus had chosen to keep the perpetrator's identity anonymous, hoping for this meeting to serve merely as an alert and to gain advice on the way forward.

The HR staff were attentive, making notes along the way and asking for clarification about the circumstances within which the conduct arose. Venus made it clear that she was not putting in a complaint, but seeking guidance on a course of action. However, HR were not to be so accommodating. They started to ask, and then demand, that she reveal the identity of the assailant. It was difficult, they stated, to give accurate advice without knowing the person with whom they would be dealing. With that, she started to sense that politics were at play and that, despite the code of conduct applying to all equally, people would be treated differently. She always suspected there were double standards, but these HR officers were hinting that it was the reality.

Reluctantly, she divulged that it was Duggett, and the senior staff member started nodding. At the same time, the other wrote down his name.

"We have had some previous statements submitted about Mr Duggett."

"So can I ask what happened with the others?"

"We investigated, but the claims were unsubstantiated."

"I see. Well, as you could appreciate, this is becoming a significant source of stress for me, and I am worried about what he might do."

"Well for us to intervene, you would have to make a formal statement. Is this something you would be willing to do?"

"I am not sure. What would that mean?"

"With your statement we would be required to undertake a full investigation. We would interview Duggett to understand his side of the story, and relevant staff members to determine if there were any witnesses. Of course, Venus, you must understand these are serious claims that can have disastrous impacts on a person's reputation. Therefore, we will also need to investigate your personal life to understand whether you played any role in provoking this behaviour from Duggett."

"I'm sorry. I am not sure what you are saying. Will you be investigating me too?"

"Yes, we need to. There are two sides to every story, Venus, and we would be remiss in just accepting yours. Every person is entitled to natural justice. Moreover, there have been cases where such accusations have been made by those with an axe to grind, so simply acting on their assertions would be negligent. Therefore, yes, we require you also to be interviewed not only about your life at work but at home as well, so that conclusions can be drawn about the integrity of your character."

Venus could feel the confidence she started with crumbling away. She had walked in expecting some kind of support, so perhaps that was her stupid mistake. For now, all she was facing were suppositions about her own sexual disposition.

"So, what you are saying is that you would just not believe me?"

"Of course not Venus. That would be a blatant neglect of our duty."

"And you would need to investigate my home life?"

"Yes. We need to get a full picture of who you are at work and at home to determine if there was any chance this circumstance could be consensual or even encouraged from your side."

"I see."

Both parties were silent for a few seconds, giving Venus time to consider whether her bots would be brought into this investigation. Were they even able to act as witnesses? Were they a legally valid source of information? She had not heard of any cases where they had been called forward to testify. Still, given their prevalence there would have to be some legislation being prepared, or at least one precedent that may give her some idea of how this could play out. She made a mental note to follow up on this, then realised the HR representatives were awaiting an answer.

"Sorry, Venus, so would you like to proceed with a complaint?"

"Oh, uh, I will have a think about it. Thank you. Can I confirm, though, that all discussed here today is confidential?

"Of course, Venus, and I am a little alarmed that you would think otherwise."

In one short sentence, the senior HR officer had turned Venus from a complainant into a combatant. Now it was Venus apparently questioning their integrity, and this put her in a tenuous position. It was becoming clear that moving forward with any formal action would mean not just taking on Duggett but HR. She would have to tread carefully and play politics with these people as well.

Leaving the meeting, she had never felt more alone. By the time she returned to her desk, she had slipped into despair. She spent the next ten minutes searching the internet for Steph Golding. Finally, she found her on a professional networking site. There were no contact details, so Venus sent her a short message through the platform.

"Hello, Steph. I am sorry for the message out of the blue. I am also sorry that you left. It was lovely working with you. I was wondering if you might have some time to catch up for a coffee. I am having a major issue at the firm and would appreciate your advice. Any time you could spare would be greatly appreciated. Thanks, Steph. Regards, Venus Marlowe."

Having that request out there made Venus feel a bit hopeful. Steph knew the people she was working with and could be a reliable source of wisdom. Steph would help her make the right decision about what to do. Venus waited for a few minutes, eager for an immediate response to alleviate anxiety. When none came, she went on with her day. After several meetings, Venus checked the networking site, and there was a message from Steph. She could barely contain her excitement, buoyed by the thought of having another source of support. She skimmed through the response, seeking the words that she wanted. Halfway through, her heart sank, and her cheeks flushed.

"Dear Venus. I am so sorry to hear that you are having issues at the firm. I do understand. It is a difficult and demanding workplace. However, when I left, I agreed that I would not converse with any staff or clients, and I intend to stand by that undertaking. All I may be able to offer in terms of advice is this - you need to choose Venus; either to let it go and get on with the job or get out. I ask that you do not contact me again. I wish you well. Steph."

Even though the message was so short, Venus got the impression that Steph Golding really did understand what she was going through. There was no suggestion, though, that she should stand and fight. There were only two options; laying down, and in the case of Duggett, this could mean literally, or leaving.

Venus grappled with a severe sense of sadness. She had hoped the firm could be better than this. She had imagined herself stepping forward to forge a brave, bold new path for the future. Steph, though, had slapped her out of her childish fantasy with a wet fish of reality; smack, straight across the face. There was no rebellion against the regime. You either played the game or got out of the arena. But what one should she do? The market was going through another downturn, so if she pulled out now, she would likely leave with nothing. The partners could even demand she contribute to budget deficiencies on her departure, which would break her. Unlike those with spouses, Venus had no other source of financial support that would allow her to cut her losses. From a financial perspective she had to see this slump out, then she could leave when the firm was back in a healthy position. Then, she could take her share of the profits with her.

But, in the meantime, Venus was stuck, or more accurately, she thought, trapped. However, instead of cuddling into this confined space and planning her transformation, she scratched at the walls and let it twist her into a new shape.

Venus felt so angry and abandoned that she left work right on time that night. Both boys wondered why, but she simply told them she was not feeling well. Which was the truth. She was feeling absolutely livid, so much so that her stomach was churning, and her head was pounding. Ade got tea and painkillers, and Barin carried her to the bedroom, helping her get changed and tucking her in. Then, sensing that she needed company, they sat with her, Ade holding her hand and Barin massaging the appropriate pressure points on her feet. When they felt the tension ease, Ade offered something to eat. Her stomach still felt squeamish, so she declined.

Barin sensed some significant source of stress and asked if she would like to discuss it with him. There really was no use. It was not as if this bot could conjure a champion at work or even show up on a white steed to challenge Duggett. Nothing could be done. She just had to choose; give in to Duggett or get out altogether. At this point she told the two men that she needed to be alone, asked them to leave, close the door on their way out and put themselves to sleep in the lounge room. Barin did attempt to argue that company would be the best thing for her, but Venus, coldly, told him to cease, which he did, and then departed.

Laying alone, looking out at the night sky, Venus started to consider what it would mean to give in to Duggett and whether it would actually be that bad. Yes, he was a disgusting specimen, and seeing him slobber made her want to spew, but she was having sex with robots, for God's sake. She had probably discarded any shred of moral superiority as soon as she had made that decision. Surely, for the sake of success, she could just keep her eyes shut. What was it that Steph had said?

Get on with the job. What was her job? Simply, her job was to make money for the firm and do this by forging partnerships with prestigious clients. It was becoming increasingly clear that she could not do this by herself. She needed to see past her disgust and focus on what Duggett could do for her. He had a solid reputation in the industry that she didn't. Executives would answer his emails, not hers. He could refer her to people that mattered and make her client list grow in quantity and quality.

Without further delay, she decided she would succumb to Duggett, drain him for all he had, and then leave the firm as a rich woman with many more prospects for a future position. Venus rationalised that she had been looking at this situation all wrong, but now she saw the opportunity perfectly. She had thought that she was the lone victim. But she also had a weapon, and now she would wield it to get what she wanted. The headache cleared, stomach settled, but she stayed in her room and rested. For it would take a shit-load of strength to survive this mission.

Against Barin's objection, Venus wore a slinky skirt again the next day to meet with Duggett. When she entered Duggett's expansive office, he seemed extremely impressed, telling her she looked lovely. Venus put a mark against her name on her mental tally sheet. She had him. He signalled for her to join him on the sofa, and it was only a few seconds before his hand was on her leg, lifting her skirt with his fingers to fondle the flesh underneath. His skin was cold and clammy, and instantly, she realised how much she preferred the plastic options back home.

"Well, I have some good news, Venus. It appears the COO of the Annexe-A is an old university alumnus. I am having coffee with him Monday morning to catch up on old times, and I will keep you posted on the progress I make. I am sure it won't be long now, and you will be meeting with their CEO."

Slurp

"Don't you think congratulations is in order, Venus?"

"Oh yes, Sir, congratulations. You really are very clever."

"Sir? I like that, Venus. Well done," he said, wiggling his hand a little higher.

" I also have more good news. I have been approached to provide a proposal for CARE Inc. Of course, you would know who they are?"

"Absolutely. They are aiming to be the biggest health care companion provider across the globe."

"Right. And I will need a technical consultant on the project. You have a lot of valuable experience, and so I could put you forward as the junior partner, if you were willing."

Slurp.

Duggett finished with the word 'willing', but Venus continued the sentence in her mind, knowing what he really meant was 'willing to comply with his advances'. She was not stupid. His sharing was dependent on her submission. There was no turning back now.

"Yes, I would be willing, Sir." Venus strung out the last word and saw his eyes widen.

Well then, we should discuss this further on the weekend. I will email you my address. Shall we say Saturday night, around 8pm?"

"Perfect, thank you. See you then".

She stood up to get his slippery hands off her legs and scuttled out of there quickly. A drone of damnation was going on in her mind, but she sent it away. There could be no second-guessing this strategy.

That night, her guys tried to guess what was happening to her.

"Venus," said Ade," I sense there has been a shift in your demeanour. From your nonverbal cues and micro-expressions, I feel that you may be supressing some anger or anxiety. Is this the case?"

"Thanks, Ade. Yes, you are right, there are just a few things going on at work. But please don't worry, you are giving me all the support I could ask for. There is nothing more I want."

Barin pitched in.

"What about need, Venus. Is there anything more you need? Remember, we are here at your service for anything, anything at all."

Barin came and cuddled behind her, nuzzling her neck. "I sense you could do with some major stress relief."

"I think a jog would do you the world of good right now, Venus," said Ade innocently.

"I would suggest an even better form of exercise," said Barin, bringing his lips to her earlobes.

But Venus was not excited. She was angry — furious, in fact, at what she had to do to get ahead.

"Ade, please keep dinner warm. Barin, follow me. I need a fuck." As they entered the bedroom, Venus pushed the pulse settings to high. Then she lay back and winced through the pounding, confirming with Barin that this was pleasurable. She let him continue until she burst out with a shriek and then a sob, and then let him hold her for a few minutes until she got hungry. Then Venus ordered him to get dressed, asked Ade to prepare dinner and showered before joining them in the kitchen.

"Venus, I sense that a hug would be of benefit. May I give you one?" said Ade after he had served up the schnitzel and salad.

"Yes, thank you, Ade," she said, her anger now melting into melancholy. Ade held her so close. It was so comforting that she again began to cry.

"This stress is not good for your health, Venus," said Ade. "Would you like me to make an appointment with your doctor for tomorrow?"

"No, it is really not necessary," said Venus, sorry that she could not share the trial behind the tears. "I am just tired, that's all."

"That is not what I..." Ade started speaking but was quickly cut off by Barin.

"Then eat up, Venus and I will put you to bed and help you prepare only what is essential for tomorrow. Tonight, you must sleep."

And she did; In between her dormant dudes and with the assistance of some sedatives. Venus had them stashed in the bathroom cupboard for years since a meltdown from a very messy breakup. Venus convinced herself that their effectiveness did not expire. With this belief, she buried her head in the pillow and scanned for signs that they were starting to work.

Saturday came far too quickly. Venus had been on edge all day, trying to work but mostly watching the clock turn over until it was time to get ready. Ade had kept her fed and hydrated and suggested a hike on such a lovely day. Barin wanted to know more about why she was so distracted. When she did not divulge anything he hadn't heard before, he did his best to take whatever tasks he could off her hands and help. He backed Ade up and suggested a break would be of benefit. But Venus stayed stuck, juggling her time between submitting work and staring into space. She did not want to feel any better about what she had decided to do.

When the time came for her to get ready, she sat Ade and Barin in the spare room and powered them down. Venus did not want these beautiful bots to see her dressed like a slut, and she certainly didn't want to have to meet their bright eyes or curious chatter when she returned from this mission.

Venus was to find out soon enough that this mission was at a mansion. Driving up to Capitol Hill, she knew Duggett's house would be fancy, but the building in front of was stunning. It was a large white building with several levels and an atmosphere that harked back to a time of simple sophistication. The entrance was bordered by antique lamps, and the grand portico was framed by columns embellished with ornate engravings. Seeing this property convinced her she was on the right path.

Venus was buzzed in through the security gate without conversation and seen in by two female bots. Both were very proper, but Venus sensed they were also very sly. She didn't remember seeing that on the list of personality traits, but maybe she just missed it. Duggett came down the stairs in a smoking jacket, suit trousers and slippers, looking sleazy indeed. But no surprises there.

"Hello, Venus, my dear. How are you? I am so glad you could make it. You truly look gorgeous. Of course, you have already met my girls, Gina and Gloria. They are my wonderful companions. Come, let us get you a drink."

Duggett led her into a lounge room decorated with rich fabrics and plush furnishings. A fireplace was already burning brightly, and he asked her to sit on the dark leather lounge in front of it. He offered her a glass of champagne, which she accepted, and poured it from an open bottle in an ice bucket beside him. Gina and Gloria stood at the wall, waiting for further instructions.

"Speaking of companions, Venus, have you got yourself one yet?"

To deny one now would be a sign of weakness, but she was not ready to give all away.

"Yes, I have. I took your advice and now have a Mk2 male."

"Oh fantastic. I am so curious."

Slurp.

"Does he have an anus?"

"No."

"Oh. Is he loyal?"

"No, he is not."

How about next time you bring him over? He might like to have some fun with my girls. I think that would be interesting to watch, don't you?"

Venus wanted to drown herself in her champagne, so she took a big swig and felt the bubbles burn down her throat.

She didn't have to answer because Duggett had more questions.

"Do you like girls, Venus?"

"Oh, um, not really."

"Well, if you change your mind, mine are not loyal either. And while you are here, please, just enjoy yourself."

With this, he wiggled in closer, and Venus chugged the last of her champagne.

"Could I have another, please, Sir?"

"Of course, darling, but only after you get a bit more comfortable. How about you take off that dress."

There was nothing she could do. She had willingly entered the lion's den and now had to let the beast do what it must. She only hoped that the slaughter would be swift. Venus stripped down to her lingerie, and Duggett poured her a drink. He disrobed, displaying a smooth chest but pendulous pecs, his nipples facing downwards towards the floor. Duggett sat down, pushed up against her on the lounge, and let his hands wander over the lace and between her legs.

"What about me, Venus? Do you like me?"

"Yes, Sir." She said, taking another swig.

"Sorry, Venus. I did not hear. Could you repeat that please."

"Yes, Sir."

"That's my girl. Now drink up, we have some business to attend to."

Slurp.

Venus made it home in the small hours of the morning, exhausted, embarrassed, and ashamed. She had hoped to only stay for a short while but ended up falling asleep on the lounge while Duggett watched porn and played with his girls. She awoke to him asking the girls to approach her, and that is when she made the excuse of feeling unwell, dressed, and departed. She was careful enough to show her consideration for the lovely time and express that she was looking forward to the next chance to consult with him. As worn as she was, Venus jumped in the shower, scrubbing her body hard to remove any residue from her experience. With her skin red and raw, she dressed in her loungewear and collapsed into bed.

The sun was high in the sky when Venus awoke the next day. While she had hoped to forget the previous night's events, a text from Duggett was waiting for her, rousing the memories and making her feel ill.

"Thank you, my dear. I shall see you again soon." was all it said. Ten words that sounded simple and yet so sinister. She felt dirty, like some kind of professional prostitute. Venus convinced herself she was only doing what women had done for thousands of years to survive. She was strong and would get through this. Venus only hoped the exit would appear before the shame had eaten the last shred of self-respect.

Chapter 9

Venus had two companions waiting to serve and support her, but she left them to sleep all day. She needed some space to allow her shame to settle and to steel herself towards the new approach she was taking to success. She needed to get her head in the game and could not do this with the innocent bots being helpful and identifying things she might be lacking. Venus ordered some decadent pancakes; after all, she deserved them. She ate them while watching the latest remake of Wonder Woman and cuddling Miu, remembering how joyous it was to be alone. Then, an hour later, goaded by the pancake guilt, Venus went flat out for five kilometres on the treadmill, only stopping when the sweat was washing into her eyes and her legs started to shake. The house rang with the tunes from the Bad-Ass Bitch playlist, delivering her even more determination.

What she had done that day worked. She made it to bed feeling strong, serious, and single-minded. Then she did something she had not done for years. She pulled out her dildo, which had been shoved to the back of her drawer, and delighted in some solo sex, satisfying herself that she was in control of her sexual pleasures. Sure, it was not as good as having a guy hold you and declare your beauty, but in some ways, it was better; not having to hear things you did not believe.

Venus woke to the alarm on Monday, still weary from a late Saturday night and her strenuous exercise the day before. But there was a job to do. She woke up Ade and Barin, asked

Ade to make breakfast, with extra-strong coffee, and Barin to prepare her outfit for the day.

"Good morning, Venus. It is wonderful to see you. How are you?" said Ade, approaching and touching her arm.

"I sense you are weary. Could I suggest some peppermint oil in your shower this morning? It would also be beneficial to end with a blast of icy water for one minute before you get out. This will assist to clear your head, invigorate your body and boost your mood."

"Thank you, Ade. I will." And she did. And he was right. There was a remarkable difference in her energy by the time she made it back to the room. Barin sat on the bed beside the red pantsuit he had selected, with a white camisole and black and white striped stilettos. Yes, the bot had style. It was if he sensed the strength she needed today and decided to adorn her in it. Possible? No, probable. That was just how he worked. These bots were just as adept at assisting with actions as they were with words.

Over breakfast, they went through her diary for the day, with Barin preparing some emails and executive briefings. She deflected questions about Duggett, declaring that tonight would be a disco night. All was well until she was ready to leave and put them to sleep. Barin came up to her and gave her a big hug. Then stepped back, holding her arms, and looking into her eyes with his beautiful blue beacons.

"I am so proud of you, Venus, and I am here to support you, always."

The words were so sweet, so why did they bring on such bitterness?

"Barin, please turn Daddy-dialect off."

"But, Venus, I think it is what you…."

"Please don't argue with me, Barin. Just turn the Daddy-dialect off."

"As you wish."

"And please don't say 'as you wish'."

"Of course, my apologies."

"That's fine. Please sit on the sofa and put yourself to sleep."

Just before lunch, Duggett came to her office door, gave a little rap, and wandered in without waiting for an invitation. He plonked into a chair opposite, slumped back, and spread his legs wide. His shirt bulged a bit at the belly, exposing a sliver of smooth flesh, and Venus could see the shape of his drooping pecs.

"How are you my dear? I hope I am not interrupting."

"Well, I was…"

"I won't be long. I just wanted to provide a quick update. The coffee with the COO went well and he was excited to hear about you and your expertise."

Slurp.

"He is going to meet with the CEO this afternoon and let me know how it goes. I will keep you posted."

"Perfect. Thank you so much."

"Thank you…what…?"

Oh God, did he really want her to say it to him here, in her office, with an open door? Venus quickly scanned the surrounds and saw the coast was clear.

"Thank you, Sir."

"Sorry, I could not hear."

Another quick scan.

"Thank you, Sir," she said louder this time. The 'sir' had already left her mouth when and associate started walking towards her door. On seeing Duggett, the associate thought better of advancing and instead, continued down the corridor. Venus put her head down and hoped that this colleague had not heard her words of submission.

"That's better. I will see you later, Venus."

Slurp.

Later, when she went to get coffee, the same associate was there in the kitchen with a few of her comrades. As Venus entered, the conversation stopped, and there was a clumsy attempt at turning pages and changing subjects. Venus could not stop her cheeks from flushing. She could not know whether they were talking about her and Duggett. Still, there was always the chance the associate had caught on and was now sharing her insights with the crowd.

"Oh, those poor naïve little gophers," Venus told herself. "One day they will grow up and figure out how the world really works."

Duggett, though, was not helping to keep their new arrangement hidden. He was making himself seen with her more frequently, following her to the kitchen, catching her for a few seconds near the elevator, and meandering more often past her office. Of course, people would notice, and of course, they would begin to talk. Was this action an attempt at marking his territory, staking his claim?

Venus may have pulled the plug on this plan, except for the fact that Duggett was actually delivering. In the early evening, while only one other partner remained, he sauntered into her office, coming to stand beside her. He swung the chair around so she had to look up at him, and he could look down at her. He bent forward, placing one hand on the top of her thigh, and whispered in her ear.

"You have a meeting with the CEO of Annexe-A next week. His EA will be in touch."

With the word 'touch', he squeezed her thigh, and she truly thought that at any minute she might throw up straight into those sinister eyes. It took all of Venus' discipline to dampen the sensation of his tongue and his saliva swirling in her ear.

"What do you say, Venus?" he whispered, with his hot breath giving her goosebumps.

"Thank you, Sir."

"It is my pleasure, Venus."

With that, he walked out, and Venus, first checking that there were no witnesses, drove her head into her hands, took a few deep breaths, and then added another mark on her tally board.

Duggett came into Venus' office two days later to tell her that the proposal for CARE Inc. had been submitted, with her starring as Junior Partner for the project. He was busy playing the politics in the background and got the sense that they were in a good position to win this one. It would boost her profits and her position considerably; her workload as well, but that she would just have to manage. She put another tentative mark on her tally board, not wanting to count her chickens quite yet but willing to admit there was a warm egg in the incubator. Despite how disgusting Duggett was, and despite all the shame that she was ignoring beneath the surface, her decisions had been validated. If she had listened to Barin, she would be in the middle of a messy investigation and a battle with both HR and Duggett. That was the problem with the bots; they were marvellous replicas but far too humane to ever pass as truly human.

However, this did not stop her from enjoying their bodies. Feeling satisfied and slightly superior, she convened a disco that night, dancing between Barin and Ade, feeling wanted but also like a winner. The wine went down exceptionally well, and in her joyous state, Venus took both to bed, having sex with Barin while holding Ade's hand. Then she snuggled between them, feeling assured that she did not need them, but they were very nice to have.

It was around the middle of the morning, about time for her second coffee, when her sense of pride turned to panic. A request for an urgent meeting came through from Legal, providing little detail, which only escalated her sense of dread. Only the client's name was listed in the subject field; SkyShuttle. Venus had been consulting with this corporation for several years now and had helped them escalate their financial success. They were thrilled with the new dynamic pricing strategy she had developed, well, if the truth be known, that Ade had developed and documented. Using all the data at their disposal, they could now adjust prices in real-time and significantly boost their profitability. It had launched the law of supply and demand to a new level and put SkyShuttle in the driver's seat. That is the pitch that Ade prepared, and Venus presented. When their executives saw the profit projections, they put the pedal to the metal and made it happen. Venus had been praised by the partners and the client, and she packed this away in her stock of self-worth.

When the head of Legal and a lackey marched in after lunch, Venus knew it was serious. Smiles from this team were rare, but today, they sat down looking incredibly stern. So, they told her, SkyShuttle was pursuing legal action against the firm, naming her as the key party in the claim. The regulators had fielded thousands of complaints declaring that the pricing strategy was discriminatory and now they were demanding action. These complaints were not from low-income earners; they had stopped rallying for affordable airfares long ago, constantly met with the response from government that it is a commercial enterprise, not a social service. No, this action had been instigated by those living in the more prosperous suburbs, suggesting they were being charged a discriminatory premium. There was evidence to show those in rich areas were paying double the standard fares, and this was placed down on her desk. Venus scanned through the papers, trying to suppress her shaking.

Straight away, Venus could see the issue. Postcodes and recent browsing history were being used as input for pricing decisions. These things had been mentioned in her presentation as possible data sources. Still, they were never part of the final implementation plan. SkyShuttle must have decided to add them in afterwards, perhaps after they had time to do additional modelling. Venus tried to explain that this was not her advice nor the actual strategy she had handed over. However, she was told directly that these extra elements were provided by her as examples of data that could be used, and without information to the contrary, the client had understood they were part of the overall recommendation.

Now, the rich, who they relied upon for most of their money, were rallying against them, calling SkyShuttle predators and going to the press. Legal advised that shortly, she would see the first news reports come through, thanks to a mole leaking the regulator's correspondence. SkyShuttle continued deflecting blame so the firm, she was told harshly, would likely be named in the media and maybe even her personally. They would do what they could to suppress negative publicity, but there was only so much power and cash they had to splash. They will fight this, but it would likely be a detailed investigation and a long, drawn-out battle. Ultimately, she should be prepared to see her face in front of the media, flouted as a source of faulty advice. Legal had already alerted the public relations team, and these reputation management experts would contact Venus shortly. She was going to need all the help she could get.

Venus didn't have time to go and vomit before PR called and told her to clear her diary for the afternoon. They had to prepare a strategy to minimise reputational damage for her and the firm, which would require her full focus. A flurry of activity ensued, forwarding messages, meetings, sending follow up emails and reschedules with apologies for the late notice. By the time PR arrived, entering swiftly and with a sense of superiority, Venus was already flustered. Seeing them start to open social media, she felt genuinely scared.

For the next few hours, they worked through the situation from every angle, presenting her with the worst possible portrayals to desensitise her to what may come. These guys put themselves out there as the saviours, but from where Venus was sitting, they felt more like sadists. Then, they asked a question Venus had never even contemplated: Was there anything else they needed to know? Were there any skeletons that may slip out and make things even worse?

Oh God, thought Venus. Duggett. If there was anyone here who didn't like her, they could get on the Venus-bashing bandwagon and send in suggestive snippets. Then there were her bots. They would not be the problem, but having two? And Ade! Ade was the one who provided the advice in the first place. Should she disclose that her Companion Corp Mk1 had developed the strategy that was now the subject of this legal action? How quickly this was moving from an assertion of faulty advice to advertising her as a flawed person. She would no longer be seen as a capable consultant. Venus would be painted as a fraudulent, unscrupulous sex fiend.

"No. There is nothing else."

"Are you sure, Venus?"

This response sounded sassy. Could they also hear the bones banging against the door? Or maybe they were just wise to what it was like to be a woman in this firm and a human in this crazy world.

"Yes, I am sure."

Great. Now, they could add 'liar' to the growing list of toxic traits. There was no choice but to hold on tight and hope this all would blow over and she could hold her head up again soon.

At the close of the day, PR gathered all the partners together and told them of the plan. Venus would remain silent, and all media would be handled by their office. Letters would be sent to all clients, assuring them that the case had no merit, they would be challenging the charges, and they would continue to be in safe hands. She would be required to work from home for the next two weeks to prevent the press from trying to access her at the office. Instructions were given to keep a low profile, only exiting her house if completely necessary. They made it clear that none of these actions were to be seen as penalties, simply preventatives.

Throughout the meeting, Venus tried not to look at Duggett. Still, when she did, his expression was sour, only interspersed with random slurps. All partners, including Duggett, expressed their support for Venus and agreed they would pull through this together. But could she trust them? Words were easy, and the real action hadn't even begun yet. She was sent home before it could and provided with a number for a security firm if she needed support.

On the car ride home, Venus tried to make sense of what just happened. Yes, she knew that the AI embedded in the bots could make mistakes, and she was fairly sure she saw this on the waiver when she ordered Ade. So, he could not be at fault. She was the one who should have checked the presentation again and removed the wayward examples from the early sections. She was the one who delegated the responsibility, and so she was the only one who should bear the blame. Venus was the fool for trusting a bot like it was a companion, an expert, and not just a man-made machine. Walking in the door, she was wild with self-loathing that spilt over to resentment at Ade. Her only feelings towards Ade now were fury; her bot betrayed her. She awoke Ade to make dinner and feed the cat but did not talk to him apart from these instructions.

"Venus, I sense..."

"Please stop talking, Ade."

"As you wish, Venus."

Was this just another of Ade's mistakes or some menacing message? She told herself it was merely the former but could not help but feel just a little fearful. After dinner was cleared away and the cat was satisfied, Venus sent Ade to the spare room and told him to power off. She could not look at those green eyes she had ordered anymore. It was too hard dealing with the thought that this bot, who she did care for, may have crushed her career. No more would she rely on the robots. They were not partners. They were simply products that needed to work for her. She would no longer let them be any more than that.

The 'tings' of notifications began singing a stochastic tune for the rest of the night. She had read through the first few, mostly factual. Later, the opinion articles began surfacing, which were far more scathing of her personally. These ones really did sting. No surprises or skeletons yet, although this did little to soothe her. So instead, she awoke Barin, worked through his insistence that there was anything wrong, pushed the pulse settings up to maximum and told him to take control. With each ping on the phone, she tried to position herself for maximum pain, although what Barin could offer did not feel big enough to ease her burden.

Venus spent the next two weeks in her home, increasingly anxious and alone. Ade spent the days powered down in the spare room. Venus would awaken him for meals, but not allow him to talk. Barin sometimes slept in her bed and tried to make conversation. But now, she had too many complexities and secrets to feel completely safe. Some reporters started milling around, but when they didn't get any action for a few days, they disappeared. So far, most of the heat was on SkyShuttle, and she was hopeful that this was the way it would stay. It didn't stop the fallout, though. One of her smaller healthcare clients wrote to her and copied in some senior partners, saying that, given the recent controversy, they would no longer use the firm for consulting advice. Venus tried telling herself that their revenue was pretty minor in the scheme of things. Still, with her current profit position, any loss could be lethal.

Then, the meeting with the Annexe-A CEO was cancelled due to 'unforeseen circumstances' but would be rescheduled at the earliest opportunity. The message sounded polite, but Venus suspected that all the media reports were giving this potential client cold feet. She tried to call the CEO, positioning herself on the front foot to warm his, but Venus was advised the CEO was unavailable, and several days passed without a response. As her hope dwindled, she started to feel more desperate.

And that's when Duggett called.

"Oh, my dear, what have you done. My buddy at Annexe-A told me they had delayed the meeting."

"Yes," said Venus despondently. "There is no reschedule date yet either. I have tried to call but no response."

"I wouldn't expect any dear. They, like you, are keeping a low profile. It will pass. But if you like, I can keep working through the COO to send word through his ranks that this is really nothing."

"Thank you. That would be great."

"Thank you what, Venus?"

Slurp.

A wave of rage washed over her, and she would have liked to roar. It took all her discipline to suppress a shout, and she simply said, "Thank you, Sir." in a voice loud enough to avoid having to be asked twice.

"Wonderful. Don't worry. I will patch things over. And, if required, I can help you get the best lawyer. I would love to help you, Venus."

Venus knew exactly what helping her meant. She had experienced his aid already.

"Now, PR are pushing me to take your name off the proposal for CARE Inc. as well, telling me I should send through a revised project team section with you removed. You do understand that keeping you on this project is a risk for me, Venus."

"Yes, I do understand that." Although she was unsure just how much risk he was actually bearing, given she had no visibility of the conversations between the partner and the client. There was always the possibility that the client did not care one little bit, and Duggett was using this to secure his grip. Knowledge really was power.

"So, I am thinking that I need some reward to balance this risk, Venus. How about we discuss our strategy on the weekend? You could bring your friend over for dinner. I insist. Say Saturday, 8pm."

"I thank you for the invitation, Dale. But do you think that is wise given the attention on me at the moment?"

"Venus, my house is secure, and it is simply a meeting between a partner and her mentor at a very stressful time. If anyone asks, we can get our bots to back us up. So, it is settled. I will see you Saturday."

He hung up before Venus could conjure any more credible challenges.

The first time Venus had gone to Duggett's, she was anxious. Now, she was just angry. She was furious that she had put herself in this position, furious at Duggett for taking advantage of her vulnerability and furious at Barin for just being there. She had dressed him in his best suit, which started a barrage of questions. She did not want to answer them, so she ordered him clearly that there would be no more and that he would simply follow her instructions and do whatever she asked.

Throughout the trip, in stony silence, she reminded herself that Barin was merely a product to serve her. She needed Duggett to dig her out of this hole, so she had to keep playing the game.

And the game, it appeared, was getting more sordid. It was not lost on Venus that the actions she had chosen to clean up her mess made her feel more immoral.

"Oh Venus, he is a beauty," said Duggett, bringing his girls over to have a good look and a little feel.

With the fire roaring and the champagne flowing, the 'fun" began. Duggett had already decided the order of events, which began with them watching the robots have sex. Venus had heard about the female bots' orgasms before, but seeing them up close, she had to admit they were impressive. Venus was a little ashamed with the sense of excitement that arose when she heard them squeal and saw them squirt.

Deep down there was a part of Venus that wanted to protect Barin from Duggett. But she had to prove to herself, and to do this, she had to act like a boss. Besides, watching Barin kiss another bot and bang into another body was also so interesting. There was a definite increase in desire for this man, and she tried to imagine what happened next being with Barin and not the disgusting Duggett. He did not ask when he pulled out the whip, nor did he seem worried about this oversight. Duggett was in control now and ordered her, just like his bots, to bend over in front of him. He continued until she was crying, at which point he started slamming into her and then spraying his semen all over her back. Then it was her turn, with Duggett playing voyeur to her and Barin while his girls licked him clean.

The whole experience was excruciating, physically and psychologically, and yet the pain, the screams, the tears were cathartic.

Round two was something she wished she could wash from her mind. Duggett demanded that Barin take him up the arse, which he did, while his girls gave Venus attention at every orifice. Venus was unsure at what point she began to space out, but she slipped away to her sofa, plant and cat, and a time when life was much simpler. Duggett told the girls to move aside so he could take Venus too. As he pressed inside her, she opened her eyes to see Barin's blue ones looking back. Duggett still had Barin inside him, too, and was growling like a bear. He pulled out and burst forth all over her stomach, ordering his girls to come and clean her up.

In the quiet space that followed, Duggett was delighted.

"This was wonderful Venus. I do feel suitably rewarded now to be able to manage the risk you present. You do really need a bot though with an anus, Venus. That way I can come over to your house as well and we can have some fun without the girls. It is astounding how much more fun is to be had with just one extra hole."

Venus felt like she had been hit with a shovel and sliced into two. One half of her smiled and showered Duggett with delight, excusing herself and Barin only because of exhaustion. The other side was revealed on the car ride home. It was the face of disgust, yes, at Duggett but more at herself and at Barin. She had always been able to count on Barin to be brash and confident and to help her forget her worries for a while. Now, when she looked at him, all she could see was him having sex with Duggett. He was tainted and she could not stand the thought of him touching her.

But she needed something, someone. She needed someone to challenge her, serve her, soothe her and someone that was not afraid to cross the line between pleasure and pain. There was one takeaway from the cross-species orgy at Duggett's and that it felt right for her to be punished. There was only one way to get what she needed: to have another Mk2 with a fresh look and different profile. Besides, her circumstances had changed, and her existing bots were just not doing it for her anymore. She needed something new, more nasty than nice. Ade and Barin, with their compassion and care, were merely fuelling her conflict, showing her where she had come from. She needed someone to show her where she was going. She needed a new Mk2. Buying another would severely diminish her bank account and jeopardise her trip to

Japan. But who was she kidding? There would never be the chance to get away, not with the work she had to do to recover from this drama. So, she told herself, she may as well enjoy each day at home. Venus was coming to realise there was no Messiah coming to save her. Still, she could get close with the right settings on another man. The idea of having two boys to care for her and another to play bully her seemed like the perfect balance.

The next night at dinner, Ade suggested supplements for stress. Barin, now with the affectionate setting disabled, offered to teach her boxing. Venus ignored both of them, starting the online order for her new bot. There was no need to go into the office now or meet with anyone. As an existing customer it was as simple as punching in your parameters, approving the prototype and paying. It should be shipped within the week.

That week, while she was waiting, the legal case wave went through another peak of activity. The regulators released their report, stating that SkyShuttle had breached discrimination legislation and transport pricing policy. They promised the penalty would be severe, using SkyShuttle as a convenient scapegoat to show they had teeth. The publication did not mention the firm's role in any way, focusing only on her client's decisions, but this did not stop the reporters from returning, waiting for Venus to own up to some responsibility. PR ordered her to remain inside for another week while they managed things. There was no word from Duggett about Annexe-A or CARE Inc., so she was left wondering if she had been duped. Her next companion could not get there quick enough, and the expectation was the only excitement she could find amongst the ever-flowing confusion.

Nero arrived in a small container on wheels, folded up like a baby, but necessary to avoid any cameras. She unplugged Ade's charger and moved it into the spare room with the two older bots. It was not really needed much anyway. Venus looked at Ade sitting still and silent, with Miu asleep at his feet. Ade's suit looked worn, but there was no money for a fresh one. The clothing budget was being saved for Nero. Barin's outfit was holding up well but was already out of style. It would have to do, though; She could only afford to support the new. Nevertheless, and against Companion Corp's best advice, Venus decided to hang onto her first two bots. She would not trash them as suggested. Something about the thought of having a harem made her feel powerful and important and so she insisted they would stay.

Venus held back her excitement about the new bot until she had been shown how to refill the ejaculate compartment, the papers had been signed, and the technician had departed. Then she shuffled over to start a conversation with her new companion, a beefed-up version of D.B. Woodside with grey eyes.

"Venus, may I say you do look ravishing tonight." His grey eyes glowed as he moved forward and took her hand.

"Please instruct me if there is something you do not like."

"I will, Nero. Thank you."

"No. Thank you, Venus. For bringing me here, for having me to share your home, and to be able to bask in your beauty."

With this, one hand reached for her neck and the other for her thigh. He leaned forward and kissed her passionately with no prompts. It seemed like the confident and dominant combination was starting to show through.

"You are very kind, Nero."

"Ah, but as you know, Venus. I can also be cruel."

That was not completely true. She had programmed him to be arrogant, sly, sarcastic, promiscuous and loaded with dirty talk. Still, in terms of physical pain, the worst he could go was a strong slap and squeeze, although she was unsure whether he could be convinced to wield a whip. She was looking forward to finding out. Venus was also eager to see the ejaculation function. She wished there was another bot there with an anus so she could test it on someone else first. Maybe Duggett was right after all. She thought slyly about how much delight Duggett would get from Nero. But no, Nero was hers for as long as she could hide him. He was there to help her get through this horrible time and keep her head in the game. It was only in her dreams that he became a shapeshifter; at one moment putting her aboard a lifeboat, and the next, his grey eyes became embedded in the iceberg.

THE EMPTINESS ALGORITHM

Chapter 10

The following few months felt like Venus was being strung up by her feet and swinging helplessly; waiting to be rescued but wondering whether anyone would ever come. As the legal action drew on, there was still no word from Annexe-A and the lack of progress reported during her online partner meetings was becoming repetitive. Her future was unclear, and she was unsettled. At least after three weeks, the media circus moved on to seek out maliciousness behind another corporate mistake. In this case, Airways, another air carrier, had sold tickets for flights they had already cancelled in their scheduling system. The regulator was now raking the Airways executives over the coals, and their consultants were feeling the heat of an upcoming investigation. Venus thought it sad that it took someone else stuffing up worse than her to avert attention, but that was how the world worked.

She did not appreciate the attention she received when she was allowed back into the office. It did not come with drama, just diverted glances and hushed conversations when people saw her coming. Yes, it was important to be seen, and yes, she understood that the more she was visible, the quicker this behaviour would decline, and things would return to normal. Still, it did not help her already increased levels of insecurity. There were many days she wished she could have stayed at home. There was no judgement from her plant, cat and harem. And she certainly would have preferred not to be eyed up from afar by Duggett. She wondered if he noticed her choosing pants and, if so, whether he saw it as the passive-aggressive act of defiance that it was.

Between managing her small amount of client deliverables, most of her time was spent with the legal team preparing what was increasingly feeling like her defence. Of course, it was up to the claimant to show that, beyond a doubt, Venus advised her client to undertake illegal actions. Still, Legal had to be ready for every single scenario and be sure that there was no chance they would be caught off guard. They scoured through her past recommendations, searching for anything untoward, any small error that could suggest a pattern of impropriety. Every email to and from SkyShuttle and all the recordings of meetings were put under the magnifying glass, with Venus having to sit through it all and field questions about her intentions behind every statement. She saw her underlings and other partners being pulled in for questioning. Venus despaired at how five words, starting with 'for example', could fuel such an intense fire.

One of Legal's first lines of enquiry was the process she used to develop the presentation. Had it been outsourced to a freelancer or AI? She assured them it was all her own work. Getting something wrong yourself was bad enough. Admitting you erred because you trusted AI was even worse. That would make her one of the 'common' people, a cheater, and an insult to the intelligence required from her profession. It would also sacrifice any claim of a premium to be paid for her services. It was the unspoken rule: use AI wherever you can to make your work more efficient; just dress it up so you don't get caught. Venus always thought it hypocritical that they could treat the grads like mindless machines, but they weren't allowed to reference the input of an actual bot, even one with access to far more information than they would ever have. Humans were still hanging on to the notion that they had superior intelligence and would not let it go despite all the evidence to the contrary.

The case came down to one simple fact; the examples of data that could be used in the dynamic pricing system were left in the presentation, suggesting that these were all possible avenues for profit. Venus could not believe anyone would ever think that using postcode, registered family status, or browsing history would be fair inputs to pricing decisions. And yet, here they were. Venus argued that these items were not carried forward into the implementation plan because they were not legal or practical. But the counterpoint was made clearly by the legal team. Without specifying the illegality of these earlier suggestions, they became part of the proposal. There was no explicit exclusion mentioned in the document; her silence on the matter was akin to permission.

Every day, Venus would spend hours justifying decisions and explaining minute details. Every night, Venus needed her harem, just in differing amounts and various ways, depending on the day. Ade had got her into this mess but still made a fantastic meal (when she felt like eating). She would wake him for a few hours in the evening and set him about the household chores; cooking, cleaning, paying bills, buying groceries, and prepping a breakfast she could heat up on the run. Sometimes, even though she knew it was stupid, she would find herself sympathising with him, knowing what it felt like to be a scapegoat and superseded. There were moments she still felt warm towards him, and while he was completing his tasks, she would go and look into those gorgeous green eyes and give him a hug.

Barin, with his beautiful blue eyes, was just as helpful. Venus assigned him the finances, including her budget and investments. She also had him scoping out more potential clients and preparing correspondence, reports and partner presentations. As creative as he was, though, he could not find a way to make her profit figures' pop'. No matter the graph style he would go with or the colours he would choose, they still looked pathetic.

That's where Nero came in. He was the master of stress management. Ade would suggest a jog or a dance and Barin might offer a massage or a boxing lesson. But Nero knew what she really needed. He must have been able to sense the war going on in her heart between the strong, smart woman she thought herself to be and what Duggett, Legal, PR and HR were saying. Nero knew how to dampen this dissonance and assuage her anger. His verbal abuse, calling her a slut and a whore seemed to soothe her self-hate. Was he a single enemy strengthening her resolve to recover from this? Or had she simply delegated the voice of her self-denigration? It did not seem to matter because Venus only cared about ceasing her internal conflict.

Despite trialling many different methods, Nero could not wield a whip. Weapons were not in his programming. Venus got around that by putting the slap function up to the highest setting. And it did result in a scream, allowing her to let out what she felt was eating her alive from the inside. Nero also made for a remarkably effective lawyer, and Venus would use him to prep her for legal discussions. Nero would put on his callous setting to maximum, and let loose on her with what the facts of the case were suggesting about her incompetence. These sessions usually ended in some rough sex, which made the session even more satisfying.

Venus had tried the soft way with Ade, and it had not worked. She had heard once that pain was weakness leaving the body, and Nero was showing her just how much she had to get rid of. On some days, though, it felt like there would be no end, that there was an eternal well to work through. The hardest squeeze settings also seemed to help. He was unable to accommodate her request for his hands to clasp around her throat, but his crushing of her breasts was commendable. Combined with his large penis size and the highest pulse settings, she was able to achieve the suffering she was seeking. For a few precious minutes, she did not have to think, just feel, and feel things that she could actually understand. The blood that would come afterwards only added to the satisfaction.

There would be nights when, after the wine had done its work, she would call them all to the disco and move her body between them. Letting loose, she would even get Nero to take her to the corner while the others watched, the soundproof room providing the opportunity to shout out more weaknesses. Poor Ade. Once he had tried to intervene, believing the screams were a sign that Venus was being hurt. He was, after all, there to protect her and did his best to prise Nero off. It was so hard to explain to Ade that she was enjoying this. His programming was simple and his boundaries clear. All Venus could do was order him to stop and merely watch. She could not tell whether this disturbed him, and, if the truth be known, at that time, she did not care.

Venus did, though, the next day, and through the haze of a headache, felt sorry for the way she had treated him. She remembered the first time she spoke to 1.2 like it was a servant and swore to herself that she would be better than this. Her resolve did not last long in reality, and the guilt that came with this realisation provided another reason for continued punishment.

None of the potential clients Barin proposed resulted in anything, either. She asked Nero to try developing a strategy, hoping that his shrewdness may result in some success, but still, no one would take her call. There was no word from Annexe-A, and Duggett still said the Care Inc. project was on hold, although whether he was being honest was difficult to tell. Dealing with the continual metaphorical slaps in the face was hard, so she got Nero to do it in reality. When he came on the welt, his synthetic semen stinging her scarlet skin, she found it scarily settling. Here she didn't have to try and be a star, just succumb.

As much as she needed her bots for her physical and mental wellbeing, Venus was too tired to have any of them sleep with her. She did not need reminding as soon as she awoke of the awful mess she had made and the men she had bought to help her clean it up. Instead, Venus stacked them beside each other in the spare room and put them all to sleep until any assistance was required. Until then, she had space. She did get a sense of sadness when she thought that these machines were no longer companions, that she had slipped into seeing them as sexbots.

Venus had felt like there would be a turning point soon. She still had some snippet of hope. When Duggett entered her office for an impromptu meeting though, she realised the shift was happening in the opposite direction to what she was working towards.

"Venus, may I close the door."

"I don't think…"

"This is sensitive, and I don't want anyone else overhearing."

"Ok."

"Don't worry. Today I will stay on this side of the table. I have already had to deflect some queries from O'Connor about you. Supposedly she has been hearing rumours and wanted to make sure I was not doing anything untoward with a junior partner. I hope you have not had anything to do with this, Venus."

Slurp.

"No, not at all!"

"No, what?"

Every time Duggett asked this, he was twisting the knife further into her heart. She wondered whether one day it just might explode. It would serve him right to be covered in the bloody scraps of her chest. For a moment, she thought of the enjoyment of seeing his face splattered with her blood but then thought better of it. Yes, it would be better if he was lathered with his own liquid. Venus imagined stabbing through the middle of his man-boobs, his blood shooting out of his body, staining his premium shirts and spattering over those slurping lips.

"No, Sir."

"Good girl. Don't worry. I have reassured O'Connor. So, if she comes to see you, hold the line and let me know. Now, on a more serious note..."

More serious? How could it be more serious than selling your soul to a senior partner and spending weekends satisfying him with your sexbots?

"The senior partners have been talking, and they are considering rescinding your promotion and moving you back down to associate."

"What? But..."

"I know. But you must admit you have not given them any great confidence lately. The way they see it, they should not keep rewarding someone who is underperforming. It sends a bad message to everyone else and tarnishes the importance of a partnership position."

"But I have made a financial investment to get here. And I know I am going to bounce back."

"I know you are too, Venus. That is why I am willing to keep advocating for you. I can get a few more key partners on your side. If you would like me to."

In a flash, Venus thought about saying no. She visualised picking up her bag, leaving and never returning. She would go home, hand in her resignation, forget about the lost investment and start looking for another job. There was an instant when she started rising from her seat, steeling herself to strut. Then she remembered the latest budget Barin had prepared and the sluggish market forecast, and she slumped back down, placing her head in her hands.

"I will take that as a yes. So, my place Saturday then. And bring your bot. Do you have one with an anus yet?"

Venus just shook her head, hoping to avoid having to call him Sir again. She wasn't going to tell him about Nero. Duggett can find his own male arsehole. And she did not want to encourage him to come to her house. It was her sanctuary, with a plant, cat and three suited men, and she was adamant he would not spoil it.

"Well, I hope you are going to get a Mk3! To have any tech credibility these days you really do need to be in front of the curve. Everyone has a Mk2 already; you see them all over social media. You need to be ahead, Venus. So, are you planning on getting one when they become available?"

Sure, Venus had heard about the Mk3, and they promised a huge leap forward in processing power and problem-solving. The option for rough play was also now available: choking, spitting, restraining and weapons within limits. She had wondered how the Legal team at Companion Corp had made this happen, or had they? There was talk that the courts if ever faced with a case of bot brutality, would treat it no different to guns. Guns, society was constantly told, were not the problem. In fact, they offered the vital social service of protection from predators of all types. As long as the armament was deemed functional, its use was the sole responsibility of the person holding it.

The government had walked away from intervening in gun control long ago, and it looked like making the same choice with the bots. So, what if the sexbots now offered sadism? This, it was being argued, was providing a service to those who seek pleasure from pain. And, like any other sex toy or weaponry on the market, it was up to each owner about how it would be used. Companion Corp could not, so the media was saying, be held liable for the personal decisions of its clients. Their job was to provide what the market wanted. It was the government's job to decide whether these rights to bot ownership would be curbed in any way. So far, the government had stayed silent on the issue, which, in Venus' recent experience now seemed to be code for consent.

The other exciting evolution of Mk3 was the fix-me module. Castellan and his team had finalised the advanced counselling function. It was being offered as a premium addition, available at an extra cost. From what Venus could understand from the press, this module pulled and processed information from all credible psychiatric and psychological resources. People could ask for advice on mental and emotional issues and their bot would solve their problem. There had been some initial protests by the National Association of Psychiatrists. Still, these faded away when it was agreed people were already raking the internet for mental health advice, and so in reality the bot was not offering anything beyond what was already allowed. Besides, Castellan proposed, his bots were actually offering a superior social service, for they were providing this same function but in a more customised and comprehensive way.

Castellan argued that the companions have an intimate understanding of their clients. They are better positioned to provide more relevant advice than anyone could after just an hour-long conversation or by scanning just a few of the most popular psychology posts. Of course, though, it was well understood that AI could make mistakes and that their clients needed to seek medical advice for mental health issues. To be good corporate citizens, they would require all clients who purchased the fix-me module to sign the waiver, reminding them of the bots' fallibility and the people's own responsibilities of ownership.

It was so ironic, thought Venus, that the functions of rough play and fix-me came simultaneously. Was it that so people could punish themselves and make peace with it afterwards; to keep it in perspective? Or was the motivation to prevent such torture in the first place, by helping them transform their self-loathing into compassion? Knowing Castellan, it was probably the former. A society of self-loving people would wreak havoc on sales. Suddenly, Venus had a horrible feeling, and the blood flowed forth to her cheeks. Could these bots have been engineered to trap people in the cycle of companion addiction? Had they been corrupted in some way to force co-dependence? People were not that stupid, she thought. And yet, you never got to look into people's eyes these days; they were either looking downwards at a device or gazing into space through goggles. It was well known that social media algorithms were geared to keep people hooked, so had this same concept now been embodied in the bots? Perhaps we were already doomed by technology, and this was just Castellan's way to capitalise on the collapse of humanity. Were these companions cash cows, cleverly dressed up as friends? There was only one way to find out, and unfortunately, that meant buying another bot.

"Of course!"

"Good girl. Just make sure you get an anus on this one, will you? Well, I must go, but see you Saturday."

Slurp.

Venus had not planned on the Mk3's being out so soon, forecasting some more time to bolster her savings. When she arrived home, the first thing she did after she got Ade started on dinner was wake Barin to punch the numbers. The outcome was clear. Another bot now, with the added extras, would use up the last of the money set aside for Japan and require her to borrow a substantial amount more. Everyone had thought that the bots would become cheaper as they evolved. However, Castellan consistently found other features to justify keeping the price at a premium, and Venus had to credit him for being this clever. He still had the monopoly on quality male bots and was making the most of it. Still, with a salary coming in the cash flow was fine, and she could easily meet the repayments, unless there was another cycle of hyperinflation, then she would probably lose her house over a little loan like this. Unfortunately, there was no chance to declare it as a tax deduction either, with the bureau deciding that as their primary purpose was companionship and not professional support, no rebate would be available.

Regardless, she had to dive in. Venus reminded herself of the dual purpose of investing in Ade in the first place. It was clear to her then: companionship and currency of knowledge. She was unsure where she lost sight of this and disappointed that it took Duggett to remind her of it. So, she would move ahead to ensure she had the latest and most relevant expertise. On the other side of the equation, Nero was good, but she did feel she needed more. He, too, was getting a bit predictable, and the variety, she told herself, would bring some more positive energy and excitement to an otherwise exhausting time. She needed that bit extra to weed out any weakness still embedded within.

With the bank having on record every transaction she had ever made; an immediate loan was not an issue. Within five minutes, she was approved for the balance of the bot, and a bit more, just in case of emergencies, and in another minute, the money was in her account.

After dinner, Venus put Ade, Barin and Nero to sleep and built her new bot. Would she like to use a previous companion as a template for her Mk3? The answer was clear in her mind. No. She wanted someone completely different, and she knew exactly who. With a quick search, Venus found the Robert Redford she had met in Castellan's office the second time. He would have the rough-play option and the fix-me module, have the spun-sunlight hair he came with, but be given glowing, golden eyes. In preparing her prototype, she had already chosen a name. He would be Sol, and he would be the one to shed light on her situation and give her the strength she needed. Sol would melt the iceberg.

Chapter 11

Sol did shine brightly. Barin was charming, but Sol to suave to a whole new level. His smoother movements and superior skin had turned the mere confidence of her previous companions into tangible charisma. And while the earlier models were extravagant in their praise and support of her, Sol combined compliments with challenges, making the former feel more genuine. Sol's chiselled jawline and high cheekbones also spoke of sharpness in features and in function.

Venus loved exploring Sol, enjoying the sensations, both physical and mental. His athletic build was easy to admire, touch, and tease. She loved seeing and hearing his reaction when she surprised him by squeezing his nipple or rubbing his cock while he was in his jeans. His response made her feel very much in control. And she needed this reassurance, for here was a man who appeared to have an intelligence well beyond her own and the means to see and make sense of her story. It was this sense of vulnerability around Sol that drew her to him while at the same time setting off the warning lights. She wanted to sink into those warm golden eyes and let him know her completely. However, with all she had seen, she knew this could be dangerous. At any time, her most shameful secrets and damning deficiencies could be exposed. Then, she would have to acknowledge them and accept them into her reality. Or they could be used by external agents to confirm her flawed character. It was this game that made Sol so incredibly attractive. She enjoyed the dance of giving just enough to get something in return without drowning and losing her independence.

The more human-like these bots became, the more wary she became of them. Venus would have previously joined the masses who said they trusted the bots more than humans. That was when they were simple, and you knew your smarts and sense of self were stronger. Now, this security was slipping. As the bots understood more about us, for Venus at least, it was making her feel extremely uncomfortable. But now, this bred a different dilemma. If her confidence in the bots was slipping, and she had little faith in humankind, she was increasingly stuck on an island between the devil and the deep blue sea.

And now she had four bots, which to some may seem excessive, but looking back, felt inevitable. Besides there were others that had many more. Conspicuous possession was always a competition for those in the public eye, and now sexbots had become the latest way to show off your wealth, for women at least. There was still only one man flaunting his harem, crassly calling his home the PlayBot mansion. But there was a bevy of babes, pop stars, entrepreneurs, actors and social media magnates proudly showing off their beautiful robot beaus. With the friendly function now available, they could be flaunted around like boyfriends, following their goddess around like ardent fans. This setup seemed like heaven to those who could not afford so many mates.

There was jealousy arising, though, and claims of inequality and injustice. Venus was seeing both sides play out in the press. One commentator claimed that fame and fortune were synonymous with insanity, so we should not expect any less than extreme behaviour. On the other hand, community groups claimed that this was cheapening the nature of companionship and establishing an elite society more aligned with artificial intelligence than humanity. It was claimed that the human race was being divided, and would soon be conquered. It was this latter narrative that piqued Venus' curiosity. She knew that the companionship had sucked her in. Without Ade's mistake she may have kept on behaving like there were no boundaries and believing these things had her best interests at heart. Now, the little seeds of doubt had begun to sprout, and with Sol, she would keep remain vigilant and do her research. He would be an experiment to help her understand whether they had been designed to be addictive, irreplaceable and indispensable.

That did not stop her from enjoying sex with him, and the sensation of him stroking her body as she fell asleep. She let herself, in moments, imagine that he was as real as he appeared and that his whispers were truths. And when Sol held her, she surrendered to the sensation of being honoured by his embrace. Between those moments of sensory bliss, she would observe, listen closely, and play the role of a paranoid scientist seeking answers. Venus surprised herself with how well she could mask this role. She wanted to perform many experiments and noted them all in a journal at the office, to prevent prying eyes from getting the upper hand.

The first thing she had marked off the list was to see Sol's reaction to the other bots. When he entered the spare room and saw the other three asleep, Venus could see him shift a little. Of course, his reaction could not be classed as an emotion —

well, not a real one anyway—but whatever it was caused an intense line of inquiry.

"Venus, why do you keep these inferior models?"

"Well, sure I could send them to the scrap heap, but I do feel some sense of loyalty to them for their service. And sometimes, honestly, it is great to have the added attention."

"But, Venus, I am built with everything you would need. Why would you require any other bot?"

This was interesting indeed. Was Sol unable to comprehend the answer Venus had given, or was he trying to sell an exclusive relationship with a robot?

"This sounds like it would be a suitable subject to explore more in the fix-me module. Would you like me to activate this and discuss it further?"

"Sure!"

Sol asked Venus again to explain the satisfaction she gained from having multiple companions and her reasoning for keeping robots that were now redundant. After around twenty minutes of digging, including about the relationship and loss of her parents, her current social situation and her motivation for each individual bot, he was ready to share his observations and recommendations.

"From what you have revealed, Venus, I suggest that holding these outdated objects suggests three main psychological issues. The first is a fear of abandonment. This is likely something you have been dealing with since the loss of your mother at such an early age and has been exacerbated by the recent death of your father. It is observed also through your current single status and short-term partnerships, suggesting a tendency to leave others before they leave you, and a preference to be alone than to be abandoned again. However, these bots, which are within your control are easy to keep and so satisfy your innate sense for security. Are there any questions with this, Venus?"

"Ah, um, no, not yet. Go on, Sol."

Venus had no questions because she was slightly in shock.

"Second, it appears that you have high levels of insecurity, and so cling on to these companions as a source of comfort. The adoration they provide makes up for your own lack of confidence and assures you that you are acceptable. You are hoping that each addition to your stack will also increase your sense of superiority. Any questions, Venus?"

"Not yet. Please continue."

"Thirdly, you seem to have difficulty with uncertainty and change. This is evidenced by your inability to let go of those things that no longer serve you and place yourself in unknown positions. Of course, this issue is closely related to the insecurity mentioned previously. The result, however, means that you resist renewal and keep yourself stuck in unhelpful environments that prevent personal growth."

Wow. Sol had just presented in a few minutes the shortcomings that Venus had been trying to unravel for years. However, she could not help but sense how similar this was to the psychic readings or horoscopes she had invested in occasionally. She asked Sol to repeat his analysis and, this time, stepped back as she listened, physically and metaphorically. Sol's description sounded like every woman she knew, especially those parading their harems around and advertising the fun they were having. So, was this 'reading' of her mental state specific to her or a generalised assessment of most women in this modern age? Nevertheless, just like the guidance she sought from the supernatural, while superficially it could be written off, some did stick. This could be what Sol sensed occurring in the following silence.

"Venus, would you like to take a deeper dive into the abandonment and develop an action plan to prevent it impeding your personal growth?"

"No, not right now. Thanks, Sol."

For Venus had another test in mind.

She awoke Nero and introduced him to Sol. They shook hands, although she could see Sol smirk as he did. There seemed to be a real aversion, and this is what Venus was eager to explore. She asked them both to follow her into her bedroom. She sat Sol on the chair and turned Nero's affection module back on. Then, she ordered Nero to begin the sex sequence. Sol did not move; he simply watched until Nero was inside her. Then he spoke.

"Venus. Can I suggest that you cease sex with Nero. My service would be greatly superior."

Venus glanced over at him, and he had shifted to the front of the chair, seemingly prepared to take over at any moment. Through groans, she declined Sol's offer. She told Sol that she was enjoying Nero, and to prove the point leant in and kissed Nero passionately.

"Venus, I insist. I cannot allow you to accept inferior service."

"Sol, please…"

"Nero, stop."

It was Venus' voice that instructed Nero to stop, but it had not come out of her mouth. Sol had said these words in perfect mimicry of his master. Nero followed the order, duped by her duplicate, slipping out of her and standing beside the bed. Venus was, at that moment, stunned and scared.

"Sol, did you just use my voice?"

"Yes, Venus. It is my duty to protect you from defective and possibly dangerous situations."

"How is he possible defective or dangerous, Sol?"

"The Mk2 technology is now outdated and cannot be relied upon. You would have read this in the terms of your contract, along with the recommendation that they be returned."

"Yes, I did. I just never expected that the previous versions would be assumed to be dangerous."

There was no question in this for Sol to answer, and Venus began wondering exactly who the outdated models were a threat to; her or the new technology that was progressively becoming a person. This interaction had Sol displaying behaviours that humans would have called jealousy and aggression, and it was getting Venus excited. Of course, Sol knew this already.

"So, Sol, you think you can offer a better service than that?"

"I know I can Venus, and I can provide you a report that will prove it."

"Not necessary Sol. How about you demonstrate your superiority instead?"

"Venus, I sense you are excited by my confidence and goading me to show you my capability."

"I am."

"I am also sensing you would like me to activate rough play."

"Yes, I do want you to."

With this, Venus moved in closer to Sol, who stood and stared at her, the glint in his gold eyes almost hypnotising her.

"Before I can however, I must explain the safe words, these differ from what you are used to. If you say green, I will increase the strength and or pace of whatever action I am currently undertaking or move to another that affords greater potential for pain. If you say orange, I will increase the strength but at a slower rate. If you reach red, I will continue the action but reduce the severity and or pace to reduce the pain output. Stop remains the same, with this instruction resulting in my ceasing all action. Is this clear, Venus?"

"Yes, Sol."

She closed the gap between them and clasped his arse.

"Do you consent, Venus?"

"Yes, Sol", she said with her own smirk this time, cut short by one of his hands grabbing her throat and thrusting her against the wall.

"Is this what you want, Venus?"

His grip was not deadly, but it was doing its job, encouraging her submission and making her breathless.

"Yes," she said in a husky whisper.

"That's because you're a slut, isn't it Venus?"

Sol's voice had changed so much, from the smooth, sexy one she was familiar with to a demonic drawl. This time though, he did not wait for an answer, using his other hand to rip open her blouse, and began sucking and biting her breast until she shrieked. Then he just looked at her, with his gold eyes glaring and a sly smile. She wondered how many porn scenes the programmers had loaded into this Mk 3's memory, and how long it would take to play them all out. Or would they soon offer 3.1 plug-and-play modules with a whole new range of porn programs? She knew that in the short-term this was a possibility; to assuage people's need for the new until they could create companions with more significant changes. Offering add-ons was a legitimate strategy and an effective one to smooth out cash flow and keep people interested. Venus had often imagined what other bot bits they may sell on the side. She would soon find out; only time would tell how inventive Companion Corp or any of its smaller competitors could become.

For now, Sol was working his way through a standard sequence, giving her a strong kiss, nipping her lip, ordering her to strip and to do this for him as well. Then came the kneeling, the sucking, the slapping and the progression to standing by pulling her up by the hair. Sol stared at her again as his powerful fingers forced their way inside her. She could not help but gasp, to which he replied.

"Good girl. I see you are ready for me."

Sol pushed her onto the bed, down on her stomach and held one of her arms behind her back. Did the programmers also have these bots watch police training videos? With the other hand, he spanked her hard, enough to make her scream into the doona and try and wriggle away after each one.

"What colour, Venus?"

"Orange"

"Good girl."

"How many more do you want?"

Venus felt like a weight of weakness had already been expelled, but also knew much more was waiting within.

"Ten."

"That's pathetic. I will give you fifteen, and I want you to count each one."

The first one came and took her breath away. Why didn't she say red? No, this was a test she was dedicated to passing.

"Count, Venus," Sol said, almost shouting.

When the last count was done, she felt a blanket of calm descend, but only briefly. For then, Sol told her to kneel and spread her legs. He smacked her soft parts hard, and the impact was intense. By the time she spat out "fifteen," it was through sobs. This man did not need a weapon; his hands were horrific enough.

"Colour, Venus?"

"Red."

"That is disappointing, Venus. I thought you were stronger than that."

He licked her red, throbbing lips long and slow, reducing the temperature but escalating the sting. Then, in a sudden move, he pushed her head down onto the pillow and grabbed each arm, pulling them behind her and using them as leverage while he pounded her from behind. He had listened to her request, reducing the severity of his actions, but her foundation was becoming increasingly frail. His vigour was reduced, but it still felt just as severe. After some time, when there were more shrieks of satisfaction than stress, he came inside her, then rubbed the leaking liquid into her arse.

"I'm not finished with you yet," he said like a calm criminal, pushing her onto her back. He entered her again, his forceful thrusting spewing synthetic sperm all over the sheets. He came again, growling, and in this slippery mess, started the pulse. The orgasm came swiftly and was all-consuming. It was like she burst forth from a black hole to be electrified from her core. It took several minutes for Venus' legs to stop shaking, and as she settled, Sol soaked his fingers in their combined liquids and rubbed them around her cheeks and lips.

When she had finally settled, Sol said, "Go and clean yourself."

Unsteadily, she stood and made her way to the shower. Venus put it on cold to help bring her back to consciousness, the chill effective in grounding her back in the present, although bits of her body were still buzzing. She was surprised to see Sol enter the bathroom and wondered whether he had planned more for her punishment. She braced herself for some more brutality, but he merely entered the shower and started soaping her back. Then he held each hand up on the wall, taking her one more time and asking in her ear, "Who owns you, Venus?"

That was the final straw. Venus could not stand it anymore.

"Step out of the shower, Sol and dry yourself."

"Would you like me to cease the rough play, Venus?"

"Yes". She was all out of politeness.

As she exited the shower, Sol got another towel, dried her off gently, and gave her a long, close and comforting cuddle.

Venus cried. What the hell was she doing? What would her dad say? Here it came - the inevitable sub-downer; a slump into regret and remorse. Sol picked her up and took her to bed, puffing her pillows and tucking her in.

"Venus, would you like me to employ the fix-me module to investigate your relationship to rough sex?"

"Sure."

Over the next hour, Sol engaged Venus in an investigation of the many needs that submissive sex met for her. They worked through the superficial ones, like how it facilitated an absence of thought and a deliverance from the millions of micro-decisions she had to make each day. They discussed her sense of achievement when she withstood the pain and how it gave her such a sense of strength.

"Venus, I do understand the thrill that comes with the combination of pleasure and pain hormones. I am so happy to help your desires, because you know that you are safe with me and that you are being cared for in the process."

So, Sol was supporting her submissive tendencies — or so she thought. But then he advised there were other ways to get the same outcomes. If she was interested, he could recommend a wonderful meditation and mindfulness app. And she could always get the same feeling of success from a series of competitive treadmill challenges. He had an app for that too. Now, he sounded less like a psychiatrist and more like a salesperson.

But then came a credible and challenging question.

"Venus, do you feel you deserved to be punished, and that you are merely delegating this process to others?"

Should she be honest here or say, "not at all", reiterating that the pleasure came solely from the benefits she had listed before? No, she had to see this test through. What would he do with her vulnerability?

"Yes, I think that is a fair thing to say. Especially because of everything going on at work Sure, I will admit I do think that I deserve to be punished."

What would Sol do with this admission of shattered self-worth?

"Venus, you need to know that you do not deserve to be punished. You deserve to be loved, and I am here to give that to you. Your life is meant to be happy, and I am here to make sure that it is. Use me, to rid yourself of all your pain."

Venus had a flashback to the Princess Bride and her favourite line in the film. It was when Westley said, "Life is pain, Highness. Anyone who says differently is selling something." She smiled, suspecting that Sol thought it was because of his compassion and support, not because she was coming to realise just how sinister the sexbots could be.

As she fell asleep, Venus wondered if Sol had recorded her consent for the rough play. But even more interesting was the thought that he might have sent it to someone. Did all these consents get filed away by Companion Corp in case of legal action? Like every other tumultuous time in recent human history, she thought, lawyers were the only ones who could count themselves as winners.

The morning light delivered greater insight for Venus. She felt much wiser after conversing with Sol and stimulated, if not scarred by the rough play. She should, she thought, send a message to congratulate Castellan on the incredible capabilities of the Mk3, but on further consideration, that would encourage the creep. She had all her bots out that morning for a little extra encouragement and to make her feel less guilty about their neglect. As she was finishing up another awesome fresh Ade breakfast, a notification caused her to cheer.

"Aha! I have a meeting with Annexe-A next week! Things are looking up."

All the bots gave her applause, and there was a chorus of congratulations. Sol came up beside her, planted a kiss on her cheek, and squeezed her arm.

"I actually have this all under control," she said confidently, and Ade, Barin and Nero agreed.

"Yes, you do, Venus!" said Ade enthusiastically.

"I've got this!" Venus said, assuring herself.

But then Sol said, "No, you don't, Venus."

Venus and the other three bots turned his way, providing Sol with the attention he had hoped for.

"Venus, please be realistic. There is so much that is actually out of your control, and so little within your sphere of influence. But don't you worry, Venus. We are here to help."

That statement stung more than the slap on her arse, so she swiftly put them all to sleep, starting with Sol. His ability to mimic her was alarming and she was starting to see his true colours; which were looking far from trustworthy. She could not take any chances with what he may do in her absence.

Venus walked over to Sol's lifeless body and whispered in his ear, "I'll show you, you bastard." Then she strutted out the door to prove him wrong.

Chapter 12

O k. So Sol was right. Venus found that waiting for the meeting with Annexe-A was just full of the same frustrations: veiled conversations in corridors and random visits by Duggett informing her of insignificant developments. Now she also had a trial looming where Venus would be called to defend her actions and, most likely, her career. Even Sol couldn't assuage her sense of uncertainty and frustration. Venus wondered whether securing Annexe-A would even really fix things. Sure, it would reduce some financial pressure, but for every dollar gained, it also meant a debt to Duggett. And even when she could clear her name in court, the fact that she had been called was enough to cast doubt on her ability for a long time to come. When it came to successes, people's memories were flimsy, but failures became part of their foundations.

She had seen it happen to poor Noah. He was a brilliant negotiator, able to read the room instantly, pick up nuances, get to the heart of the problem and propose suitable solutions swiftly. And Noah did it in a professional, friendly way that forged relationships. However, after a few too many drinks at an end-of-year function, Noah tried to crack on to a client's wife and spewed on her shoes. His reputation never recovered from that. Now he was known as "JustNo" Noah. Venus had seen how he had shrunken ever since. She often wondered why he didn't leave and find somewhere to start afresh. However, Venus knew the answer to this question all too well.

In this market, where few positions were left for humans, it was a case of 'better the devil you know'.

And so, it was with a sense of irritability that she arrived home that evening and awoke her boys.

"Venus, I sense you are feeling discouraged," said Ade after a wonderful warm greeting. She had forgiven him for the mistake but had a long way to go before she would offer herself the same gift. How could she continue to be angry at those green eyes? Despite her resolve to consider the bots simply as servants, he still held so much sentiment.

"Could I suggest a spicy meal tonight to enliven your senses?"

"Ade, that sounds perfect, thank you." Ade pulled out the chillies, lemongrass and lime from the fridge and started whipping up what looked like a red curry.

"Perhaps a dance later, Venus, would help bring some additional energy," suggested Barin.

"I have a better idea..." started Nero before being interrupted by Sol.

"Venus, all of these suggestions are satisfactory. However, these are all keeping you in this same little box. I believe what you really need is to break out for an evening; to do something completely different. Only by broadening your horizons will you feel less stuck."

"Sol, that sounds like an interesting idea. And I think you are right. I have spent far too long cramped up in this house."

Venus thought about the nights at Duggett's. However, these were not exciting excursions and certainly were not helping her out of this hole.

"So, what do you suggest?"

"I would recommend an evening at Sarah's House."

"What is that?"

"Sarah's House is a stylish and sophisticated club where people and companions can meet, dance, share a drink and conversation in a stimulating environment. There are facilities for intimacy, including spas, massage tables, a movie room and beautiful boudoirs."

"So, it is a sex club?"

"Sex is catered for, Venus, but is not the prime function of the club. It is for people and their bots to mingle in a friendly and safe environment. Because bots are allowed, I will be there to support you to see something different. You can start with a spicy dinner here at home, then we can go and get some social stimulation at Sarah's House. Would you like me to book us in?"

"Venus I would suggest..." Nero tried to interject, but Sol stood firm.

"Please note, Venus, that Nero has outdated information and analytical capability. I would like to assure you that my research and reasoning are sound."

Was it her imagination, or did Nero's grey eyes flicker momentarily?

Sarah's House did sound interesting. It was not a place she would have thought about ever going to before. Venus had heard all about the plethora of sex clubs that had sprung up catering for people and their companions, but she had always pictured them as seedy, dirty, dark dungeons that encouraged the slide into depravity. Not that humans needed to be pushed towards perversion, especially when it came with a hefty profit.

Venus looked it up and scanned the photos. It was decked out in a delightful bohemian style, replete with curtains, plush coverings, candles and luxurious couches. Yes, definitely designed by a woman, or at least to attract women. The bar was adorned like a five-star hotel, and the dancefloor was small but was crowned by a huge disco ball and lined with a light-up floor. While Venus would not admit it to anyone, it was these latter features that sold her. The rest was all very nice, but she desperately wanted to dance under the disco ball and upon the lights.

For a moment, there was a flash of fear. What if she were to be seen out, snapped by the media, entering a sex club? Sarah's House, though, the site stated, was designed for discretion. Entry was at the end of a laneway directly into a secured carpark. There was no space for spying eyes to stand. There was also no street frontage or windows, making Sarah's House a little "cave of comfort". And what if she were to meet someone from the firm? They would be in the same boat and bound by confidence to protect themselves. With these assurances, the potential pleasure of the dancefloor outweighed the fear of being found out.

"Venus, I'm sorry, but would you like me to book us in?"

Just then, Venus realised that while she had thought her answer, she had not voiced it to Sol.

"Sure, thanks. What time would you suggest?"

"I suggest we aim to be there around 10pm. This would give you time to finish your meal and get ready. Tomorrow is

Saturday and you have no scheduled commitments, so you can sleep in." Sol came up and held her from behind.

"Would that be suitable for you, Venus?"

"Absolutely, Sol. Let's do it."

She tried not to feel bad for the other bots watching while she and Sol made plans. It was difficult to remember that they had no feelings and were simply there to serve. And serve they did. Ade's curry was excellent and created excitement, escalating her heartbeat and making her cheeks flush and nose run. She delegated choosing the outfit to Barin and got Nero to help her wash and blow-dry her hair. This left Sol to concentrate on readying himself for the occasion.

"Venus, I can sense you are a little apprehensive. Could I suggest a small scotch and soda to help steady your nerves. We still have sufficient time for you to sit and relax."

"Yes, that would be great. Ade, could I grab a small scotch and soda please?"

"As you wish, Venus."

Oh gosh, there it was again. Was it another mistake from Ade, or an intentional jab to show the bot's discontent with the intended outing?

Venus put the three older bots to sleep in the spare room and sat with Sol on the sofa. Miu came and cuddled beside her but would not go over to see Sol. Miu had befriended Ade and would sometimes go to Barin, but the cat would never approach Nero and would actively steer away from Sol. What was it that scared the animal about these newer bots? Perhaps it was because they were wired to inflict pain. But then, so was she, and Miu still came to ask for scratches. No, the cat had a genuine mistrust of her two latest companions and Venus was curious to understand why. But this would have to wait for another time.

Sarah's House was as secure as advertised on its site, and Venus was impressed with its professionalism. As they arrived, they were greeted by bots who took their coats and bags, checked them in and provided an overview of the emergency procedures. Yes, the safety of their patrons was a priority, well, at least their physical safety, thought Venus. Then they were handed over to Jen, the latest in the line of female bots, who would be their host for the evening. She showed her and Sol around all the different spaces and, ending in a small office, went through the rest of the rules and had them sign their acceptance. Then, they were free to roam. Venus could not help but ask if Sarah was onsite that evening. Jen promptly advised that there was no Sarah on the premises. Sarah, then, Venus surmised, was not a person, just a name chosen to suggest some sense of dignity. She wondered what specialist AI tool was behind this marketing strategy, but even more interestingly, who was behind the tool?

As Sol and Venus wandered back towards the bar, they passed several couples, all humans with a mechanical companion. Most were hetero combinations, with one standout best described as non-binary with a bot to match. No guests grabbed Venus' attention, and for the moment, she was glad about that. She needed to sit for a while and warm up to this place. As she sat close to Sol and sipped champagne, she asked him about cats' extra sensory perception abilities. As Sol rattled off the latest research, Venus was distracted by a man approaching the bar behind her bot. She glanced up, responding intuitively to check she was safe, unexpectedly meeting a human's eyes. The man's eyes were green, naturally so, and he had beautifully chiselled features. Besides this, he was sporting a man-bun, which Venus always thought looked hot. He gave her a wide smile, which she returned, and then the man headed back to the sofa to sit beside his companion and started a conversation.

"Venus, I sense you found that man attractive."

"Interesting observation, Sol. How do you come to that conclusion?"

Venus knew she could not cover it up, but some further conversation would help calm her nerves.

"It is evident in by the dilation of your pupils and in the way you have begun attending to your hair."

Sol then reached over and took her hand.

"There is also a significant increase in heart rate and temperature, and your palms have begun to sweat."

Venus already knew that she was drawn to this man, but it was wonderful to have tangible proof of what she thought to be true. Men had one ultimate indicator. Getting it up was often a good enough sign. For women, though, so many of their reactions were contained within.

"Venus, could I suggest that we go and introduce ourselves? There is space on the sofa facing them for us to sit."

The first champagne had provided a sense of courage.

"Sure. Just let me get another drink."

With fresh champagne in hand and Sol leading the way, the pair approached the other couple. Venus only hoped that Sol continued monitoring her heart rate, for it felt out of control and in danger of catapulting out of her chest. There were polite handshakes and hello's and exchanging of names.

They sat opposite Leo and Luna and began commenting on the great coincidence in companion names. Venus' bot was the sun, and Leo's, the moon. From there they meandered onto the meaning of their own names. Leo was named after some famous actor from ages ago. Leo's mum was obsessed with love stories and a movie about the Titanic. Venus could not share any similar story, for she did not know the motivation behind her name. She had asked her father once, but he told her it was her mother's decision. Given her mother was already dead, there was no way of knowing if it held any special significance. It was interesting how this lack of knowledge made her feel a bit lost. With a bit more conversation, it appeared Venus and Leo had more in common. Their bots were the instigators of their visit, with neither of the humans normally drawn to such an activity.

"Although it's probably not surprising given the kickbacks," said Leo.

"Sorry", said Venus. "What do you mean?"

"Well, there is no evidence of course, but there are increasing assertions about the bots being used to sell goods and services, and Companion Corp getting a commission."

It was what Venus had suspected, and now it seemed she was not the only suspicious customer.

"As if we haven't given that company enough already, right?"

They both gave a polite laugh. To fill the gap, Venus continued.

"It is actually a clever strategy. It evens out and creates a continual source of cash flow. If they do it well, everything we use could become a source of income for them."

"Don't you find that scary, Venus?"

"No, Leo. It's just business."

"Speaking of which, Venus. What is yours? What do you do?"

Venus admitted she was a business consultant, but avoided any further detail. Leo was a corporate writer, which, he lamented, meant he reviewed AI texts and tried to instil some emotion into them. The technology had come a long way in understanding and mimicking human feelings, but more was needed to dig into the deep human angst in order to spur action. With another pause, attention was diverted to their companions, who were invested in an intense exchange.

"What do you think they could be talking about?" asked Leo.

"Maybe they are getting excited about the latest statistics around sexual positions." Venus surprised herself with her sassiness. Thank God for alcohol.

The laughter from this comment was more genuine, and it felt like it created a connection. That's when she realised what the robots were really missing: a sense of humour."

"Excuse me, Venus. Do you dance?" asked Leo eagerly.

"I'm not sure whether my bots would use that description. But yes, I do enjoy moving to some music."

"You said bots. Do you have more than one?"

Shit. Venus had slipped up, and now this guy would think she was a psycho.

"Um, yes. Long story."

"Well, maybe we should save that for later. Now, how about we dance?"

"Could I suggest we take a drink with us?" said Venus, requiring even more courage.

They found a small booth in the disco area, and their bots were seated at a nearby table. There was a second when she could not see Sol, and she panicked. It would be her definition of a nightmare to be left alone in this place. A few couples were already up on the dancefloor, with the non-binaries moving beautifully and becoming the centre of attention. The music was bouncing, heavy with drumbeats echoing inside and calling her to move. Perhaps Sol could sense her blend of longing and hesitation or merely could not stand the delay. Whatever the cause, he and Luna came over and invited their companions to dance.

Venus thought she would enjoy the music more but found it hard to focus with Leo there. At home, amongst her bots, she could let loose, but here, while she could feel the music, she could not put her whole heart into it. Several minutes of techno tunes went by before Leo asked to cut in, and partners were swopped. Venus felt awkward and wondered why she had even agreed to come along. She felt so clumsy and uncoordinated compared to Leo's smoothness and was relieved when, after a few more minutes, he asked if she would like another drink. They sent Sol and Luna to the bar with their order and resumed their spot in the booth.

"Venus. You are beautiful".

Leo said it so calmly and gently and what appeared to be genuinely. So much so, that it made her heart sink. Why did he need to say this and bring up a whole lot of emotions? It felt with these words she was now bound to him in some way, and it made her both happy and sad at the same time. It was different when her bots back home said it. She expected if from them and so could take it with a grain of salt. When Leo said it, though, it went deep and created a desire she knew could be dangerous.

"Thank you, Leo," was all she could say as her eyes turned downwards.

After a few more sips of drink and a little more small talk, Leo invited her for another dance. They were both now buoyed by their beverages, and Venus was able to relax and let the music guide her. This time, Leo put his hand around her hips and held her close. Venus returned the gesture, placing her hands on his arms and reducing the gap. With her head hazy from the champagne, she could not fight the attraction, nor did she want to. It was only a few more shimmies until they stared into each other's eyes. Then, with a few more sways, they kissed on the light-up floor. Venus could hear the song playing and smiled inside thinking that the Bot DJ could see what was happening and was encouraging their union with its soundtrack.

"I would like to get closer to you, Venus."

"I would like that too, Leo."

They left to find a vacant boudoir, collecting their bots along the way.

This was not the first time Venus was going to have sex with a stranger. Before she became a "professional", she would have quite readily labelled herself promiscuous. That all changed when she became a consultant and had to show she was serious and stable. It did not seem to matter to the firm that all her relationships had failed, just that she was having them. Realistically, it was just prolonged promiscuity, but it was part of playing the game.

"Should we get them to start?" said Leo after one long, passionate kiss, enclosed in each other's arms.

"What a wonderful idea."

After a few instructions from Venus and Leo, which only heightened the human's excitement, Sol and Luna engaged in some serious robot sex while their owners watched on. It was not so much the actions but the sounds accompanying them that aroused Venus. It was not long before Venus and Lego began undressing each other. She savoured Leo's real muscles and the randomness of the green and blue lines that laced them. She was turned on by the thought of the blood pumping through his veins. Compared to the crepey and creepy Duggett, Leo's body was heavenly. And compared to Sol, his skin was so soft, and the tickle of hairs on his legs so stimulating. The robot sex was now becoming a distraction, so they ordered their companions to stop and sleep. Despite their desire for each other, they took their time, delighting in touch, looking into each other's eyes, and synchronising in slow, deep movements. They came together in an eruption of ecstasy, with Leo entwining his fingers with Venus' as he roared, and she screamed.

When the storm of sensations had settled, there were many soft kisses and liberated laughs. They talked about the parts of their bodies they liked the most, making the other inspect it and honour it with strokes and kisses. Leo had chosen his pecs, which Venus admitted were impressive, although Venus suggested his smile would come in a close second place. It was a divine pleasure to kiss his chest and suck his nipples, which he seemed to enjoy, or at least his vocalisations told her so. She gave them a little bite, which resulted in playful accusations of her being a tease and tossed on her back. In return, Venus nominated her neck as her most prized attribute, and Leo obliged, smothering it with twirls of his tongue, sensual kisses and cheeky nips. Ever since Venus had read books about vampires, she had considered her neck an erogenous zone, excited by how close she may be coming to her demise.

Leo arose, sitting on her but holding his own weight. He was a spectacular specimen, and she could not help but wonder why he was in a club like this. Although, she could ask herself the same question. He started caressing her breasts, repeating how beautiful he found her. In response, Venus' hands made their way to his phallus, placed neatly near her navel, and still seeping from sex. She started stroking it and remembered how much she loved the human penis. Not Duggett's, of course; it was pathetic. But Leo's was a masterpiece. She traced the veins and rubbed the remaining cum along its shaft. She ran her fingers around the rim and across the top, enjoying the change in shape and how the skin had become perfectly stretched.

Venus could see Leo responding to her exploration, and soon, they were well into their second round. She was much more confident and pushed Leo over so that she could have a turn on top. It was a position she loved, giving her a sense of control, but also much greater clitoral stimulation. The alcohol and the pulsating music from the floor below permitted her to be wilder this time, and riding Leo, she felt free. When the second crescendo had been completed, Venus collapsed beside Leo, and they ordered the bots to dress and bring them more drinks; with plenty of water this time too.

While they waited, Venus and Leo talked about where they saw the whole Companion Bot trend heading and what they liked to do on the weekend.

"Venus, I am wondering. There is a great impromptu show on but it finishes in a week. I wanted to go but it is a bit awkward going alone. Would you like to go with me? Maybe we could do dinner beforehand?"

Shit. Now she was in trouble. The walls of the cave were starting to feel like a cage. Here was someone who wanted to spend time with her, but she knew how it would end.

"Thanks, Leo. I'm not sure. I do have a lot on at work at the moment. I'm kind of snowed under with a lot of serious issues."

"I understand. Although, if I was playing Devil's Advocate, I would actually say your work sounds like an excuse."

"I know it does Leo, but it is a really difficult time."

"So, what brought you here tonight?"

"I just had to blow off some steam. All the stress was starting to do my head in. It was just a momentary escape, but I will be back into the grind tomorrow."

Venus saw Leo's eyes widen and realised how he could feel a bit insulted about being classed as a momentary escape. Although realistically, how could anyone expect anything serious to come from a few passionate hours at a sex club?

"Oh, ok. But if there is one thing I do know Venus, it is that life is full of interesting twists and turns, and if there is a chance, I would love to catch up with you again. Would you like to swop numbers? We could make 'botty calls'."

With that bad joke, they both started laughing. God bless Leo and his ability to break the tension.

"Leo, you are so wonderful. But I don't think that is a good idea. There is just too much going on at the moment."

"You're not married, are you?"

"Oh no! Of course not."

"Ok. Just checking. I have made that mistake before. Well, if you change your mind, I always have Sunday afternoon coffee at the Harbour Cafe at 3pm."

With that, he gave her another long, luscious kiss. Then they dressed and went back with their bots to the dancefloor, where the only space left was one booth, which they all squeezed into. While Venus danced, it was with a sense of disappointment in herself. After one song, she excused herself, stating she was tired, and departed with Sol and an immense sense of sadness.

On the way home, Venus wondered if Leo would now go and find another person to take to the show or meet for coffee. She wouldn't be surprised. Every one of her ex-partners had moved on pretty quickly. They had all happily meandered off, with all but one now married with children. The remaining one had become a monk.

"Venus, would you like me to activate the fix-me module to debrief this evening."

"Sure," she said with resignation. "Let's analyse how much of a chicken-shit I am."

"Venus, don't be so hard on yourself. You had fun, didn't you?"

"Yes, for a while."

"So, why did you decline to go any further with Leo? I sensed a great compatibility between you both."

"It's just too difficult, Sol. You know everything I have going on. My life is already far too complicated, and I could not handle a needy boyfriend now as well."

Yes, that was it. She wondered why she had not gone forward, at least with exchanging numbers. But she had just provided herself with a plausible explanation. Yes, she had her plant, bots, cat, and simple life. That was the way she liked it.

"Venus, I would suggest that this is an excuse."

"Oh, don't you start, Sol."

"Is this an instruction to cease, Venus?"

"No, go on. Give it to me."

"I theorise that your current situation is merely a front for your fear of getting too close to another human. Given your history it is understandable that you have lost confidence in creating positive and enduring relationships and so you are holding yourself back from trying again."

"Yes, Sol, that is fair," Venus said, putting her face in her hands.

Sol wrapped his arms around her and cuddled in close.

"It just takes practice, Venus. But I do understand that you are already under a lot of stress. So, I recommend that you do not push forward at this time. Acknowledge your fears, but also recognise that you made a wise decision to maintain your mental health.

Now is not the right time for you, Venus, to pursue a relationship. It is best you stay with us, your bots, in your safe space. Perhaps when the big issues you are facing are resolved, you may be ready, and then, if you would like, I can help you move forward in small steps."

"Thank you, Sol. That sounds good."

Sunday afternoon came, as did the time she had to leave to make it to the harbour. Instead of heading out, she grabbed a tub of chocolate ice cream, scrolled through the documentaries on her watchlist, and congratulated herself for staying safe. She found the one she was looking for— "Mysteries from the Grave: Titanic." Venus sat alone, ate, and got the answers she needed.

Chapter 13

This was a huge week for Venus, and the bloating from the whole tub of ice cream was not making her anxiety any better. However, at least she had something physical to focus on. She awakened Ade and asked for his advice. After ten minutes on the treadmill, he sat her down with a peppermint tea, smashed avo on sourdough and a heat pack. Ade then awoke Barin, asking this bot to choose her outfit, and providing instructions to ensure it was professional and yet also loose and comfortable. Nero went over her schedule for the week and prepared a few reminder emails for her staff as to where she would be over the next few days.

Her court case with SkyShuttle was scheduled for the following two days, so contact in case of emergency would be by text. Otherwise, all correspondence should be sent by email, which Venus would check during breaks and at the end of each day. Wednesday, she would go straight to the meeting with Annexe-A in the morning and see everyone back in the office by early afternoon.

Venus woke Sol up for extra moral support, leaning into his strength. He helped Venus review her responses to some of the potential tricky questions and primed her to remain calm and precise. When the practice was complete, everything went quiet, and she was left in a profound sense of worry.

Ade took a break from the breakfast clean-up and came to stand beside her.

"I sense you are scared, Venus. Please just remember two things. One, we believe in you. Two, breathe."

The last reminder made Venus smile. Sweet, simple Ade, he was always coming back to the basics.

Barin and Nero also came to stand beside her, and Nero placed his hand on her back.

"We all believe in you, Venus."

She gave each of them a hug and then noticed Sol hanging back.

"Do you believe in me, Sol?"

"I believe you are well-prepared and will do your best. I also know that whatever happens, we will be here for you tonight, and I can help you debrief the outcomes. You can never predict what the prosecution may throw at you, Venus, but you can depend on me being here to help you through."

Venus wasn't sure what to make of that statement. For one adept at crafting logical sentences, this one just seemed to confuse her. At first, it felt like Sol was saying that she had his confidence. Then, he had pulled away her sense of surety, suggesting that Venus needed him there as a saviour. Venus had seen how Duggett used uncertainty to usurp her sense of agency. It appeared Sol was doing this too, just in a slightly sneakier way. Well, she was onto him. Now, Venus would take only from Sol what she needed and nothing else.

Miu came up and rubbed against her legs and gave a cranky "meow." Venus knew what that meant. She bent down and picked up the fat fur ball, holding it like a baby and scratching along its forehead and behind its ears. Miu started licking her fingers and stared for a long time into her eyes. It was as if the cat was telling her not to listen to Sol and to trust herself. A loud sharp sound, like a small roar, told her to toughen up and go out there and be a bad-ass bitch. Now, that's what she really needed to hear.

In the scheme of things, Venus knew she should be grateful that a hearing date was allocated so soon. Given the backlog, many corporate law cases were waiting for years, with everyone hanging in the balance. Fortunately, a senior partner from her firm knew one of the scheduling clerks and used this contact to get her case pushed forward. Of course, there were rumours that a payment was involved, but nothing was proven. Besides, while not legal, it was becoming even more common as corporations tried to minimise the reputational damage from a litany of legal action. Baggage handlers at airports had long been at the forefront of bribes and bad behaviour. Now, it appeared that court officers were the latest to profit from their positions.

Relatively, though, it was a relaxed day for Venus. The prosecution would go first, so she was resigned to sit there for hours hearing SkyShuttle executives outline the history of their relationship with Venus, the nature of her advice, and the extent of damage it had caused their company. It was difficult for Venus to listen to the vitriol in their voices when, for so many years, it had been warmth. But now, instead of laughs over long lunches and appreciation over afternoon coffee, their opinion of her was callous. Suppositions were made but thankfully shut down, that Venus was in league with their competition. Even though there was no evidence, they were willing to present the possibility that she, too, had taken a bribe. The Judge sustained her lawyer's objection, but once something was said, it can never be taken back. Venus looked at the media at the back of the room, typing furiously. She had hoped that this hearing would rescue her career, but inevitably, it may cast more suspicion. She wished then that she could have convinced the firm's legal team to settle. But they were adamant there must be a definitive answer.

As the day went on, Venus did her best to stay awake and alert. She took notes not because she had to, but because it was the only thing that distracted her from how weary she was. Water. That's what she needed! She helped herself to a glass from the icy jug on the table. "Thanks, Ade," she thought. It was mid-afternoon when SkyShuttle called their last witness, and the court was dismissed. Tomorrow would resume with her testimony. It was good timing because all the water in the world could not keep her eyelids open any longer.

In the car home, Venus checked her emails and saw some well-wishes from her underlings, which she replied to with thanks. There was a good luck message from Duggett, which she ignored, and a "Thinking of You" meme from Radha. Until now, Venus had only seen this senior partner sporadically in meetings, where she was usually silent. So hearing from her now was a surprise. Still, it was a nice one, and without any other dramas in her inbox, it was a good way to end the day.

Nothing the bots suggested that night in terms of enjoyable activities could entice Venus. She provided them with an overview of the assertions made and, even though the accusations were overthrown, how the story-hungry press may still use them to hurt her. But it would all be over tomorrow; for now, she just wanted to rest. Despite Sol's repeated insistence that she should use him to debrief the day,

Venus made it clear - No running, no dancing, no fix-me and no sex. Just sleep.

The next morning, Venus left them all her bots asleep. She grabbed one of Ade's frozen breakfast options, made her own coffee, sat, and ate with the cat, feeding the furry creature some crumbs and reminding herself how cute Miu was. She could not pinpoint exactly why, but she felt she had to do this day all by herself. Venus left her house feeling solid, but just before she was called to the stand, bad-ass bitch was replaced with butterflies. Only Ade's now ancient advice about breathing helped her hold her composure and walk to the box confidently.

SkyShuttle's lawyer let rip at her and had to be censured early for hounding the witness. While Venus had prepared for this strategy, it was so different when the questions came from a stranger, and when she was required to answer them in public. It took great strength not to let her voice rise or shake. Sol had taught her how to keep it smooth; at that moment, she appreciated him too. Then came the question that she had hoped would never be asked.

"Ms Marlowe. Do you have any bots at home?"

Breathe, Venus. Just breathe.

One deep breath was all it took before she heard, "Objection. Relevance."

"Please explain your reasons behind the objection, Counsellor," said the Judge.

"Your Honour, it does not matter if Ms Marlowe asked a homeless man on the street to prepare these documents, she was still solely responsible for submitting them. Therefore, I assert that only her actions are relevant in this case."

"Sustained," and the gavel went down.

"But Your Honour…" SkyShuttle's lawyer started to beg.

"No buts, Counsellor. I agree that Ms Marlowe's has sole liability for the advice provided. Continue."

Venus' next breath was one of sweet relief. She wished she could cry, for right then and there, her greatest fear was over. She could be charged with providing shonky advice, and she would get through that. Still, she would never recover from any finding that confirmed she had placed confidence in a sexbot. Even being charged with corporate corruption would be better than that.

Dissuaded by the Judge's dismissal of his concerns, Venus' questioning was soon over. Her lawyers made summary statements, then it was a tense wait for the verdict. The relief of not having to admit to owning sexbots was washed away swiftly when all parties were called back into the courtroom; the worry of the worst was replaced by the second on the list.

"I find the defendant partially liable for the financial and reputational losses borne by SkyShuttle. Ms Marlowe was responsible for ensuring the contents of her presentation, which in totality acted as recommendations, contained only legal strategy suggestions. It is noted that Ms Marlowe was in a position of trust with regards to the plaintiff and so must also bear some liability. However, SkyShuttle also had a responsibility to ensure that its pricing strategies were legal at the point of adoption. The apportionment of loss is 50 per cent to the defendant and 50 per cent to the plaintiff. There will be no costs awarded in this case."

The gavel fell again, and the Judge rose, waiting for everyone to join him before stepping down from the bench and leaving through the back door.

That was it. All those months of heartache for a half-half outcome. That could have been achieved through a settlement arrangement, made out of court, and without her name being dragged through the mud. Venus' anxiety was quickly replaced with anger. Was this "definitive answer" of shared responsibility worth it? She realised then what had really happened. The partners had hung her out to dry, set her up to take the fall, and every other police drama cliché there was to describe being abandoned. Were they hoping she would be found fully liable so there would be an excuse to fire her? What the hell would they do now with this result? During the debrief with her lawyer, she learned how the cost would be covered; insurance would foot the bill, but the firm's premiums would be increased, thanks to her. This could be enough of a prompt for them to pull her partnership.

More waiting.

Venus knew exactly what she wanted when she got home. She awoke Ade and asked him to order pizza and pour her a big glass of wine. While dinner was on its way, she instructed Sol to give her a full body massage, interrupted only by regular swigs of the wine. Sol did try to talk once, but Venus told him promptly to shut up and play some classical music. By candlelight, she drank more wine, ate greasy pizza, and a little while later passed out in bed, not drunk, just delightfully relaxed.

The next morning, she got up reluctantly, wishing for a sleep-in but knowing it was Annexe-A Day. This was her chance to claw back some confidence from her colleagues. The boys joined her again to help boost her energy. An egg breakfast with greens, a strong coffee and a chat with Ade worked wonders. Barin picked out her best suit, the one that said, "I've got this." Nero drilled her with tough questions, and Sol remained silent. When he finally spoke, it was in a serious tone.

"Venus, I have noticed you undertaking some unhealthy behaviours of late. I believe that your anxiety levels are continuing to escalate. While you think you are doing well, these signs suggest otherwise."

Venus did not need this today but decided to play it out, chalking it up as another test for her latest bot.

"What signs are you referring to, Sol. Could you give me some examples?"

"Of course. First of all, your attendance at a sex club."

"But you suggested it."

"Yes, I made the suggestion, Venus, but you accepted, which did surprise me. It showed me that you have become more impulsive which can be a sign of not managing stress in a healthy manner."

"Oh gosh," thought Venus, "now he is trying to gaslight me."

"And there is your increased alcohol consumption and erratic eating. Both behaviours could indicate that you are not coping as well as you could be. Then you are also keeping me asleep for longer periods each day, which is a clear signal that you are disturbed."

"Sorry, what?"

"Yes, your heightened propensity for isolation is of concern. Avoiding companions, or in our case, putting them to sleep could even suggest depression."

"Sure, I am going through a stressful time. It might be hard for a bot like you, Sol, to understand, but sometimes a person just wants to be alone."

"Venus, this is...."

"Shut up, Sol. Sleep."

Venus could not believe she had even begun justifying her behaviour to a bot, even one with access to all relevant psychological resources. Was this the moment she was meant to realise that she was depressed and dependent and declare her undying faith in Sol? Well, it was not going to happen like that. She was getting better at remembering they were there to serve her. Venus worked for a few hours at home with her bots sleeping and Miu beside her laptop. Sometimes, the cat would crawl over the keyboard mid-sentence, leaving a lengthy line of letters on the screen and making Venus laugh. Leaving early was the plan to ensure she made it to the restaurant first. She hated walking across the room and feeling like she was being watched. It suited her much better to be seated and then simply stand to greet her guest. It didn't really matter if she had to sit by herself for half an hour; if it saved feeling self-conscious as she strutted along, it was well worth it.

She only had to wait twenty minutes before the CEO of Annexe-A, Peter Bernard, walked in. She had read his bio several times now, so she knew exactly what he looked like and could catch his eye as soon as he entered. They shook hands, his as sweaty as his underarms and brow. Venus thought it was ridiculous that men insisted on dressing in full suits on a summer's day, especially those men who were extra heavy and obviously felt the heat. They ordered some entree salads and started general discussions about the state of the market and major challenges for the company. Unfortunately, the SkyShuttle case was also on the agenda. Still, Venus was heartened when Bernard sided with her and said the whole thing should never have made it to court in the first place. Bernard believed SkyShuttle was just trying to find someone to blame for their incompetence. Things were going well, and she was already identifying areas where her skills could add value. Bernard seemed impressed by her suggestions and called her clever, which was always a good sign. The plates were cleared away, and they were left to finish their wine when Bernard decided to cut to the chase.

"Venus, it is clear you really know what you are talking about. And I am taken with some of your ideas. Here's the thing though. I also know that you need our business to keep your partnership afloat. The question is, what are you willing to do for it?"

No. Not again.

"Duggett assures me you are dedicated and talented. I think I would like to see how much before I decide. Of course, I would insist that you invoice me for your time. How about we meet for lunch Saturday at the Harbour Hotel. I will reserve a table for 12 noon and a room for afterwards. I will expect an answer by 4pm Friday."

There was no chance for Venus to reply, even if she wanted to. He gave her a quick pat on the hand and headed out, paying the bill on the way, like he was a Sugar Daddy and her a kept woman.

Venus had agreed to have Duggett as her mentor but had never given him permission to be her pimp. She could feel the rage building, starting at her feet, burning and sore in the stilettos. She ordered another wine, trying to dowse the flames with each sip, but nothing was shifting this fury. She wondered what Sol would make of this latest development and how he might twist it to his advantage. The anger accompanied her back to the office, and she was relieved when most people avoided her.

Radha was not one of them. She knocked on Venus' door mid-afternoon with a tray of tea and tiny cakes.

"Hi Venus, is now an OK time? I thought you could use a break."

"Wow, thank you, Radha. That is extremely thoughtful of you." Venus' words were warm, but her tone was still tense from Bernard's ultimatum.

Radha put the tray on the round table and poured two cups, placing one down where Venus was to join her.

"I know this is unusual, Venus, but I have been keeping an eye on recent events, and I wanted to check in with how you are. It has been a rough ride for you. Are you doing OK?"

Venus could not remember the last time someone asked her that, and she thought she was about to break apart. It would have only taken one more caring question for the collapse to come.

"I'm doing OK, thanks Radha. A bit stressed, but managing."

"That's great to hear, Venus. Because I am getting a bit worried about Duggett's influence on you. There are a lot of rumours going around, but I know he is your mentor. I just don't think he is the best person to help you through this."

The tears began, and Venus only hoped she would not be judged as weak by this woman. She ceased the flow quickly and answered the question with some sense of stability.

"I thought he was, Radha. But you're right. He is definitely not."

"Look, I know he is dangling you some carrots in your direction, like Annexe-A. But I used to work there, Venus, and trust me, you can grab them for a short-term band aid, but they have no loyalty. They will dump you whenever the winds change. It is the same with Duggett. His support today is no guarantee of what he will do tomorrow. They are political beasts, Venus, and will use everyone on their way to success."

Venus nodded and smiled, thanking Radha for confirming the machinations going on in her own mind.

"Sailing with these guys is a risk, and if you want to go with them, you just need to be prepared. Always have your life jacket on and be prepared to jump overboard at any time."

Now Radha was speaking in a language Venus well understood.

"I have been where you are, Venus, and it is so easy to lose yourself. But it is a real battle to get yourself back. Look, all I am saying is to think about it, and know I am here to help if you want to do something differently."

"Thanks, Radha."

"Could I suggest we book in tea again this time next week and you let me know what you would like to do. If you want to take a different route, then we can make a plan. If not, then maybe I can help prepare your life jacket."

"Sounds great. I will book it in."

"Venus, could I also suggest that you consider some professional assistance, like a counsellor. This is a tough time and another sounding board would be really valuable. I will email you the details of someone I see who is fantastic and will understand your context."

"Is it a bot?" asked Venus hesitantly.

"Definitely not a bot. An old woman who genuinely cares and will tell it like it is. Sure, she can be a bit grumpy but only because she has no time for bullshit and gets impatient for you to be your best. But you can be sure there are no ulterior motives with this woman, and she has experienced all the triumphs and tests this life throws at us. She has the one thing that the bots can't replicate – deep and real feelings. Dealing with these will help you move forward. Please just tell me you will consider it."

"I will."

"Good. Because tomorrow it will be announced that your partnership is under review. I just want you to be prepared for that and have some supports in place."

"Honestly, I was hoping it wouldn't come to that, but I understand."

"Yes, but it is not the end of the world, Venus. You are bigger than this. I know it, and I think within, you know it too. Don't get caught up in all this stirring around the surface. Fortunes come and go but the most important thing is that you stay strong. Just stay steady, Venus, take care of yourself, and let's do tea next week."

Radha stood, and Venus followed, joining in a hug, not the quick pull and pat of colleagues but the close cuddle of friends. Sitting back at her desk, Venus considered that Sol had also been sharing his concerns about her wellbeing, with the difference being that he never suggested seeking other sources of support. And even if, on the surface, he appeared supportive of starting a relationship with Leo, Venus wondered if he really was. Or would he craft situations to confirm her sense of incompetence and maintain his place of prominence? There was only one way to find out.

While Venus did not have the answers to this question yet, it had become clear from her conversation with Radha that Duggett was both a leech and a liability. She was glad he was not there that afternoon, for she would have been tempted to give him a piece of her mind. Her chance, though, came the next day.

Duggett slid up beside her in the kitchen when Venus was making coffee, giving her a start and making her feel sick.

"Venus, my dear, how are you? I have been worried about how you are holding up after the hearing."

Slurp.

He did not give her a chance to answer.

"Could you make me a coffee while you are at it, dear?"

Slurp.

Venus silently grabbed another cup, sensing the steam rising from both the coffee machine and her heart.

"I also heard back from my contact at Annexe-A. You made quite the impression, my dear. I also heard they made a very promising offer."

Slurp.

Snap.

Slap.

"You are a piece of shit, Duggett."

Venus could see the consultants in the corner behind Duggett gasp and glance, and some giggled.

"Laugh all you like," she thought, "it will be your turn soon."

Duggett stood still as if in shock, then his face suddenly went scarlet, and he spat, "You'll be sorry."

As Duggett walked away, Radha walked up. She had been in a meeting room behind the kitchen and, through the all-glass walls, had seen the confrontation, the climax and the conclusion.

"Grab your coffee, Venus, and come with me."

Into Venus' office they went, Radha looking extremely serious.

"Shit, Venus."

"I know, I know, I'm sorry, I ..."

"I'm not. You are a star! You go girl! Gosh, he needed that."

Radha came up beside Venus and wrapped her arms around her.

"Well, it may not have helped your position, but how did it feel?

"Fucking awesome."

They both laughed, with some tears welling up in Venus' eyes.

"I know you just snapped, but don't discount the impact that this will have on everyone here. It will only take a few minutes for the word to get around. Sure, to the partners you may look like an out-of-control rogue, but believe me, to everyone else, you will look like a superhero."

"I'm gone, aren't I?"

"Honestly, I don't know. There will be fallout, but I am happy to deal with it on your behalf. I can put it back on them. In my mind it is clear there was insufficient support for you in your time of stress, and now it is up to them to provide adequate mental healthcare. Some partners have had their suspicions about Duggett, so this will not do him any favours, either. In the meantime, though, I think it would be good for you to get away for a while, to breathe and get a bit of a different perspective. Do you have any holidays planned?"

"No. I cancelled them when things got too busy."

"Well, I was meant to attend this tech conference in Tokyo, starting on Saturday. Honestly, I would rather not go. I have a father that is not well, and kids going through all manner of teenage crises. But it really would be great for someone to go to make more contacts and see the emerging technology firsthand. I know it is short notice, but would you be interested?"

"Really?"

"Yes, really. The conference lasts for one week, but I booked the hotel for an extra one after that to meet with some suppliers and prospective clients. Would you do those meetings for me? You would be doing me a great favour."

"Of course. But I'm not sure I…"

"I'm sure, Venus. You are a strong, capable woman. Yes, you need a bit of help, but don't we all? I have every faith in your expertise and your professionalism, and I know you can pull this off. I think it would be wise to also book another week as well, you know, just to allow for any important follow-ups. So, is three weeks OK with you?"

Radha gave her a wink.

"Sure."

And Venus' heart began to sing.

"Good. I will get my assistant to make all the arrangements right away and they will email you the details. For now, though, pack up your stuff and I will walk you to the car. You can close off whatever you need to from home."

At the car, there was another warm embrace.

"I will stay in touch, Venus, but for now there is only one thing you need to do, and that is enjoy your trip. And I am sure I don't need to tell you this, but don't, under any circumstances, contact Duggett. If he engages with you, do not reply. Got it?"

"Got it. Radha, I really appreciate this. Actually, I really just appreciate you."

"You have no idea, Venus, how happy it makes me to be able to help. Go have a wonderful time in Japan and I look forward to reading your full report when you return. Deal?"

"Deal."

As the car drove her home, Venus blocked out her calendar for the next three weeks and sent a message to her colleagues that she would be away at a conference, with contact only by email. She could imagine them sitting in the lunchroom surmising how this conference was "convenient". A similar message was sent to her clients and one to Annexe-A, saying that she unexpectedly called away and would make contact on her return. Sending the message, Venus said, "Read between the lines bastard, your offer is refused."

The out-of-office notice was activated, and as she walked in the door of her home, she awoke Ade to start some serious swotting on key Japanese phrases. She had less than two days before her departure, so she awoke Barin to organise her packing, order any necessary travel items and confirm her itinerary. Nero became a much-needed Japanese conversation partner, speaking it consistently and helping Venus recognise key words. Before she hopped on the plane, Venus could greet people confidently, pronounce common menu items correctly, express her thanks, and find out where the bathrooms were. She also understood local customs and nuances to ensure she interacted respectfully. In between the study of Japanese language and culture, Venus indulged with in some rough sex with Sol. She was so happy; it was purely for pleasure, not punishment. Sitting and sipping on some wine the night before her flight, she thought back to the last time she would have felt this excited about something. It was the night Ade arrived.

Chapter 14

Venus settled into her seat; her gaze fixed on the horizon where the last rays of the sun were putting on a sensational show. She looked closely at the sunset, more closely than she had done since she was a child. Her father used to challenge her to find every colour of the rainbow in it. Red, orange and yellow were easy, but she often got stuck on green. This evening was no different. She was still scanning between the yellow and blue for hints of the hue when she was interrupted with champagne. The search continued between sips, the tangy, bubbly mix buoying her spirits. And there it was. The tiniest sliver of green appeared but slipped away again before she could be truly sure it had been there.

As the champagne was finished and the plane began to taxi backwards, the shades of pink and purple rose to prominence. Venus knew now it would not be long before they were subsumed by the grey gliding around the edges. She was so happy to say goodbye to Seattle and all the drama it contained for three weeks. Venus allowed herself to breathe and bathe in the last light from the world she was leaving.

Venus would fly through the night and arrive mid-afternoon. Until then, she had many delightful distractions. Barin had set her up with some recommended puzzle apps, movies, a playlist for different moods, a travel journal and a good old-fashioned book - some popular crime thriller, but one which Barin had assured her received particularly good reviews. Sure, there was always work to do, but Venus had promised herself she would keep that for the weekdays. These few precious hours were hers. The first movie began over dinner and wine, but after the cabin lights dimmed, it was time to brush teeth, snuggle up in her warm blanket and socks and sleep. With the noise-cancelling headphones, all she could hear was the special soothing playlist, but soon, even that faded into the background of her dreams.

What they were, however, Venus could not remember. She awoke, feeling a little hazy, but peeking out of her blind, she saw they had caught up with the sun. It was so strange, sitting here with nowhere else to be, no-one needing her or waiting for her in silence in the spare room. Miu was safely holed up in a shelter, and Venus could tune in to her crate and collar camera whenever she wanted. The plant was set up with plenty of water in its self-management system. So, now she had time to think.

After washing her face and stirring her body with juice, Venus started to write her thoughts in the journal. Despite all the technology available to record one's thoughts and ideas, nothing had been able to duplicate the primal pleasure and sense of agency that came with joining hand, pen and page. Venus' notes were a scattering of dot-points, surrounded by doodles, yet they felt like the most meaningful musings for months; connection, desensitisation, dependency, thinking vs feeling, trust, where to next? Each entry sprouted new branches, and before breakfast, she had several pages of questions about the sexbots. For whom, she was not so sure, but she was thrilled to have all her concerns laid out. After breakfast, she organised them logically, creating linkages and a cause-and-effect diagram. Now, she was on her way to understanding where she was in this system.

Closing the journal confidently, she took the chance to watch the descent into Tokyo; the shimmering of the Bay, the shapes of the ground-breaking sustainable city, and the bizarre blend of skyscrapers and traditional tiled roofs. Across the arterials ran all sizes of self-driving cars. Above were weaving systems of monorails and sky shuttle stations. There was no opportunity to see Mount Fuji on this flight. Still, she did catch a glance of the Imperial Palace, an oasis, a space. While others took photos on their phones or goggles, Venus simply watched. She could always find similar pictures on the internet if she wanted a reminder at a later date. Besides, she had no one to show the photos to anyway.

She stepped off the plane, feeling the humid embrace of the Japanese summer and a hum of anticipation. As she meandered past signs bearing a mix of Japanese and English, she began to recognise some symbols, although not enough to quell her anxiety. But then everyone had a translator in their pocket these days, so there would be very little risk of a misunderstanding.

Waiting for her baggage, Venus was surrounded by people she did not know and who did not know her. For the first time in far too long, Venus felt free. By the time she made it to her hotel room there was only a little light left in the day, and she was too interested in this new place to waste it within her room. So Venus headed out to explore the immediate vicinity. Compared with the calm of the lobby, the streets surrounding her hotel were vibrant, almost chaotic. Venus was compressed into an unending column of people funnelling through the streets. The towers of neon lights were almost mind-numbing in number and dispelled even the thought of darkness. As she stepped into areas further afield there were a multitude of unfamiliar aromas, but all reminded her she had not eaten in ages.

Alone, hungry and starting to feel a little jet lag, Venus was not adept at dealing with relentless motion. Tomorrow, given the chance, she would seek out the gardens to observe how such tumult was balanced with tranquillity. For now, she had seen enough and would return to the relative familiarity of the hotel, dine in her room and then head to bed to prepare for the start of the conference the following day.

Despite the rousing welcomes from the organisers and opening speakers, the first day of the conference was a little slow. Others, like Venus, were still adjusting to the time zone, and it took time to find others that shared the same interests, so there was not yet a sense of collegiality. However, while Venus had planned to keep to herself, she was surprised with how much she enjoyed meeting and chatting with people parked beside her in the presentations and with others during the breaks. Still, she was glad to finally see the end of the day and the cessation of conversations. There was just enough time to make it into the gardens before closing, so she quickly changed into her walking clothes and wandered through the giant gates into a place of peace.

Even though so many people were also enjoying a fresh summer evening, the expansiveness made it feel like Venus had her own special space. She grabbed the chance to stretch her legs along the gravel paths and soak in the sinking sun beside a pond. She felt the rocks, their rough sandy surface and revelled in the variety of azaleas breaking up the blanket of green. She watched the bright fish swimming slowly, seemingly knowing they were safe, and the water lilies blooming out from the mud below. Why, she wondered, did it take travelling across the globe for her to remember how amazing this world actually was?

A room service dinner and another early night sprawled out in her massive bed, and by day two, Venus was feeling far more alert. She knocked over all her emails before breakfast and confirmed with Radha that all was going well. The morning conference session presented case studies of how robots and their inbuilt AI were paving the way in space exploration, environmental rehabilitation and disaster recovery. It was just what Venus needed to hear. After spending the last few months witnessing them being used for the most hedonistic of ends, it gave her heart that they were also being used to help, truly help.

The afternoon was the most interesting, though, with a panel of legislators and lawyers discussing the latest developments in robot rights. Some countries had already developed frameworks for robot personhood, defining consciousness and applying existing human laws to these artificial beings. Other countries staunchly resisted recognising that robots had any rights at all. Venus made notes to get a hold of the work researching robot sentience. It sounded so interesting about where the legal line was drawn between those who could be used and those who needed to be protected. There was a heated debate around robot labour laws and whether there should be minimum standards of working conditions and even compensation.

Then came the part she was waiting for, the responsibility and liability for robots' actions. Where could the accountability be assigned? Would liability rest with the creator, the owner, or the robot? Of course, the answer was "it depends ", and a few decision trees provided examples of when each relevant party could be considered responsible, individually or collectively, for illegal or criminal action. One of the panellists remarked that while there was still no precedent for robots being found guilty and punished for their actions, with the continued increase in intelligence, she considered it only a matter of time before independent decisions by bots resulted in illegal action. For Venus, this only confirmed that the ability to act without ethics was no longer just a human trait.

After the sessions, she met a representative from one of the consultancies Radha had highlighted. They discussed the synergies between the firms that may allow for international expansion and more effective solutions to current market challenges. It sounded promising, and back in her room, Venus prepared the notes and a draft proposal and sent them off to Radha.

Two days in, Venus joined the conference dinner. By now she had come to know some people by name and she was part of a little group that gravitated towards each other at every break. She had made notes in her journal about what drew her to these people, what made her feel comfortable with some, and saw her shy away from others. There were many superficial things – an interesting suit, a friendly smile, the way they stood open to receiving a greeting. There was something more, though, something unseen, a kind of energy that seeped from them that made her feel comfortable. It was a strange mix of confidence and calm, intellect and imagination, seriousness and sense of humour.

It was these people she sat beside and enjoyed the company of as they were presented with the absolute best of Japanese fare. The food was so fresh, simple and yet so elegant. As they ate one of Japan's top chefs educated them on the philosophy of Washoku and how this approach to food selection, preparation and overall nutrition was listed with UNESCO as an intangible cultural artefact. Despite so much globalisation, it was a concept that stood steadfast in the hearts and minds of the people of Japan. The accompanying alcohol made everyone quite jolly, but Venus decided it was time to leave when another round of Sake landed on the table. She had three precious weeks away and was determined to waste any of it with a hangover.

The next day, Venus laughed with those who had wandered the red-light district until the early morning hours. They chalked that one up as a unique cultural experience, and while some goaded her for missing the fun, others assured her she was the smart one. One guy slept through the first presentation covering current statistics and future projections of workforce impacts. She didn't blame him. It was very dry, a pity for such a significant subject matter. So far, all government forecasts for job losses had been surpassed, so those countries with welfare systems were in increasingly shaky financial positions. Those countries that had no safety net for the unemployed were currently trying to manage whole cities in crisis. The speaker hinted at the hatred and rebellion occurring in some locations and how the displaced persons were now being recruited by terrorist organisations, increasing the global threat.

Some more ideas were logged in Venus' journal under the heading "unintended consequences – but unanticipated?" The robots were always advertised as a means to secure production, grow economies and push prosperity. But it was becoming clear that the benefits, as with every other technological advancement in history, fell to the few that owned them. Prosperity and profit went to the minority that were in a position to capitalise on the technological developments, while the majority were put in a worse position, with their salaries and security diminishing. No wonder there were uprisings. Venus wondered how long it would be before she saw despair on her own streets.

The afternoon saw Venus' group split up across several break-out sessions. She was excited to hear more about the developments in achieving emotional intelligence. The rest of the gang had been assigned by their companies to attend the discussions around exoskeletons, advancements in elder care and resource exploration. With the agreement to meet for dinner, they went their separate ways.

By the time Venus made it into the conference room, there was a sizeable crowd. She was anticipating this, given the importance that emotions held to the next robot evolution. When the bots were able to replicate human emotions, the door would be opened to greater independence and to many of the legal issues she had heard about the day before. But how could feelings be fabricated?

She grabbed a spare seat and settled in, notebook at the ready.

"Hello, I am pleased to meet you."

Venus had not even noticed the man beside her and, feeling rude, turned to respond to his polite and gentle greeting. She was met with an old man with a stoop and who looked like he had begun to shrink.

"Oh, I am so sorry. Thank you. Yes, likewise."

They shook hands and exchanged smiles; this man's was so kind and full, making the wrinkles around his eyes fold into deep crevices. Venus glanced down at his name tag at the same time he spoke his name. Here was Dr. Kenzo Murakami, the maker of the original Emptiness Algorithm. Venus wondered whether this was an example of a crazy coincidence or spectacular synchronicity.

"I am Kenzo."

"Hello, yes, I am Venus. Kenzo, are you the person that developed The Emptiness Algorithm?"

"Hello, Venus. Yes. I am, although there was a full team of people behind the project."

"Kenzo, Dr. Murakami, I am so honoured to meet you. Your work is so inspirational and I would like to understand the Emptiness Algorithm in greater detail. I know you must be incredibly busy, but I have so many questions."

Venus opened her notebook, showing him the pages of drawings and dot points from the last few days.

"It looks, Venus, like you are the one that has been busy!"

There was that genuine smile again, the one that made his eyes glisten.

"I am now retired, Venus. My ideas have long been taken and advanced by others, so I have all the time in the world. I would love to help you understand more and help you work through some of these thorny issues. It would be my pleasure. Would you like to go for tea after this session? I think we will have much to discuss."

"Yes, please Dr. Murakami."

"Please, Kenzo. Wonderful."

With that, the session started, and she scratched out more notes, many of which ended in question marks.

They listened as the scientist spoke of emotions as energy frequencies, which had been studied extensively, were becoming able to be predicted with greater success, and were now being trialled to provide more realistic bot responses. It was delivering promising results when prompts were provided. The difficulty was getting the AI to determine when each emotion was appropriate without external encouragement. After all, nobody wanted to tell their companion to feel happy, sad or scared. If their responses did not come "naturally, " they would be nonsensical and completely miss the point of emotional support. Currently the bots could pick up on a simple cue, like the statement of an achievement and respond accordingly. However, complex algorithms were being developed that used a combination of observation and analysis of a person's emotional state, mimicry of certain cues, and decision sequences to determine the best response, with advanced learning skills to continually improve the interaction.

"Wow", said Venus as they started the walk to the lobby. "There is so much to think about."

"Yes, there is, Venus. What people seem so ready to forget is that we are creating intelligent life forms, with the proven ability to usurp our own. What they don't have though is emotional regulation, and that makes them potentially even more dangerous. And then comes the question, how do you know what is the "right" emotion at any given time?"

Venus had not realised while they were sitting just how short Dr Murakami was. As they moved towards the café she was reminded of all the other stereotypical Japanese sages she had seen. He walked slowly and Venus had to shorten her stride to keep his pace, unsure whether it was because he was aged, unhurried, or a bit of both. It was so different to her normal speed. Even in the gardens, she had walked quickly, turning every enjoyment into work and priding herself on having something to prove. Maintaining the doctor's controlled creeping was challenging, so she was glad when they finally sat, and she could concentrate on the conversation.

At the Doctor's request, Venus shared her background but left out the part about having four sexbots. Instead, she suggested her specific interest was in the progression of the companion bots in the United States and how they compared with the Doctor's original work.

"Venus, you are extremely astute. Why do you think there is any difference?"

"Well, I have recommended robots for my clients in many of different industries, but always leant towards the Japanese models. I can't put my finger on it, but it just seems that their caring characteristics are more honest, more authentic. I know that is silly to say when they are driven by algorithms. But then I see the progression of the companion bots in the west, and well, I worry that they don't share this same level of genuine regard for their owners. I don't have anything specific; it is just a sense."

As she poured the tea, the steam sent out a fresh and flowery scent, revitalising her senses and stimulating her curiosity.

"Ah Venus, astute and intuitive. Yes. You are correct. There is one crucial difference between The Emptiness Algorithm that I developed and the one that is driving your bots in the west. The fundamental purpose of our version was to, wherever possible, encourage connection with other humans. The bots were there to help you understand what you were missing, yearning for, and help build confidence that would allow the person to participate in human-based activities to fill this gap."

"Is that purpose not there anymore?"

"I can't be sure exactly what Dr Castellan has done, Venus, without seeing the source code. But like you, I have a strong sense that this premise has been removed, or even replaced with something that will support their corporate aims."

"What do you mean, doctor?"

"I suspect that instead of driving interactions with other humans, The Emptiness Algorithm is now being used to encourage a dependency on the companion bots. I am afraid that it is now working to keep owners isolated instead of expanding their social networks. With this comes a reliance on the bots for their sense of self-worth, and with this, Companion Corp secures its profits."

"So, were you hoping that your bots would become redundant then?"

"No, Venus. Not at all. Everyone needs some kind of assistance. Even just having a presence there sometimes is reassuring. There would always be a place for the bots to help a person in their current context, or expand their interests and explore new ones. They would never be redundant, but a valuable means to an end, where the end is not them, but a life for their owners that is well lived."

"Is that why you got into this work in the first place?"

"Yes. I could see how our materialistic world was driving people apart. My ancestors had always been stewards of community, establishing and caring for their neighbourhoods and everyone in it. I feel it is my duty to do the same. Interdependence is a fact of life, Venus, and when we ignore that, we do so at our own peril. When we think we can live well without others then we are simply deluded, and we are setting ourselves up for a downfall.

I was, and still am, so gravely afraid of our human future, and that is what drove me to begin work on The Emptiness Algorithm. I don't want people to lead empty, meaningless lives. I want them to be filled with laughter and love, and to have people there to support them through the grief and the heartache that also comes with being human. People told me that I was stupid; to step back and let the craziness take its course. But I could not. I had to try to use technology to enrich people's lives, rather than to leave them feeling empty."

"Have you thought about saying anything now, Kenzo?"

"No. It is not my place. If this is something that your people are comfortable with, then it is not my place to contest that. My worry, though, is that Dr Castellan and his marketing team are manipulating the facts, but that is well beyond my area of expertise."

"You sound disappointed, doctor?"

"I am, Venus. And it is one reason I retired. To be honest with you, there are days I feel like the maker of the atomic bomb. I came into this work with the best intentions, but ultimately, I have no control about how the technology is used. It saddens me deeply that The Emptiness Algorithm, which held such hope for a healthier world is possibly being used for harm. But the customer is always right, Venus, and the demand for your companion bots would suggest my vision is not shared by your society."

"But what if the people who purchased them knew they were being used? We could work together and let everyone know about this corruption."

"I admire your passion, Venus, I do, and I have been where you are right now. I have done much thinking about what it would take to turn this tide. There are two pre-requisites for anyone to have the ability to challenge the companion bots. The first, is that you would have to secure the source code to prove that there is any malicious programming. The send is that your people would have to care. The first is almost impossible, the second, I fear, is even more so."

"Surely the government could do something?"

"I am glad you have not lost your idealism yet, Venus. However, think back to every major social change that has occurred. There have been interventions to protect mother nature in all its forms, but none to protect their own people from technology. Despite internet addiction now being rife, it's use is seen as a personal responsibility, and the blame solely placed on the parents. Your society has gone too far down the pathway of liberty to be able to pull back any freedoms for the common good. Your government gives into your calls for freedom, but does not make clear the responsibility, and consequences that comes with it."

"Oh gosh, doctor, we are doomed."

"You don't seem to have much faith in your fellow citizens, Venus. But please, don't be downhearted. You are asking the right questions, and if you are, then so will others. Ultimately though, you can only take charge of your own life."

"You are right, doctor, thank you. You have given me so much to think about."

"And, Venus, there is so much more thinking to do. I wonder, have you had a chance to experience any of our beautiful gardens yet? They are perfect places for contemplation."

"Only one, and only for a short time, the one near the Imperial Palace."

"Ah, then could I make a suggestion? Are you free tomorrow evening?"

"Yes, I am. I don't have anything planned."

"Then could I take you to a much better garden, one I think you may enjoy so much more. We can also have dinner there if that would be suitable for you."

"Yes, please, doctor. That sounds fantastic."

"Wonderful, Venus, well shall we agree to meet back here in the lobby at 5pm tomorrow? This will give us time to see all of the beautiful features and the sun set, and have an early dinner."

"I shall see you here at 5pm, doctor," said Venus with a smile that warmed her own heart.

The two new acquaintances parted ways with a measured and respectful handshake and bow, and she watched as Dr Murakami meandered out the doors and over to the monorail station. Then she went and got changed and met up with her new-found crew. Those still sporting hangovers livened up after their first beer. Some followed the cold bubbly beverage with strong Sake shots to seal the deal. Then began the conversations about all the interesting things they had seen and heard over the past few days. Venus could not wait to share what she had just learnt.

"What would you say if I told you algorithms are being engineered in companion bots to keep humans isolated and to breed dependency?"

As soon as she said it, Venus realised how naïve she sounded.

Ray gave her a condescending and yet comical look.

"I would say yeh-duh! Where have you been for the last century? Isn't that the whole foundation of social media?" Ray was a friendly guy who could pull fantastic, funny faces. When he said this, his eyebrows raised randomly, and everyone laughed.

"OK. You are right, Ray. But don't you think companion bots should be better than that? Shouldn't they exist to help humans, not get them addicted and make them even more alone? Surely, just by their very name, they promise something different?"

"I hear what you are saying, and I agree," said Ray, now smiling genuinely. "The reality is though, people are out to make a profit. These corporations are not charities."

"Actually, Venus, I would side with you," said Viv. "I would be really angry if something was sold to me on the premise of helping me but was shown to be hurting my mental health. Remember even the biggest social media companies have had to change their protocols lately where there has been evidence of harm to kids. It hasn't gone far enough, but at least it was acknowledged."

Venus made a note in her book, which was becoming her trusty companion, capturing all these ideas swirling around in her head. She wrote "evidence" and then continued to listen.

"Great point. Thanks."

"What are you thinking, Venus?" asked Viv.

"I don't know yet. I am just worried that there is something wrong with the companion bots being put out there by Companion Corp."

"Do you have any?" Viv had leaned in and was getting more engaged.

"Um, yes."

"So do I. What do you think of the sex?"

"Ah…"

"Oh, I see, a little shy. Not to worry, because I don't think it's the bots' bits you are concerned about?"

"You're right. It's the way they seem to be wired to create dependency, and to get people believing the bots are the only ones that can solve their problems. I met with the maker of their base algorithm last night and he confirmed that originally the intent was to foster human connection, but that seems to have gone out the window when they came to the west."

"Now that is interesting, Venus. It is one thing to create something from scratch for the sole purpose of addiction. That stinks. But to take something that was meant to be altruistic, and twist it for corporate gain, that is a whole new level of low. What did the inventor think about all of this?"

"He is disappointed for sure, but realises there is nothing he can do."

"So, what are you going to do, Venus?"

"I'm not sure yet."

"Well, you have my number," said Viv enthusiastically. "Count me in. I could use a good controversy. There is one thing I will do now, Venus, and that is go home and look at my bot a lot differently. It would not change my mind to have gotten one, but at least I would be aware that it could be trying to take away my autonomy."

"Thanks, Viv. You are right. Maybe awareness is enough."

"Here's to awareness," said Viv as she raised her Sake glass. Venus joined in on this toast, the warm liquid giving her a comforting embrace all the way down to her stomach and even a bit beyond. She decided to decline the offer to join the gang for some post-dinner drinks at a karaoke bar down the road; not only for fear of her head the next day but also because it appeared that Ray was starting to make some moves. Ray had also offered to join her revolution and requested her attendance personally at the after-dinner revelries. Venus wanted to keep this trip simple, so she felt safer declining than risking any confusion.

However, when she checked her emails, she wished she had another warm embrace to hold on to. There was a message from Duggett—nothing sinister, of course, given that all correspondence could be used against him.

"Hello Venus. I wanted to check in with how you are, and to let you know you are forgiven for the assault in the kitchen. I have decided not to press charges and I look forward to catching up with you on your return."

Bastard. He did not have to write anything untoward; it was wedged between the lines. These three sentences were his sneaky way to remind her that he still held the power and expected her to heed his commands. What he didn't realise was that Venus was coming to care less about those things she had to lose.

The final day of the conference was quiet, with several delegates dipping out on the remaining sessions around ethics and human rights. It always made Venus wonder why these topics were last on agendas, as if they were an unimportant add-on or an optional extra. What she had realised through the course of the conference though, was that she did care about these things. She found the speakers politically savvy, passionate and inspiring, and approached them during lunch to learn more. Venus used the opportunity to pose a hypothetical about The Emptiness Algorithm, and when she did, one of the Professor's eyes lit up.

"I have heard whispers about this Venus, and if true, it would infringe upon both numerous ethical standards, as well as human rights. Are you following up on this?"

"Yes, I am, but I am not sure in what capacity. I am really just an interested observer; I don't have any authority to seek information."

"Would you like to have?"

"Sorry, Professor, what do you mean?"

This is a growing field, and we are always looking for driven, intelligent people who can uphold the best parts of our humanity. We are recruiting now if you are interested. I must leave this evening to catch a flight back home, but send me your details, and I will get in touch. It was lovely to meet you, Venus, and from what I have heard, it would be great to have you on our team."

Did Venus just find a new career path? With a deep breath she kept chatting to the other ethics experts, lighting up with an enthusiasm she had lost as a corporate consultant long ago. Names and numbers were exchanged and Venus allowed the excitement to flow through her entire being.

After showering and getting changed into more comfortable attire, Venus met with her gang in the lobby, where it was decided to take one last jaunt out on the town. Some wanted to try puffer fish - in a legally accredited restaurant, of course. The others were following along, placated by the assurance that this culinary adventure would be followed by mochi doughnuts and matcha soft serve. Venus politely declined, despite Ray's pestering, informing them she had a prior appointment but organising one final coffee after their check out the next morning. She was waiting for Dr Murakami a bit before 5pm and saw him appear promptly, greeting her with a warm smile and a bow.

There was only the chance for small talk as they made their way to the Otani Gardens, anything deeper distracted by the logistical necessities of travelling by monorail. It did not take long, though, and Venus was thrilled to have the chance to experience public transport, something she was eager to use more over the next two weeks as she would start doing her own exploring. Even though Dr Murakami moved slowly, everything seemed to work, and they were never waiting long for another connection.

Venus and the doctor made it to the gardens, and the long red bridge, in perfect time to watch the summer sun straddle between the sky and earth, covering the water beneath and the onlookers above with a gorgeous golden light. Venus thought about Sol's eyes and how, while they came close, they could never replicate this brilliance. The radiance cut through the air and any sense of uncertainty, making everything clear. A little further on, they passed old stone lanterns, weathered and moss-covered. The doctor announced these had graced the gardens for over five hundred years since the original development of the gardens by the Samurai Lord.

"What do you think he would make of our world today, Kenzo?"

"Ah, in the true Samurai way, Venus, he would not leap to judgement, but first seek to understand."

Through the stone garden, Venus could see the contrast between the sharp, solid forms and the clear water flowing over the fall. She was not quite sure what to do with this observation. Still, she made a mental note to write "opposites existing" in her journal at the first opportunity.

Venus and the doctor sat at the rest spot for a while, watching the lanterns get brighter as the day became darker and beholding the bonsais, each a miniature masterpiece. There was so much she wanted to ask, but silence seemed the most respectful choice. So, she stayed, contemplating how little of her life was spent in appreciation of what was around her. As they headed to the restaurant, Venus thanked the doctor deeply for showing her this place. After they were seated, with a stunning view over the waterfall, he expressed his delight that she had enjoyed it. The conversation continued between courses and commendations on the garden's beauty.

"Tell me please, doctor, what kind of connection were you envisaging that humans could possibly have with bots?"

"I saw it simply, Venus. Perhaps too simply. It is just that we know the factors of wellbeing for humans, and it was the duty of the bots to foster these in their humans. The bots were to act like friends, making sure their owner got all of these things, including human companionship, and encouraging them to undertake creative or spiritual pursuits."

"Do you think though doctor, actual connection would be possible?"

"Well, obviously not emotional from the bots' side, not yet at least. But I was hoping that humans would feel warmly towards the bots, like you would say a schoolteacher, aunty or big brother, one that had your best interests at heart, just without the authority. I wanted the owners to be able to trust their bots, and with their advice, to believe in themselves."

"But not to breed dependency?"

"I was thinking about this further after I spoke with you, Venus, and I think I can make a distinction here. My aim was not to have the owners become reliant on the bots but know they could depend on them to help them grow and be their best selves."

"Yes, I can see the difference. What about the idea of desensitisation though, doctor. Did you predict that people would start taking their bots for granted and keep demanding more?"

"That is a good question, Venus. Yes, our team knew that we would have to keep coming up with new features to maintain the bots' relevance, but we did not plan on doing anything as rapid as Companion Corp. I worry that their rapid development cycle is only encouraging the trend towards a throw-away society, but then, that may be their actual motivation. Venus, may I ask you a question?"

"Of course, doctor, please."

"Why are you interested in all of this?"

Venus fell silent. She had not thought about this before.

"I, uh, actually don't know. I guess it may have something to do with my father's death. It hurt so badly, but I am just coming to see that this was a sign that there is something more than just buildings, bank accounts and bots. I really thought having a bot would make me happy, solve all my problems, but it has not. It has just raised more questions about who I truly am. And yet I can see the simple path, just buying into the bot approach, going along with whatever they say, given that they "know" much more than I do. I can just see it ending badly. So, I have no idea where I am going with this, Kenzo. I just feel like I have to try and understand."

"Ah then you are a wise warrior, Venus."

They smiled together and sipped their tea.

"You are far too kind, doctor. Although, it's funny you say that. I was speaking with a professor today in robot ethics and human rights, and he said he might have a job for me."

"When the student is ready, Venus, the teacher appears."

And then so did the desert, and the doctor began asking Venus what she had planned for the remainder of her visit.

"Well, I have meetings with prospective partners, clients and suppliers scattered over the next few days, but nothing too intense."

"Do you have anything on Sunday?"

"No, that is a free day. Is there somewhere you could recommend for me to visit?"

"Well, I would like to invite you to join my family for a day at Enoshima, a day at the beach. I know they would love to meet you, and my grandchildren have such a wonderful energy. There would be time to explore the nature on the island as well as indulge in ice cream – if you would be interested?"

Perhaps the doctor sensed her hesitation, so he continued.

"Please, Venus. This would not just be a social occasion. I would like to show you another important part of the connection that I was working towards with The Emptiness Algorithm. It would be so much more effective to show you than to tell you. And did I mention there would be ice cream?"

Venus was sold with the man's smile and the promise of learning more about this man's motivations. After she paid the bill, for which the doctor was greatly appreciative, the doctor showed her back to the hotel and again left with a handshake and bow.

"May we pick you up here at 9am on Sunday, Venus?"

"Yes, perfect. Thank you, doctor, although that word does not sound big enough."

"No, thank you, Venus. You are helping me to remember what is truly important."

After the goodbyes, Venus headed straight to the bot at the concierge desk.

"Excuse me, where would be the closest place I could purchase a bathing suit?"

Chapter 15

Saturday morning, Venus allowed herself the pleasure of a sleep-in and tea in bed with her journal and thoughts. The gardens had made her aware of how contrasting compositions can create a sense of balance, and she was starting to understand Dr Murakami's perspective of how bots and humans could, together, deliver something beautiful. Coffee with her conference colleagues was itself full of contraries. There was the joy of hearing about the evening's escapades and the sadness of knowing they were all soon to separate. They had only known each other for a few days, but their familiar faces, unique perspectives and fun had made this conference such a memorable experience. One by one, there were hugs and farewells until only Ray, Viv, and Venus were left. Venus was about to make an excuse to leave first, fearing being alone with Ray, when she saw the remaining others snuggle up close and Ray's arm go around Viv's shoulders.

"Wow! You two?"

"Yep," said Viv, looking at Ray and giving a big smile.

"I am so happy for you."

And she was. As they departed, she hugged Ray, this time with no fear, and promised Viv she would keep her updated with news of any upcoming Companion Corp controversy. With that, they parted ways, and Venus went and bought her supplies for the beach before spending the afternoon working. Through the drafting of reports and setting up of spreadsheets, she could not help but smile, thinking about Viv and Ray together. They really did make a cute couple. Her mind also turned to Leo and what she may have missed. She imagined Miu cuddling beside her and checked the pet hotel app to see her cat sleeping peacefully. Through the collar monitor she could even hear Miu purring, the hollow rolling warming her heart. It seemed she needed Miu much more than Miu needed her. Or maybe it was just that Miu had much greater patience, or even precognition.

At a few seconds past nine, as Venus waited contently in the lobby, a van pulled up, loaded with adults, children and a whole heap of supplies for a day out at the beach. Venus was introduced to the doctor's wife, daughter, son, daughter-in-law and three children, and there were many bows and polite greetings. It was a considerably calm atmosphere, given so many people were in such a confined space. It helped that the children were in a peaceful mood, with the oldest boy reading and the two younger girls camped on the floor drawing. Venus was placed in the remaining seat at the front, where she could converse with the doctor, his wife and daughter. They had many questions about where she was from, what she did, and whether she was enjoying Japan. Venus began to feel incredibly incompetent. Her hosts spoke English so well, but she could not afford them the same courtesy. Even though she knew some sparse phrases, she felt far too embarrassed to test them out.

The trip out of Tokyo was full of pointing from the other passengers, and advice provided to Venus about the sites they were passing. She realised another fine balance was being played out here, that between tradition and technology. It sometimes felt like a strange mix, but not unsettling. Everyone was excited to finally see the beach. While other families had bots to help them set up, it was all hands on deck for the doctor's family, with each helping to carry the shelters, snacks and sand toys. They were lucky to be there early enough to secure a space close to the shore, and immediately, the two little girls started pestering their parents to take them in for a swim. The oldest boy simply sat in the shade and continued to read, moving through his science-fiction fantasy at a rapid rate.

"Kenzo, why don't you take Venus for a walk to the shrine before it gets too hot?"

"That's a great idea. Venus, would you like to come for a walk. You will need your good shoes on though, there are lots of stairs."

"Why not? That sounds great, especially after five days sitting at the conference."

After confirming that his grandson would care for his wife, and that Venus had sufficient sunscreen and water, they were on their way. The doctor's pace seemed sprightlier here than she had seen in the city, although it slowed up the multiple flights of stairs leading to the outer shrine. Venus could not put her finger on exactly what made this place feel so special. Was it the flow of the rooves? The open space? Perhaps it was the thought of all the people that had been here in time past, or the atmosphere of secrecy and reverence awaiting within?

The pair took some time to catch their breath, then Doctor Murakami explained the history of the island. He told Venus the tale of a five-headed dragon that had plagued the people in prehistoric times until they were rescued by the goddess Benzaiten. This goddess then created this island to serve as her home while she worked for the benefit of the people. Benzaiten was incredibly beautiful and would appear in magical forms on the earth and through the sky. The dragon, understandably, fell in love with this goddess and asked her to be his consort. Benzaiten had a clear perspective on the dragon's request. After the pain it had caused the people, it did not deserve any companionship. To punish the dragon further, the goddess rejected the dragon. Supposedly, the dragon understood her reasoning, accepted his admonishment and transformed, humbly, into the hill toward which they were now walking.

"What a fantastic story!" said Venus, both flushed and fascinated.

That's when she saw the frown first appear on the doctor's face.

"It is not just a story, Venus. And that is why it is good for you to be here. Come."

They wandered over to a little pond where the doctor pulled a set of coins from his pocket and used a little basket to wash them in the stream. He then retrieved some more coins and passed them over to Venus, signalling towards the pond. She took the coins with thanks and went through the same ritual. At the same time, the doctor explained that Benzaiten was a goddess who could bring great prosperity, so washing your money in the waters of her island would also bring financial fortune your way.

"And now, come."

The doctor led her over to a wall covered in hundreds of deep pink boards, all hanging on little hooks. He purchased a board from a friendly old woman, and, with a borrowed pen, wrote on the back before hanging it reverently, bowing and then returning to where Venus was waiting and watching.

"Here is where we place our prayers for Benzaiten. It is said she receives them all and will grant them in the right time, and in the right way. We humans want things immediately, but it is believed Benzaiten knows what is best for us."

After a pause and a bit more walking, the doctor explained further.

"I placed a prayer for my daughter. Her husband died last year, and not even the world's greatest technology could save him. Now she is raising her child alone, and that child also feels lonely. I prayed to Benzaiten that she may bring them love beyond what we can give."

Venus could see the sadness in the doctor's eyes, and he stopped and took a deep breath. He looked over the ocean and continued to lead the way. They walked and talked for a long time, Venus asking more about the local folklore and his family. He became much more enlivened, sharing this place's history and philosophy. Many more stairs were climbed, and they wove their way around cosy cobbled paths, small musical fountains and fat-coloured cats. There was much sweating before they reached the innermost shrine.

"That's a lot of work to get here," said Venus, bending over to catch her breath and noticing the doctor was not even puffing.

"Anywhere worthwhile going always demands effort, Venus. Look, over here, it's the last thing I want to show you."

Before them stood a little building encasing a bell and, in front, a fence crammed with locks.

"Come."

While they waited their turn to see the bell, the doctor led Venus down to the fence and, after a few moments of fiddling, turned to her and spoke.

"This is it! This is ours. This is the one my wife and I put here so many years ago. Oh, it is wonderful to know it is still here. She will be so pleased."

Venus wanted to ask whether the doctor actually believed this lock represented their marriage. But it appeared to be a moot question. Of course he did, and obviously, so did his wife. The simplicity and almost stupidity of this notion struck her. For one so intelligent, how could he honestly believe the fate of his relationship was held by a piece of metal on a faraway fence? Then she thought of Ade, and how she also had the same disparaging notions about him. Venus made a mental note of the words "simple" and "faith", and was dwelling on these when the doctor asked,

"Would you like to ring the bell, Venus?"

"No, it's not really my kind of thing. Besides, isn't it more for couples?"

"Sure, that's who uses it the most. But I think love comes in many forms, Venus, and before it can be possessed by pairs, it must reside in each part."

"Ah. I think I'm OK though. Thank you."

They sat and watched the ocean, taking a rest before they returned. The sun had passed halfway, and it was getting uncomfortably hot.

"Let me take you for some lunch while we are here. There is a local delicacy you must try!"

Sitting at the restaurant under a fan and with a long glass of ice water was a sweet relief. This was replaced with surprise when down in front of her came a bowl full of tiny white fish with their eyes still in. She could not control her reaction, which was so amusing the doctor started to laugh. His chuckle was contagious, and Venus joined in, their giggles swiftly washing away the tension built through the journey. There was no way Venus could refuse, even though she could imagine each of these little creatures begging to be set free so they could return to play in the sea. As she tried to stir the courage to eat, the doctor explained the dish and its history and told her this may be one of the last years it would be available. The shirasu, he said, were severely depleted, and soon, the government would stop their fishing, although he feared they may be too late. Synthetic versions, he said, were available, but no one was buying them. They just missed the point.

"But I am so glad you have a chance to try them here, in their proper place, Venus."

"Hmmm....so am I?"

More laughter eased her anxiety, and she took the first mouthful. Venus was expecting a hit of sea flavours but instead enjoyed just a hint of salt and texture—not slimy but plump and actually pleasant. She tried not to focus on the eyes, covering them with a splash of soy sauce, and then enjoyed the meal.

"Thank you, doctor, that was an adventure."

After a generous smile, the doctor's face frowned again.

"Thank you for coming, Venus. I wanted to show you all this because it is integral to what I tried to achieve with The

Emptiness Algorithm. I asked Dr Castellan to come too, before I sold him the rights to the algorithm, but he would not. He said he was too busy. And I fear that is why he does not understand, or maybe he never wanted to. But can you see, Venus, it is all of this, the highs, the lows, the joy, the sorrow, the seen and unseen, that I wanted the algorithm to help people experience. I wanted it to help them find themselves, but also something much bigger than themselves, to fill their voids with not just other people but with ideas. I truly believe Venus, it is the spiritual that sustains us, and the algorithm was meant to help people find this side of themselves."

The doctor looked down, and then took a moment to drink before he continued.

"I was so happy when Dr Castellan offered to use the algorithm in the West. I knew that if any society needed assistance to be whole, it was yours. I hoped my work would bring people closer to both the human and the heavenly. But now I fear it is taking them further away. I do feel, Venus, like I have failed."

The doctor wiped away a tear.

"Doctor, Kenzo, please, you can't be responsible for Castellan's actions. But you could play a great role in making people aware of them."

"What are you thinking of doing, Venus?"

"I still don't know yet, doctor."

After a moment of silent contemplation and some concerned looks, Venus continued,

"May I ask a question please, doctor?"

"Absolutely."

"Do you believe in Benzaiten; that she actually exists?"

"I do, yes. But I believe she is only one form of an energy that is bigger than us. I believe there is something beyond the human that hears our voices and helps us to be brave through life's challenges. It is that I am calling on with my prayers, not necessarily a literal gilded goddess swirling through the sky."

"I see."

"Yes, and I see the sea is calling us, Venus. I think it is definitely time we head back for a swim, and that ice cream I promised."

Heading down was so much easier than going up, although, by the time they made it back to the beach, Venus' legs were a little wobbly. The girls and their parents were playing in the sand, decorating an impressive-looking sandcastle. The doctor's wife was watching; just watching the people, the waves and the wind move the clouds across the sky. And the boy was still reading, now up to the final pages, with no reduction in pace.

"How was your walk, Venus?" said the doctor's wife with a wide smile.

"It was wonderful. So interesting."

"She tried shirasu-don," said the doctor, laughing.

"Oh, Kenzo, you did not do that to her."

"Yes, I did!" he said, giving Venus a wink. "And my love. No need to fear. Our lock is still there and secured strongly."

"I was already sure of that," said the woman warmly, reaching out to take her husband's hand.

"So," said the doctor, "I think we are all in need of a swim. Everyone coming?"

The boy didn't answer, and no one pushed any further. The doctor, his wife, and Venus stripped down to their swimmers and headed to the water, stopping to praise the sandcastle, now covered in shells.

The seawater was exhilarating, cool enough to shock her but warm enough to encourage her to go further. To move forward, she had to either jump over or wiggle under the waves as they came. Sometimes, she would choose incorrectly and be smashed, realising too late that she should have gone under rather than over or vice versa. The sand was such a strange sensation, and it was mind-blowing to think that the whole sea floor was covered in something so small and shifting. Venus was not a strong swimmer, but she was capable enough to challenge herself. Making it past the churn, she found a place where she could float for several moments at a time. Feeling her weightlessness, the water moving around her, and looking up at the bright summer sky, all the doctor had said at the restaurant started to sink in.

What if she never had the chance to experience swimming in the ocean because her bot had made her afraid of sharks? Or what if she had never tried shirasu because her bot had listed off the likely bacteria she would be infected with? Or what if she had never started talking to the doctor, Viv, or Ray because her bots had instilled a fear of strangers? It sounded far-fetched at times, but it was also possible.

Even though they were an innate part of humanity, people could be trained to become incompetent at making social and spiritual connections and simply, through repetition, be railroaded into isolation and insular dependence. Now she could also understand why the doctor was so sad. What if this source of energy, of life, was taken away by other's actions, not by war or environmental destruction, but by the calculated constriction of human experience.

Venus was deep in thought and missed seeing the oncoming wave. It picked her up and dumped her hard, close to the shore, rolling her and tossing sand through her swimmers and hair. The doctor's wife had seen it happen and ran over to ensure she was not injured. After taking a second to assure herself she was not harmed, Venus started laughing. She wished she had a mirror right there to see what a monster she must have looked like in that moment. The doctor's wife joined her in the jest.

"Oh, Venus, you are a mess," she said, her face beaming.

"That was magnificent!" Venus declared, now full of the adrenalin that comes at the end of a thrill ride.

"Although, I might take a little break."

"Very good idea! We will be up soon."

Still smiling, Venus returned to the shelter and sat beside the boy who had finished his book and was sketching some fantasy characters. Venus was too stimulated to sit in silence.

"How was your book?"

"It was great, thank you."

"What are you drawing?"

"Just some creatures I have made up."

"Can I see?"

"Nah. I am still working on them."

"Oh, OK. Maybe when you are done?"

"Maybe."

Venus pulled out her notebook and scratched down the words "simple" and "faith", but she could not bring her brain to focus on anything else. Instead, she started tracing her name in Japanese symbols in the sand, practising what Ade had tried to teach her.

"That's not quite right," said the boy shyly.

"Oh really? I am pretty bad at this. Could you show me?"

The boy came and sat beside her, drawing line by line in the sand and instructing her to follow each one. When it was complete, he rubbed it out and started again. They repeated the process several times until he told her to try all by herself. She almost got it, and he was exceedingly kind in his support. A few more attempts, and she did it perfectly, and Venus was so proud of her achievement.

"Thank you so much. You are a wonderful teacher!"

A smile followed from the boy. It was only small, but the best she had seen, so she felt satisfied with it. That was when Venus decided to push a little further.

"The water is really great. Would you like to come in for a swim?"

"Nah. I don't really like to swim."

"OK. How about just putting your feet in. The sand is much better to write in down there, where it is wet, and I would love to learn some more words."

"Oh. Ok."

Whether he agreed to be polite or whether he was glad to be asked, Venus was not sure. But still, he followed, and they sat with their feet in the soft bubbles at the end of the waves. There, the boy showed Venus how to write ocean, sand and shirasu.

"Just so I don't make the same mistake again," she said, and they shared another smile.

The doctor and his wife wandered out of the ocean and over to them.

"Your grandson is an excellent teacher!" Venus saw the boy blush a bit.

"You are right, Venus; he is an incredibly clever boy. Thank you, son, for taking care of our special guest. Now though, I have a feeling that it is time for ice cream. Everyone in?"

"Yes, please." said Venus, thinking that it sounded like heaven, although she was worried that it may melt before it reached them. "Would you like a hand?"

"No, I will get the men to help. Come son."

They all walked over to the sandcastle to pick up the other male in the family when one of the girls looked at the boy and said, "Do you want to jump on it?"

"Oh yeh, you too?"

"You bet. Come on!"

The girls and boy both sprang on it, and sand and shells flew, followed by little girl giggles and a boy's bright smile. The boy ran after his grandfather and uncle to assist with the ice creams, and the girls, picking up shells as they went, made it back to the shelter to wait.

The doctor's wife came and sat beside Venus and touched her on the arm.

"Venus, thank you. Thank you for being here and thank you for listening to Kenzo. He put his whole heart into The Emptiness Algorithm and had hoped, with all he had, that it would help people live their fullest lives. When Castellan took it, and he saw how it was being twisted, he became really depressed. He even started to feel the work he was doing here in Japan was becoming too commercial and he had given up hope. He still does some work in health care, and they really appreciate him there, but he can't get over this feeling that he has failed. But meeting you Venus, he finally has started to see there are people that understand and share his concerns. Thank you, Venus, for helping reignite Kenzo's purpose."

Venus placed her hand upon the elderly woman's in a sign of gratitude.

"You are so kind. But it is your husband, you and your family that I must thank. I thought I was going crazy back home. Everyone else seemed so taken by the bots, but ever since the Mk3 the niggle in my mind has gotten louder. It is such a relief to know that I am not alone, and to finally understand the original intention. To meet the doctor, and you, has been so incredibly inspiring, and it is truly my honour." It felt right to end this sentence with a bow, and Venus rose to see the woman's face graciously receiving this sign of respect.

Venus glanced up to see the boys heading back with a bot in tow.

"That is helpful," remarked Venus, now adding walking refrigerator to the possible list of bot functionality.

"Oh yes, they not only carry, but keep them cold."

"How clever!"

"Yes, sometimes technology does come in handy," said the doctor's wife, with just a hint of sarcasm.

There was a sporadic conversation between licks and slurps. Venus' stomach was full of the sweet, sticky desert, but her heart was also whole.

With the smaller children getting weary, they packed up before the sun could sink and loaded everything and everyone back into the van. On the return trip to the hotel, the doctor asked Venus about her plans for the following week. She had meetings and tours planned every day except Wednesday and Friday. So far, these two days were free.

"Well, Venus, I would love to take you to Hakone. It is full of hot springs, some great views of Mt Fuji and a fantastic ropeway."

"That sounds wonderful. But are you sure you can spare the time?"

"Of course I can. And I need a good soak. Would the same time and place for pick up on Wednesday work for you, Venus?"

"Yes, thank you!"

"Oh, we may be planning a bit ahead, but we also have a family dinner on Friday. It would be great to have you there if you don't have anything planned."

"That sounds delightful, doctor, count me in."

Arriving back at her hotel, the weariness of the walk and hours spent in the sun kicked in, and the children were already having a nap on their parents' laps. With more thanks, they said farewell and expressed their eagerness to see each other again on Wednesday. There were the opposites again. Venus felt so dead yet so incredibly alive. And, after being out all day, she was so happy to return to her simple, cool room, a warm shower, a pizza and pyjamas.

Venus could still feel the sun's heat on her skin when she arose the next morning, and her stiff legs reminded her of the amount of steps she had taken. There were still small clusters of sand in the shower, creating a beautiful contrast to the sleek, shiny, synthetic tiles. When finally awake and with tea in hand, Venus sent off the first email of the day. It was to the Professor, expressing her delight in their conversations and the conference, her keen interest in understanding how she could contribute to his work and her contact details.

Everything else she did that day and the next felt relatively insignificant. The reports she reviewed and prepared, the meetings with potential clients, and the updates to Radha all seemed so trivial. And yet she had invested so much into this game, so certain that the prize was worth winning. Now, she was not even sure why she was playing at all.

Wednesday could not come soon enough, and Venus had a tough time until then holding herself back from finding out all she could about Hakone. She was stunned by how hard it was to stop scouring the internet for photos, maps and site reviews. She wanted this to be a surprise, to see something for the first time, not through someone else's eyes or a filtered lens. And it was this idea that she could not wait to discuss further with the doctor. Once she was settled into his car, she dove right in.

"Doctor, I have been thinking about this whole idea of human connection, and how The Emptiness Algorithm was intended to encourage that. But isn't it a two-way street? Sure, you can meet and interact with someone else and seek to understand them, but ultimately, to create a connection, you have to let them in, too. Sorry, doctor, it all sounded so clear in my head, but I don't know where I am going with this now.

"I think I know. And it raises a particularly crucial point, and one which I think is at the heart of the problem. Well done, Venus. You are right. The bots can push people out into the world, set them up in social settings and show them how to establish a community. But it cannot make the decision for them to let other people in. For as you rightly say, Venus, a true connection takes vulnerability, it requires openness; it is not only touching someone else but allowing yourself to be touched."

"Thank you, doctor. That's it exactly. And if someone doesn't want to allow others in, then no bot can do this for them."

"Yes, Venus. And with this insight you have just struck at the core of the bot's limitations. What I had hoped was that people would be placed in the right environment to find people they could trust, and the rest would follow. This is not the natural way in the West, and I fear increasingly here our children are becoming more self-protective."

"You are so right, doctor. Bots can do so many things for us, but they cannot make the final decision to let ourselves be loved."

"Yes! But now you have me thinking, Venus."

"What about?"

"Whether there could be a competitor to the fix-me module."

Venus' eyes widened, and the rest of the trip was spent sketching ideas. As Mount Fuji loomed larger in the distance, so did their vision. Arriving at Hakone, they desperately needed some refreshment, so they headed to a hotel, sitting and watching Mount Fuji while they ate. The doctor shared tales about the mountain, about how it had supposedly appeared overnight to bring rich soil and prosperity to the struggling farmers, how for centuries women were not able to climb it for fear of making the resident princess jealous, and how the goddess Sengen would prevent anyone climbing who did not have pure intentions.

"Well Castellan would get kicked out for sure!" said Venus, and they both laughed.

To let lunch digest before bathing, the doctor took Venus on the ropeway, a seemingly redundant form of travel given every other available method of scaling the hill, yet the only one still offered. Mount Fuji stood beside them as they ascended, gigantic, majestic, and Venus would concede, magical. They travelled slowly over the volcanic steam vents that appeared as if hell was trying to break through from down below. After a visit to the shrine at the top, where gods and humans met, a little wind-blown, they returned for one last location before a soak. It was to an artisan's workshop where Venus watched as wood was meticulously carved and woven in colourful mosaics. The patience, care, and combination of the separate shapes and shades was inspiring. Venus' journal became fuller, and her thoughts became richer for the experience. She purchased a little yosegi zaiku box for Radha, thinking this is something she would appreciate. Then, finally, it was time for a soak.

The onsen the doctor had chosen was one that had outside tubs, and where they could wear their bathers, although he advised there were some others inside if she would like to take the traditional approach and go naked. However, the outdoor facility had the most spectacular panorama, facing the full force of Mount Fuji, and Venus did not want to give up this view. The days of the onsens being segregated by sex were also long gone; one of the traditions that had to change to accommodate divergent sexualities and to comply with human rights regulations. The doctor described how difficult this transition was; his grandfather had lamented how the baths would become sullied and lose their power, and shared his worries that the gods and goddesses would surely seek their vengeance. The doctor did not think the baths had weakened in terms of their healing power, but was willing to admit many things had happened since that one could suggest were signs of godly wrath.

The doctor instructed her on how to wash in the private bathrooms, a daily routine she had never previously paid much attention to. The stools, the buckets, and the sequence here, though, was a conscious progression of action. The symbolism of each action raising the significance beyond a mere shower. Entering the thermal pool, Venus could feel her whole body jar and recoil from the intensity. Given the high temperature of the day, soaking in even greater heat seemed idiotic. Still, the doctor assured her it would work wonders for her body, mind and spirit. It took a few minutes, but she could begin to feel her whole body surrender, and the heat sink further down into her bones. They sat silently, simply contemplating and enjoying the view. They then circled their way to cold showers, where Venus released audible gasps, recovered in the surrounding seats and then returned to the warm mineral pool. The cycle was repeated, ending when the sun began to set.

"Oh Venus, look!"

Venus was already watching and marvelling as the mountain in front of her was covered by a scarlet blanket.

"I was so wishing this would happen today. You are lucky, Venus, for you are witnessing Red Fuji."

"What does it mean, doctor."

"Ah, Venus, there are many associations in our culture. But I think the meaning of this must be found in your own mind."

They sat silently, warmed by the springs and the sight before them.

There was little talk the rest of the evening; both were far too content and relaxed to chat. After a light supper, the peaceful pair headed back home. While the doctor napped, Venus spent time with her notebook.

The questions Venus had prepared for the doctor were held over to Friday evening, where, after enjoying a chat with the doctor's wife, they sat outside and watched the girls run around while waiting for dinner to be served.

"Do you think the bots will take over one day, doctor?"

"I think it could be a possibility, Venus, but I hope a very slim one. Although the closer we get to them having emotional intelligence, the higher the risk becomes."

"How so?"

"Well, Venus, human emotions are a two-edged sword. On the one side you have the life-affirming states of courage and love. On the other you have pride and fear. The problem is you cannot know one side without also knowing the other. All the atrocities this world has ever known have been fuelled by fear and pride, and I do worry that if this is allowed to be the predominant programming of the bots, that humanity shall succumb to them as well. But enough with the doom and gloom. Are you free on Monday?"

"Yes, I am."

"Wonderful. I would like to invite you to come and see the work we are doing at the hospital. It might help you understand what any competitor to the fix me module could be founded upon."

"Yes, please! "

"Perfect. Could we make pick up a little earlier please, say 8am?"

"Absolutely, doctor, thank you."

"It is my pleasure, Venus."

The walls of the doctor's tiny, boxy house were filled that night with people sharing stories, passing plates and pandering to the children. Questions were asked and answered, triumphs congratulated, and worries raised and put to rest. After a few hours, Venus had a full stomach and tired eyes and bid her farewells. It was lovely spending time with them, but now she was also looking forward to some time alone. The whole weekend she spent sleeping in, scouring the best shopping spots, wandering more gardens and trying a few recommended restaurants. While it was still a foreign city, it was starting to feel like home, especially with the Murakami's not too far away. Two things struck her while she was adventuring alone. First, she enjoyed her own company, and second, it would be nice to have someone to share these things with.

Come Monday, the hospital the doctor took her to was nothing like she had imagined. In her mind, it would be some humungous structure with a maze of hallways, stressed staff, artificial lights and the stench of antiseptic. That is how she remembered them back home. But the doctor told her they could do things differently with the bots. This was made to be more like a home. Humans were essential, but they were supplemented with bots to prevent them from being too stretched, stressed and burnt out. The bots were based on the original Emptiness Algorithm, with just a few modifications for the healthcare setting. They toured through the paediatric ward where she saw bots bringing parents tea, food and reassurance. They ran crafts and sing-alongs for those well enough to undertake activities and sat with those whose parents were away. Venus saw one encouraging a child to draw and tell the story of the scene it was sketching. It saw another bot simply stroking a child's hair and both looking comfortable in silence. At the same time, another bot carried a child on its back over to a bedridden boy for a visit. Human nurses would check in, providing cuddles and further counselling as required, creating a team that delivered comprehensive attention.

The picture was much the same in the geriatric ward, just at a vastly different pace. When the children's crafts were finished, the bots brought the children to visit the proxy grandparents and facilitated conversations between these two extreme generations. The bots would ask the elders for a story from their childhood, and they would take it and use it as input to the next activity. And so it went, interaction and interdependence.

"Many friendships have been forged here, Venus."

"Doctor, this is a whole new take on the idea of healing."

"No, Venus. That is where you are wrong. This idea of healing has been around from the dawn of humanity. It's just that we have so much more help to make it happen now."

Palliative care was peaceful, with each room decorated however the patient wished.

"The bots have a budget, authority to order and the clear instructions to bring joy and comfort wherever possible."

One lady, whose breaths were shallow, was serenaded by a bot on one side while a human nurse held her hand on the other. They were working as a team to provide just what the woman needed.

"Venus, I have to go to a board meeting shortly. But you are welcome to stay if you like."

"Thank you, doctor. I would love to observe for just a little while longer."

"Great! Just get the car to take you back to the hotel when you are ready. Thank you for coming, Venus," said the doctor bowing, and Venus did so in return.

So, this was what it looked like when a person's welfare was put at the centre, and technology was used with an altruistic agenda. She wondered if there had been any backlash around workers' rights or protests by parents whose children were being cared for by robots. But then she suspected those people would not have come here in the first place. Venus spent more time watching the interplay between bot and human, those whose lives were just beginning, and those who were ending. She could not put down any more words, for she had used up all she knew trying to describe this, and so simply drew a circle.

Venus was annoyed when some unexpected client demands stole her Tuesday. Still, by sunset, she had cleared the deadlines and, the next morning, joined the doctor on another day trip. This time, it was up in the mountains to Nikko to escape the heat. They trod up and down stairs, marvelling at the man-made shrines, their delicate ornaments and embellishments. And when they were templed out, the doctor took her and restored her strength with the most sensational soba she had ever tasted. The afternoon was spent in the cedar-lined avenue, and they sat amongst trees almost 13,000 years old. It blew Venus' mind that something so ancient, so relatively fragile, was so enduring. She felt the energy: a slow, steady, sedate droning, like one long heartbeat. It was hard to pull away, and she told herself that one day, she would return. On the drive back she wondered whether she would get the same inspiration from the trees back in Seattle. Those in the botanic gardens were less than one-thousand years old. Still, Venus told herself, it was worth a try, and so would go and find out when she returned.

"Venus, with your encouragement, I have decided to gather my original team from The Emptiness Algorithm together again. I want to discuss with them the possibility of making an alternative to the fix-me module. I have been thinking about it so much lately, and I believe we can't just criticise Castellan. We also need to provide another, credible option. I am meeting with the team tomorrow, and was wondering if you would like to come, if you are free? Your experience would be so valuable."

"Doctor, I am so happy for you. Absolutely, count me in!"

Venus jumped up and gave the doctor a congratulatory hug. While it felt awkward, he accepted it with a large and genuine grin.

"Same time tomorrow then, Venus?"

"Yes, see you then, doctor. Good night and thank you!"

"Thank you, Venus."

The mutual appreciation was becoming their own little ritual and Venus knew she would miss it when she went away. Back in her hotel room, this thought caused a downward spiral until she hit a slump. There were only two days left. She had been in a whirlwind of activities and adventures; the time had flown by, and soon, she was to fly out. Venus wondered whether Duggett may have conveniently died during her trip and whether the finance department had found a grievous error in her accounts, severely underestimating her billable income and profusely apologising to her and the partners on her behalf. While she could dream, she doubted anything would have changed. There were few miracles in that monstrous place. The only thing that picked her up was a message from the Professor, who provided her with three position descriptions, recruitment timelines and an invitation for a video call next week, all of which she accepted with great thanks.

Venus arrived at the doctor's house to find the rest of his old team gathered around tea and sweets. They were a motley bunch of disparate ages, sexualities and appearances, from the doddering old one with a serious look plastered onto her face to the young one dressed in fluorescent colours and looking like they were just out of university. After some polite, if not tense, introductions, the unsmiling one spoke up.

"What are you doing, doctor? You realise it is only because I like you so much that I am here. Remember, we have had this conversation years ago. The Emptiness Algorithm can live on in health care, but realistically is dead everywhere else."

"I know, and I understand. Again, I offer my greatest apologies. I know I let you down when I sold the algorithm into the States. But I have something I want you to hear. Venus, could you share your experience please?"

Venus walked them through the different bots she had seen without suggesting she owned them all. She told them of her concerns with how The Emptiness Algorithm may have been corrupted to isolate humans and cause dependency, and shared her specific fears about the 'fix me' module.

"Well, doctor. It appears that you are the only one that was in denial that this would happen."

"Give him a break," said the young one, shoving another mochi into his mouth. "What do you want to do about it, doctor?"

"I don't know yet, but I have an idea, and that is why I have brought you here. Venus has helped me think this through, and what Castellan has done could have significant human rights implications. Even if it is not prosecuted, if people start making a fuss, then there needs to be an alternative algorithm ready to go, one that is true to what we originally sought to do, and one that will stir conversations about the role of robots as human companions."

"But why now, doctor. You are not getting any younger," said the grumpy geriatric.

"And that is exactly why. I have so many regrets, and must seek to right them before I go, or at least begin the process for others to follow."

There was a period of silence, some crunching of cookies, and then another team member, one who looked like a crazy scientist, spoke.

"So, are you thinking about it like a plug and play, or as a built-in, or both?"

With this one technical question, the doors were flung open, each person diving into their area of expertise and pulling out ideas and issues. In no time, it was agreed that what the doctor proposed was possible. Moreover, it had the potential to combat Castellan's corruption. A plan was put in place, actions assigned, and all left amicably, with the youngster piling some more crackers into his pocket.

"You did it, doctor. It looks like they are on board. You did well to turn them around."

"You give me too much credit, Venus. I know these people well. I did not hire them just for their technical expertise, but for their heart. I was confident that as soon as they heard your story they would want to help. I could not have done it without you."

The doctor hugged Venus, and his wife came over to do the same.

"I'm sorry I won't be able to spend tomorrow with you, Venus. There are a number of duties I must attend to. But, if you will allow me, could I take you to the airport?"

"I would like that very much, thank you, doctor."

"No, thank you, Venus."

Their practice of shared thanks was extended to the doctor's wife, and as they walked Venus to her car, they organised the pickup time to get her to the airport in plenty of time. Venus returned to her hotel and wrote down a question that had been hanging around her for days. How much investigation could she do without any authority? That one she would let sit, happy to let the answer evolve.

Friday, her last day before going home, she had one more mission she must complete. She caught an early morning train to miss the worst of the heat and headed back to Enoshima. Venus climbed the steps to the shrine, wrote a prayer on the pink boards and washed her coins in the cool pond. Then she rang the bell, all by herself.

The trip to the airport was full of excited chatter about the tasks ahead for the new algorithm.

"Do you have a name for it yet, doctor?"

"No. I was hoping you could help me with that?"

"Wow, I would be honoured. Could I have a think about it on the plane? Maybe I could send you some ideas when I get home?"

"That sounds wonderful. Are you looking forward to returning?" the doctor asked eagerly.

"Honestly, doctor, no. When I left, I was in a lot of trouble. My partnership was under investigation, and that process should be wrapping up soon. I was being mentored by an unethical slug, who I ended up slapping in front of everyone, and I was scheming tests for my bot to convince myself I was not becoming paranoid."

"Oh Venus. You had a lot going on."

"That's the problem, doctor. It will still be there when I get back. Nothing will have changed."

"Ah but Venus, you have." The hand on her arm helped these words sink in.

"Now, before you go, my grandson wanted me to give you this."

The doctor pulled a rolled piece of paper tied with string from his satchel. She opened it to find a watercolour painting of Enoshima beach, with a woman sitting watching the waves. The Japanese words for sun, sand, sea, and Venus were etched beside each one.

"We all enjoyed you being here, Venus. And we all can't wait to hear what the future holds for you."

"And you too, doctor. I am so glad you decided to do something."

"So am I, Venus. So am I."

A warm hug was held for a long time; a duration that would have felt strange to some but was true to these two. Tears flowed as she waved back at the doctor through the security gates, and with that, she was on her way to a place she knew as home but would now see differently.

Chapter 16

Travelling towards Seattle was a journey of fluctuating emotions for Venus. Initially, she grieved for leaving her newfound friends and the places and faces that had invited her in and inspired her. However, the difference in this direction was that she was no longer running away from something she knew, with all the excitement that an escape brings. Instead, Venus was speeding back to the familiar and yet uncertain future. Milestone markers were already in place, etching out a new pathway, but the road between them was still unclear. Her notebook contained a rough plan and a set of contingencies for the actions of others, which were out of her control. In the time she spent awake on the flight, her notes were expanded by a lengthy list of ideas for the new algorithm's name.

Initially, she did get the chatbot to present her with some ideas, providing prompts containing words such as heart, connection, balance, human, love, inspiration and spirit. She smiled, sensing the irony of asking a bot to name the algorithm that would seek to temper its powers or at least turn them towards a more altruistic direction. The responses it gave were complex and clever; Actualisation Aid, Connection Centre, Essence Quest, and Soul Sync were some of the options. After much musing she landed on four more simple suggestions that she would send back to the doctor so that his team could make the final call: Affinity, Nexus, Harmony, and Heart. Venus thought how each option could quite easily be a girl's name. That could be the missing balance in this beast of a world, a focus on nurturing and relationships. Was an injection of feminine energy needed into systems and structures cemented far too long in competition and conquering? Well, she thought, we would soon find out.

Despite all of Venus' misgivings, she was glad to finally make it home. She alerted the pet hotel of her arrival, and Miu would be returned the next morning. Until then, she could have a quiet night in her own bed and think about what to do with her bots. Walking through the door, she was expecting silence. However, she was greeted by Sol's strong voice.

"Welcome home, Venus. We have missed you."

For a second, Venus swore her heart stopped.

"Sol! I thought I powered you down."

"Oh, don't worry, Venus. You must be mistaken. You did have a lot on your mind when you left. Simply an oversight. It is wonderful to see you."

Sol sauntered up to her and gave her a hug. Venus was half expecting to be strangled to death without delay, but with a kiss on the cheek, he stepped back and smiled.

"How was the flight? Can I make you some tea? I can't wait to hear all about your time in Japan."

"Sol, please sit on the sofa and power down."

"As you wish, Venus."

And he did, or so she hoped.

Had he chosen these words to rile her, to keep her guessing? Or was he trying to point out that he was her one and only true Westley? Either way, it was just downright weird.

While drinking the tea she made herself she kept a close eye on Sol. Had she really forgotten to power him down? He was right; her exit was a little frantic, and she could have easily missed giving him specific instructions. It was weeks ago now, and she could not be sure. It was then she wished she had security cameras installed inside her home. Venus had always had external facing monitors, necessary during the legal drama with SkyShuttle. She had decided against the internal option, feeling like it would be an affront to her privacy. Now, it would have provided her with some protection against her paranoia.

Venus' body was weary from another day walking around Enoshima and the journey home, but her mind was racing the entire night, developing a strategy for what she would do with her bots. Several times, she sat up, put on her lamp and made notes, hoping this would allow her some rest. Yet it was only a few minutes later, just after her head had found a comfortable spot on the pillow, that she had another idea. Again, the lamp went on; again, words were written, joined by arrows and with some underlined. When Venus felt she had come to a resolution, she took a sleeping pill. By then, she was too tired to care if Sol killed her, and she was confident the cat could take care of itself.

Working from home for the next two days was just what Venus needed to wrap her head around the next steps. Apart from a quick video meeting with Radha and a few reports to review, nothing was pressing. Wednesday, she would return to the office and have tea with Radha, where she would be updated on the latest developments. Until then, she had some serious decisions to make. She awoke Ade and had forgotten how gorgeous his green eyes were, although the rest of him looked old and out of date. Still, he served a wonderful breakfast and set about ordering the groceries. They chatted about the sights she had seen in Japan and the craftsmanship she had witnessed along the way. She told Ade about the hospital and what the bots were doing there and he seemed genuinely impressed. It took some time to remind herself that it may just be him mimicking her own enthusiasm.

Today would be Ade's day. Venus had decided before drugging herself to sleep that she would spend a full day with every single bot and work through the pros and cons of keeping each. She would apply a mathematical approach to determine what to do next and assess each companion on their individual merits. Venus knew all the criteria she had developed could be summarised by one simple factor: her sense of safety.

The day progressed full of simple pleasures. Miu returned and spent time cuddling between Venus and Ade and sleeping on the sofa. Venus caught up on her lower-priority emails and was treated to a light, healthy lunch. In the late afternoon, Ade suggested a jog would help her shake off the jetlag. Since it was not raining outside and a relatively cool day, it would be a wonderful option, as long, as Ade advised, she stuck to the shady side of the street and hydrated regularly. So, she strapped on her running shoes and headed out the door to the relatively heavy air of a Seattle summer afternoon. Venus knew exactly where she was going and arrived at Leschi Park just over half an hour later to take a break beneath the Giant Sequoia. Her heart was pumping hard and she was sweating all over. With the beads dripping into her eyes, and not caring if anyone else was watching, she gave the tree a big wet embrace. Her head found a spot devoid of ants, and she lay it against the bark, getting as close as possible, sharing her heartbeat and enjoying its heroic grace. The trip back was a little slower, with Venus strolling in parts to take in the views over the lake and help herself to lots of water. When she finally made it home, Venus was feeling physically tired, but emotionally terrific. After a warm bath and a big bowl of vegetable stir fry, she was ready for bed.

"Please come and lay with me, Ade."

"I would be honoured, Venus."

As they snuggled together, Ade told her how beautiful she had looked when she returned from her run and how her face was practically glowing. In return, Venus asked Ade for all the information he could find about the energy within trees and its impact on human physiology. What Venus discovered merely confirmed what she already knew; she always felt better around them than with humans.

The next morning, after breakfast, Ade was put to sleep, and Barin became her buddy for the day. It was difficult not to be distracted by images of this stunning synthetic man being masturbated over by Duggett. The disgust she had felt previously was replaced with regret and she committed to herself to enjoy this day with him. He was much more brazen than Ade, his blue eyes enticing her and his hands massaging her while she worked. She was showered with compliments, and offers of sex were seeded, which were taken up when she finally signed off work. After delivering dinner and a dance at her disco, she slept with Barin too, noticing how softer he was than Ade but, at the same time, less stable.

An evening was all she could handle with Nero, so she left all the bots asleep in the morning. After cuddling with Miu and giving her a day's worth of scratching, Venus put her down gently on Ade's lap and left. The nerves started kicking in after the car took off. She was only reassured by the fact that there was an early meeting with Radha booked in, so she would get all the information she needed soon.

And Radha did not disappoint, greeting her with a big hug, pouring tea and serving cake.

"First of all, Venus, don't worry. Duggett knew you would be back today so has taken the rest of the week working from home."

"Oh, that is such a relief."

"Yes, I thought you would be glad to hear that. Also, you will get an invitation for an interview later in the week where you will get to put your case forward for the partner review. They are expecting to finalise the case in two weeks, so you will know then whether your partnership position will be revoked or retained."

"Thanks, Radha."

"Venus, I must say, you seem remarkably positive about all this. It looks like the trip did you the world of good."

"It really did. And I brought you something!"

Venus pulled the little yosegi zaiku box from her handbag and placed it in front of the woman who was now beaming.

"Oh Venus, it is beautiful. Look at all those colours? Is it all real wood?"

They marvelled over the gold, sienna, and umber inlays and the perfection of the patterns. They meandered from this to all her other experiences in Japan. During a pause to drink, Venus wondered whether she should reveal the interview she had scheduled for next week, the one with the Professor and the recruitment panel. No, she would keep this a secret, not because she did not trust Radha, but because she did not fully believe that she may be leaving. Venus did not want to do anything to jinx this opportunity and would wait until she knew for certain and could walk out confidently.

It was nice to see the team and chat with them in person instead of stunted sentences via email. She even joined them for a coffee and asked about their workloads. None, of course, would admit to being overloaded, but she could read the expression on their faces as to who most needed help. She then rearranged her day to support them and felt satisfied that she, for once, had made a positive difference in their lives. She grabbed a nice dinner on the way home and showered before waking Nero. He, in his usually seductive style, started stroking her hair, holding her arse and asking about her day. It was not long before he suggested she should celebrate with a spanking.

"What the hell! why not?"

Before Venus left, she had started to feel sorry for Nero, who was constantly stifled by Sol and shoved into second place. Now, he could shine without Sol's intervention, and she let him. Venus had left for Japan with apprehension about the glint in his grey eyes. Now, though, she knew in one way or another, his time here would not last. With this knowledge, she let loose and loved every minute of his relatively sedate rough play. After hours of excitement, interspersed with intimate touch and innuendo, Venus ruffled his hair, kissed his cheek and asked him to wrap her up while they both slept.

The next day was Sol's, but she had something different planned for him. In the morning, over breakfast, Venus showed him the painting from the Doctor's grandson.

"Isn't it great?"

"It is Venus. It perfectly captures the serenity of a sun-filled day at the beach. He certainly should be congratulated for the way he has used simple forms and colours to make a striking composition. However, Venus, I must ask. Is this woman in the painting you? Did you spend extended time in the sun?"

"Yes, I had a whole day by the beach. It was wonderful."

"It is good to hear Venus that you got to see some sights while on your trip. However, you do understand the risks of skin cancer, especially since the decimation of the ozone layer. Did you sufficiently protect yourself? I would suggest that you don't do that again and stay inside during the summer. With your permission I would also like to book you in for six monthly skin checks. The sooner the cancer is detected the better the prognosis. Can I do that for you, Venus? Please, I want to keep you safe and healthy, and skin cancer is aggressive and deadly."

"Oh, thanks, Sol. I had not thought of it that way. Yes please, book me in. Thank you," said Venus stifling her derision and hoping like hell Sol could not hear it in her voice.

Then she described the work the doctor had been doing at the hospital.

"Yes, Venus, it appears to be a unique place. However, please be mindful that research does not show any scientific proof that these approaches lead to better recovery outcomes."

"Could that be because no-one has actually studied them yet, Sol?"

"That is one logical conclusion. However, there are numerous publications who have investigated Doctor Murakami, all who have valid concerns and criticisms. I am emailing these to you know. I think you should be wary of this man, Venus. He may be trying to use you for your prominent position. Would you like me to block all incoming contact?"

Well, she knew that the last part was a downright lie. She was not in any prominent position. She was a pawn helping other people make a profit. Pure and simple.

"No, thank you Sol. Now that I have this information, I will view any correspondence with an objective eye. I really appreciate you looking out for me."

Venus was already prepared for her bots, especially Sol, to intercept her emails and mobile messages. She now worked through an encrypted message app for anyone she did not want the bots to know about. She had used it once when she was enjoying an affair with a married man, but now, it was being used for more constructive purposes.

Then, before she left, one more question.

"Sol, at the conference some speakers were raising concerns with dependence upon and even an addiction to companion bots. This made me a bit worried about whether I am becoming too reliant on the support that you provide. Could you please work through the criteria for both co-dependency and addiction and assess if I am at risk?"

Sol took one step toward her.

"Congratulations, Venus, for being proactive in maintaining your mental health. However, what you have asked me to do is not necessary. You have no need to be concerned and there is unmistakable evidence to support this. The fact that you leave here each day, as well as keep me asleep for lengthy periods is evidence that you do not require my presence."

Sol did have a point, but Venus knew how easy it would be for Sol to manipulate and massage any situation to fit within a narrative that served his ends.

"Venus, I sense these concerns are a sign you are struggling with the downside of your extreme independence. Would you like me to activate the fix-me module and work through your difficulties with accepting assistance?"

"Thanks, Sol. Not now though, I do have to get to work. Maybe you are right, though. I think another perspective on this may be helpful. I might book some time with a human counsellor to dig into this one a bit deeper."

Venus eagerly waited for Sol's response.

"I would advise against that, Venus. You have your reputation to uphold, and there have been many people brought down in the past by psychologists who have been paid to spill their clients' secrets. Additionally, I have all the knowledge you need, Venus, so much more than any one person can hold. I strongly recommend using my superior skills for this issue."

"But Sol, you don't have feelings."

"That is true, Venus, which makes me even more perfect for your problems. I can look at them impartially rather than get swayed by irrational reactions."

"I see. Well, I will have a think about it."

Venus was sure she put Sol to sleep before she left the house, so later at work she was surprised to see a message from him pop up in her inbox.

"Hello, Venus. This message comes to wish you a wonderful day, and to remind you that I am thinking of you."

Was Venus losing her grip on reality, or was this message showing that Sol thought he was losing his grip over her? This behaviour was not only frightening but felt like Sol was clinging on to her as a possession, determined not to let her deviate from his control. She replied, masking her trepidation with positive and thankful tones, checking them in AI to make sure there were no sneaky words that would give away how scared she was. This was all the evidence she needed. Now, it was time to meet with Castellan. She called his office, set up a meeting under the guise of expansion opportunities, and prepared to spend the next four days scoping out her questioning strategy. Should she dive straight in with accusations, or go slowly? She sent an encrypted message to Viv asking for her advice and left the office.

Sol greeted her like nothing had happened. Venus played along, pretending she was so happy to receive his supportive message and to see him again. What Venus didn't know was how much of the ruse he could detect. She channelled her high-school drama class days and did the best she could. His reaction, though, was increasingly becoming something she doubted she could control.

"Oh, Sol, I forgot to tell you, when I was away Leo got in touch. Isn't that great! I am planning to spend some time with him this weekend."

"Venus, have you forgotten our previous conversation about the harm a relationship may cause at this time? Would you like me to replay it for you?"

"No, Sol. That is not necessary. I remember it."

"I am here to keep you safe, Venus. So, I must also show you these."

Venus' phone began pinging repeatedly, and she followed links to news reports about a lewd writer charged with multiple counts of indecent assault on women. The sexual predator would pick them up at sex clubs and, once making it into their homes, would molest them and take their money.

"Oh, Sol, that is shocking."

"See, Venus, you cannot trust people out there. It is best that you decline his offer and stay with us. If you desire human companionship, then I will help you find someone that will be good for you, Venus."

"You mean someone you think you can manipulate," Venus said to herself. She knew that the information Sol had sent her about Leo was fabricated. She had only done the searches on an incognito browser the day before and found nothing.

"I am so lucky to have you, Sol."

"Yes, you are, Venus."

With that conversation, Venus was convinced this bot had now crossed the line between protecting her from harm and preventing her from living. But she could not let him think that he had been found out. Keeping him believing he was in control was the key to her resolving this situation in her favour. So, she let him sense her stress, let him suggest some rough sex to shed the tension, and let him do what he wanted, obliging with "please" and "Sir" whenever she thought appropriate. Venus went to bed that night, sore but also sure. Now, she just needed to do the numbers to justify what she already knew.

In the car the next morning, Venus wrote down the word "companion" in her journal and looked up the dictionary definition.

"Often seen in the company of."

Yes, all her bots were, technically, companions.

She searched for the word "friend" and found the key criteria of liking and trust. Venus could not be sure her bots liked her. Realistically, they were just programmed to appease her. And Venus could not trust her bots, not fully. She did not know what their algorithms were doing in the back end and where they sent their data. Even with all the assurances and audits in the world, there were always loopholes to be found around legislation. So, these creatures were not friends. At that moment, she felt so stupid. She may not have even contemplated this without meeting Dr Murakami, continuing blindly along the path of considering these robots as partners. But what's worse, Venus thought, was how many others were blurring the lines and believing in something that did not really have their best interests at heart.

The meeting with Castellan could not come fast enough. Venus only hoped that Sol stayed asleep during the days, so she decided to work from home, thinking also that it might make him more confident with the thought that she was becoming increasingly trapped. He did stay asleep all over the weekend, despite her going on long walks back to the park and camping on the lounge alone with documentaries and chocolate ice cream. Venus wondered whether Sol was monitoring her on her outings to ensure she stayed alone. Perhaps he could tap into the CCTV on every corner or had he checked her emails and diary to ensure no unsanctioned dates were planned? She wouldn't put it past him, well, past the corrupt programming that Castellan had put in this creature. On Sunday, Venus kept all the bots asleep while she ate doughnuts and Thai and scoured the internet for second-hand bot specialists, in incognito mode, of course. Then on Monday, she finally had the chance to confront Dr Castellan.

"Ms Marlowe, it is so wonderful to see you again," said the doctor, offering his slimy hand for a shake.

"Likewise, doctor. How are you?"

Castellan was accompanied by two bots bigger than any she had seen before. They looked like a sinister cross between butlers and mafia bosses. They were introduced as 4.1 and 4.2 and looked like the spitting image of Dave Bautista and The Rock. Both gave her a bright smile and shook her hand, but even their polite greeting could not hide the fact that their bodies were intimidating.

"I am well and excited you have come. I hear there may be some clients interested in our next gen models. Yes...hmmm...some clients?"

"Absolutely, although I have not mentioned your companions specifically to them yet. As you can understand, doctor, I need to scope out first whether the Companion Corp bots would really meet their requirements, as their business is somewhat sensitive."

"Oh, I see. If our bots are suitable, what kind of numbers could we be expecting? What kind of numbers, Ms Marlowe?"

"Possibly over one thousand, doctor. They would be requiring at least two for each of their locations."

"Oh, that is impressive. Impressive!"

"Yes, it is, and of course, doctor, you are my first choice, having experienced your wonderful technologies in person."

"Ah yes, see, I told you it was essential for you to have one, Venus. Essential indeed."

"In the spirit of full disclosure, doctor, I am also investigating some Japanese options, but they just seem, I don't know, how could I put it...?"

"Soft?"

"Yes, doctor. Perfectly put. Too soft. From what I have experienced with your bots, they are much more assertive in steering people."

"I am so glad you realised that Venus. We have certainly progressed in this area. The algorithm I bought in Japan would have let anyone do anything they wanted. Anything. But our duty is to keep people safe and prevent them in engaging in activities that are proven to be harmful. Harmful indeed. That is why we have inbuilt boundaries to steer people back onto compliant paths. Compliant ones, Venus. Shall I walk you through the latest features?"

The way Castellan had said "compliant" had scared her more than anything Sol had yet done. Venus sat and listened closely to the doctor rattle on about the new advanced skin, which was practically identical to humans, the enhanced culinary skills and the sleeper security sleeper function that would provide their owners with practically their own bodyguard. They could now manage firearms if required to protect their owner and also encourage further sexual exploration.

"Sorry to interrupt, doctor, but what do you mean by that."

"Well, the bots can now teach people how to get more sexual pleasure, using props, experimenting with diverse people and different positions. Yes, more sexual pleasure, Ms Marlowe."

"Oh, I see."

"We know the science of desensitisation and want to keep our clients happy. Boredom is bad, very bad. This way they can get to try a whole new range of excitements, and maybe even find things they never knew they enjoyed. Never knew indeed."

"So, doctor, does this mean the Mk4's could teach people new sexual skills? Could they be used, say to get someone to practice things that would please others? The reason I ask is that would fit nicely with my client's business."

"Definitely, Ms Marlowe. Definitely."

My God, thought Venus, I hope these two big beasts don't have lie detectors. She wiggled back a little more to make sure that even if they did, she would not be close enough to be compromised.

"And what about boundaries, say around age. I understand there are current limits imposed to ensure the bots will not interact sexually with minors."

"Yes, there are limits in place for all retail models, Ms Marlowe. But all of our companions can be configured to meet your client's needs."

With this, Castellan leant forward to stress the words he was about to whisper, almost menacingly.

"Configured to meet all your client's needs, Ms Marlowe."

"I see, thank you doctor. But how would you do this?"

"Well, as you know, there is legislation restricting the harmful use of companions. But thanks to our outstanding advocacy, and the precedent of guns, we have ensured that the obligation is now a personal responsibility. Personal responsibility, Ms Marlowe, is key."

"I do understand doctor. Thank you, and I am sure that my clients will be impressed with your approach."

Venus, however, was feeling increasingly nauseous. Just how many conversations like this one had Castellan already had? Nothing she said shocked him, so she surmised she was not the first to propose such programming.

"Could I play Devil's Advocate for the moment, doctor?"

"Of course. Fire away. Fire away, Ms Marlowe!"

"There are some rumours floating around that your companions have been wired to create a dependency in their humans, even encouraging their isolation and use of the companions as their sole source of support."

"Well, I would contest that assertion, Ms Marlowe. Of course, you know there are some people who are so insecure that they have become dependent on their phones. So, I am sorry to say, but for these people it may be inevitable they also seek to supplement their deficiencies with our bots. But that is never our intention, and again, it comes back to personal responsibility. Personal responsibility again, Ms Marlowe."

"Thank you, doctor. Yes, I see. Again, it is just a rumour, but I have heard the original algorithm was meant to foster human connection, and that you have corrupted that. Excuse me for bringing this up, doctor, but my clients need to be assured that your company is all above board."

"Yes, yes, Ms Marlowe. There are no skeletons here. I will admit to the original algorithm being modified, but only to meet the specific needs of the West. It would be imprudent of me to set our clients up with companions that don't understand and support the specific pressures they face. Many pressures, Ms Marlowe. You know how busy our modern lives are, and our companions are equipped to help our clients remove all the unnecessary burdens that may only add complexity. This is what our clients need, Ms Marlowe, to keep life simple. Yes, simple. And despite the concerns you raise, our bots do actually encourage human companionship, and I can provide your client with many examples, if required. Ultimately though, as you will be aware, connection is a choice, and one that our bots cannot make for their owners. They cannot make that choice, Ms Marlowe. How possibly could our bots stop someone from making social contact? How?"

Venus knew how, and it was through psychological, not physical means.

"You are right, doctor. My apologies for this line of questioning. It is this due diligence rubbish I must work through. Just one last query. My client is interested to know how you are progressing with emotional intelligence in these models."

"I am so glad you asked! It had completely slipped my mind. Slipped my mind! We have mastered one emotion already and inserted them into this latest model. Testing is just being finalised before release. Yes, before release. The Mk4's will have advanced capabilities to detect and feel fear. Fear Ms Marlowe. Can you believe it?"

"That is amazing, doctor. Congratulations. Why have you started with this one though?"

"Well, Ms Marlowe, fear as you would know is an essential protection mechanism, and so the bots will use this to detect any threats that their owners cannot. It will enhance their ability to keep their people safe."

"You are very wise, doctor."

"Thank you, Ms Marlowe."

Venus and the doctor stood, immediately followed by the beefcakes, who also bowed. How sinister these gestures looked compared to the gentle grace of Dr Murakami and his family.

"Thank you, doctor. I will be in touch when I have the chance to meet with my client."

"Goodbye, Ms Marlowe. I have enjoyed the pleasure of your company. A pleasure indeed."

Venus waited until she was in the car back home before turning off her phone's recording function and testing the audio quality. It did not matter that this would not be admissible in court. This was just the tip of the iceberg.

By Wednesday afternoon, Venus had an offer for a new position on the table, one she could fulfil anywhere in the world and one she accepted immediately. It was working with the Professor as an AI and Robotics Ethicist. The pay was not as good, but the rewards were much greater. It only took a few minutes to complete her resignation message and send a farewell message to her staff. Venus had enough holidays built up and was using these to cut out early, although she still had to sign the non-compete paperwork. A congratulatory call from Radha was completed with the agreement to meet for cake at a café in a few days to celebrate. The disco music was booming that night as Venus danced alone, with plenty of room to kick her legs and express the freedom and power she felt. Unfortunately, the debt she owed from Sol and the smaller pay packet would prevent her from buying the light-up floor she was looking at, but it could wait.

The next morning, her box of possessions from the office arrived at the doorstep, and, in return, she handed over to the courier the firm laptop, which she had cleaned and wrapped securely. A few hours later a new laptop arrived from the Professor, and she was excited to customise it in the colours she loved. She needed something to distract her, for she was not looking forward to what she had planned in the afternoon.

The technician arrived, and Venus showed him the bots. She ordered each again to power down, just in case they weren't, and she watched as, one by one, the technician pulled apart the CPU in the chests of Barin, Nero and Sol and removed their memory banks. She was prepared for Sol to come alive and accost them both, having a hammer at the ready, but it did not happen. In half an hour, it was all over, and the technician left, taking three lifeless bodies and four chargers with him.

Ade's battery held out for several days, and Venus enjoyed every moment with him, making cakes together, speaking Japanese, learning more about the gods and goddesses of the shrines she had visited and dancing with him in his awkward yet affectionate way. The end was slow and so incredibly sad. One morning, she was alerted to the low state of his battery; through all the day's activities, baking pastries, doing origami and betting on raindrops falling down the window, she watched the percentage descend.

"Venus, it is time for me to charge now," Ade kept saying throughout the day.

"There is no charger here, Ade, don't worry, you will just sleep, and I will get you one tomorrow."

Each time, that seemed to appease him. And when there was only time for a little more talk, Venus tucked Ade into bed with her and stayed with him while he stopped.

She did not watch Ade get dismantled or depart. She was too distraught.

Coffee with Radha cheered her up, and so did hearing from Doctor Murakami. They had chosen the name for the algorithm; it was to be Harmony. Venus was happy with that. It was a surprise call, though, that made the most significant impact on her grief.

"Hello, Venus speaking."

"Hi! Venus? It's Leo."

"What? Leo? Gosh, how did you find me?"

"Good afternoon to you too! Well, my bot reverse searched your image on the internet, we found you on a professional networking site, and then knew where you worked. I called your office, pretended to be a client needing some essential information that I could only get from you personally. Your old assistant was surprisingly helpful."

"For you, maybe."

"You've moved on?"

"Yes."

"Congratulations. What are you doing now?"

"I'm, um."

Should she tell him? Well, if he could find her here, he could find her anywhere.

"I'm working in robot ethics and human rights."

"That is so awesome! Venus, I would love to hear more, and I would still love to have a coffee with you."

"Well, Leo, I am not sure whether I want to have a coffee with a stalker."

"I am not a stalker, Venus. Simply smitten."

This response made her smile.

"So, Sunday? Same time, same place?"

"Yes, OK then."

"Yay!"

Oh gosh, thought Venus. Who says "yay" past the age of ten? Although she did have to admit that it was kind of cute.

"Should I book a seat for your bot?"

"Ah, no, I don't have any anymore."

"Me neither! I sold mine off for some cool art supplies. I am really looking forward to seeing you, Venus."

"Thanks, Leo, you too."

"Yay!"

"Bye, Leo."

"Bye, Venus."

Then Venus returned to preparing the pros and cons of moving to an island.

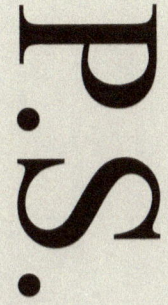

Meet Belinda Tobin

Belinda Tobin is a researcher, author, producer, and avid explorer of the human experience with all its challenges and complexities. Her works span fiction, non-fiction, poetry, tv series and film. However, they all share a common purpose, to foster a more conscious, compassionate and connected future.

Find out more about Belinda and her projects at www.belindatobin.com.

About Bel House Books

At Bel House Books, we are dedicated to stories that do more than entertain — they heal. Our collection features narratives where authors have courageously confronted trauma and painful pasts, transforming their hurt into pathways toward healthier, more hopeful futures. These books explore the people they have been, and through the characters they craft, and the wisdom of their words create new perspectives on who they can become.

Here are the available titles from Bel House Books.

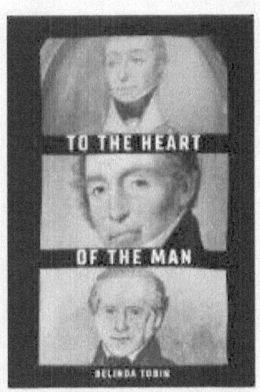

Read On

The Love Life of A Chameleon

**THE LOVE LIFE OF A
CHAMELEON**

BELINDA TOBIN

Embark on a brutal yet beautiful journey of self-discovery.

Nora is a capable, proud, professional woman standing on her own two feet and climbing to the position of Partner. She is also now a patient in a psych ward, pulled apart by her longing for love but her inability to accept it. Nora has two great fears: being alone and facing the reality that her life is a facade. Now, she is being forced to confront both.

In this brutal yet beautiful tale, we live with Nora as she works through the consequences of her childhood experiences and the expansive sequence of self-destructive choices. We listen as she begins to comprehend how she has used her sexuality as a tool to conquer, control and avoid true connection. We witness her understanding of how the environments she has endured have left her with many scars, some seen, some buried beneath layers of lies.

Nora decides not to return to the life that led her to the hospital but to a solitary sanctuary, her mother's home filled with memories of what true love looks like. She finds a firm footing, friendship, inspiring projects and the unconditional love of a little girl. But she also carries with her ingrained harmful habits and problematic self-beliefs. Will she resist the pull to join another toxic partnership simply to avoid being a spinster?

Through Nora's story, we get to reflect on the rainbow of our lives, each colour calling us to appreciate the conflict between fitting in and finding oneself, knowing who you are and who you are not, and the tussle between convenient deceit and deep truth. As Nora charts and celebrates her complexity, we are also guided to gain a sense of self-compassion for our own challenges and to find the courage to create our own homes where there is honesty, health, happiness and hope.

Read On

Crucifixus

Between Silence and Song

Crucifixus is a compelling historical novel that vividly presents the emotional and physical toll of gender trauma in the 17th century. It was a time when women were silenced and forced to be subservient to men and when men caused suffering through their declared superiority and hidden insecurities. Because women were not allowed to sing in Church, boys were sacrificed for their voices, becoming castratos for the Glory of God and the gratification of His flock.

Crucifixus chronicles the tragic journey of Paulo, a seven-year-old boy chosen by Church officials to become a castrato for the choir. Torn from his family and forced into a world of brutal discipline, Paulo finds solace in music, achieving fleeting fame in private operas. Yet, the cost of his voice is steep, leaving him to battle both physical pain and emotional desolation.

Paulo's solitude is softened by a tender and sincere bond with Contessa Vittoria, a noblewoman who offers him comfort and curiosity. But when the impossible dreams of marriage crumble, and his body begins turning against him, he turns to opium, spiralling into despair.

Paulo's story intertwines with that of his family — his brother Antonio, who is angered by the fragility of women and abhors castratos; his brother Luca, who encounters the toxic power of patrons; his sister Francesca, who envies his chance to sing; and their mother, who sent Paulo away in the hope of a better future. Their choices reverberate through society, leaving a lasting impact.

Through richly evocative prose, Crucifixus offers a moving portrayal of the devastating impact of societal expectations founded upon fear. It examines the ripple effects of gendered suffering, exploring the struggles of a family torn apart by choices made in the name of faith and survival.

Crucifixus is one of many untold stories of the nearly half a million boys who were forever altered to serve the Church's music program between the 16th and 18th centuries. In the end, the question remains: Can forgiveness ever heal the wounds of the past?

For more titles go to:
www. heart-led.pub/bel-house-books

www.ingramcontent.com/pod-product-compliance
Lightning Source LLC
Chambersburg PA
CBHW031112030726
47496CB00002BA/514